DEAD FOR A DOLLAR

DEAD FOR A DOLLAR

A FIRESTICK WESTERN

WILLIAM W. JOHNSTONE

PINNACLE BOOKS
Kensington Publishing Corp.
www.kensingtonbooks.com

PINNACLE BOOKS are published by

Kensington Publishing Corp.
119 West 40th Street
New York, NY 10018

PUBLISHER'S NOTE
Following the death of William W. Johnstone, the Johnstone family is working with a carefully selected writer to organize and complete Mr. Johnstone's outlines and many unfinished manuscripts to create additional novels in all of his series like The Last Gunfighter, Mountain Man, and Eagles, among others. This novel was inspired by Mr. Johnstone's superb storytelling.

All Kensington titles, imprints, and distributed lines are available at special quantity discounts for bulk purchases for sales promotion, premiums, fund-raising, educational, or institutional use.

Special book excerpts or customized printings can also be created to fit specific needs. For details, write or phone the office of the Kensington Sales Manager: Attn.: Sales Department. Kensington Publishing Corp., 119 West 40th Street, New York, NY 10018. Phone: 1-800-221-2647.

First Printing: February 2019
ISBN-13: 978-0-7860-4798-7
ISBN-13: 978-0-7860-4395-8 (eBook)

10 9 8 7 6 5 4 3 2

Printed in the United States of America

Chapter 1

They had the griz cornered.

Late the previous day, after interrupting the massive bear's feed on a young beef he'd dragged away from one of the ranches out on the flat, they had driven him into a widemouthed box canyon in the Vieja foothills. Before they were able to get a clear shot at him, though, he'd disappeared into the underbrush and trees back deep in the canyon.

Since going into a thicket after a riled griz ranked almighty close to a death wish, they'd decided instead to back off and settle for waiting him out. With high, steep cliffs rising out of the thicket on three sides, the bear had only one way to go when he got thirsty enough or hungry enough or mad enough at the thought of that half-eaten beef he'd been chased away from.

And when he made his move, they'd be ready . . . hopefully.

"I'd be a sight more comfortable if this canyon mouth was narrower," stated Jim "Moosejaw" Hendricks, squinting against the early morning sunlight angling down out of the east. He was a big man, massive through the shoulders, thick torsoed, six and a half feet in height. His broad, fleshy face showed its share of wear and weathering yet still belied his near fifty years of age.

Standing next to him, Malachi "Beartooth" Skinner arched a brow and replied, "Hell, if you're gonna wish for comfort, why not go all the way and wish we was home in our beds instead of camped out here in the path of an ornery grizzly we've gone out of our way to piss off?"

Skinner was right at the fifty mark, age-wise—maybe a year or two one way or the other; he'd lost exact count somewhere along the way. He stood an even six feet tall, was built lean and leathery, with a narrow, slightly wedge-shaped face tapering down to a deeply dimpled chin that seemed well suited to the wide, roguish grin he tended to frequently display.

A few feet away from this pair, straightening up from having just poured himself a cup of coffee out of the big pot simmering on the coals at the edge of their campfire, Elwood "Firestick" McQueen glanced over at his two companions and said, "Sounds to me like you two are gettin' soft. Wastin' time wishin' this and hopin' for that . . . You'd think we've been roughin' it out here for a month of Sundays instead of for only one night."

McQueen, the oldest of the trio at the mid-fifties mark, stood a shade over six feet. He was broad shouldered and solidly built with a square, stern face dominated by penetrating ice-blue eyes.

Responding defensively to Firestick's remark, Moosejaw said, "Well, it was a blamed cold night. And a long one."

"What's more," added Beartooth, aiming his cocked brow in the direction of Firestick, "I heard you doin' your share of mutterin' and cussin' over here durin' the night, too—tryin' to settle yourself and keep warm."

"Okay, maybe we're all gettin' soft," allowed Firestick. "The point is, there was a time not so very long ago when sleepin' on the ground in conditions a whole lot worse than last night was a way of life for the three of us. We went months and sometimes years without a roof over our heads or a proper bed underneath us. All I'm sayin' is that a little taste of it now and again ain't gonna kill us and therefore ain't worth so much frettin' and fussin'."

"Maybe so," Beartooth said. "But that little taste might've gone down easier if, like I said a minute ago, we wasn't planted smack in the path of that griz."

"That's right," agreed Moosejaw. "It was more than just the cold night air had me worried about the ruination of my health."

It had been close to evening yesterday when the three men drove the bear into the canyon. They reasoned he likely would stay put for the night. To help make sure, they'd built three large campfires at intervals spaced across the width of the canyon's mouth. Each man had taken a post at one of the fires, with his rifle kept at the ready and his horse picketed close by to provide early warning in case the griz decided to go on the prowl in spite of the fires and the man scent accompanying them. This bear had proven more than once to have no fear—and maybe even a little hatred—when it came to humans trying to interfere in his business.

Starting just short of a month prior, the grizzly had begun making it his business to feed on cattle and some-times horses to be found on ranches scattered over the grasslands below the Vieja Mountains. Since the Viejas didn't normally see much in the way of bear activity, it was speculated that this one, a rogue of some sort, must have wandered down from farther north right after the spring thaw. Whatever his origins, he showed up big and mean and hungry, and the ranchers soon took alarmed note of his attacks on their stock. Attempts to get in the griz's way had resulted in one death, two serious maulings, and three or four additional close calls.

It hadn't taken long before all of this was brought to the attention of the men now camped at the mouth of the nameless box canyon where the bear was cornered. Folks in the area had several reasons to look to these three for help and for them to agree to try and provide it. For starters, they represented the law in Buffalo Peak, the nearby town that supplied goods and services to the various ranches now being threatened by the bear. Firestick was the town marshal, Beartooth and Moosejaw his deputies.

While bear attacks on outlying ranches didn't normally fall in the category of what most town lawmen might concern themselves with—and technically would fall outside their jurisdiction even if they did—the way Firestick and his deputies approached upholding the law tended to allow room for a fair amount of leeway when it came to formalities like jurisdiction. What was more, in this particular case the backgrounds of the three made them qualified beyond their badges for dealing with the problem at hand.

Prior to arriving and settling in West Texas, each had spent nearly three decades roaming the mountainous regions to the north and farther west. Among the last of a dying breed, they had been mountain men living wild and free and making their way by hunting and trapping in the high reaches far from the encroachment of so-called civilization. During this time, they'd had their share of bear encounters, individually in their younger years and then later after they'd bonded as friends and partners.

It was also during those years together that they had earned, from Indians with whom they frequently skirmished, the colorful nicknames they continued to carry with them even after they quit the mountains and came to the Texas prairie. "Firestick" due to McQueen's uncanny accuracy with a rifle; "Beartooth" for Skinner's prowess with a knife that he kept as sharp and wielded as deadly as a grizzly's fang; and "Moosejaw" resulting from the occasion where an otherwise weaponless Hendricks was caught by surprise yet successfully fended off a band of Jicarilla braves using only the jawbone from a moose skeleton he found on the floor of the canyon where they had attempted to trap him.

These credentials, colorful names notwithstanding, were what prompted the ranchers in the area to look to the three for taking the lead in dealing with the bear. In addition to responding as friends and neighbors and out of whatever obligation they felt as local lawmen, the three also had a personal stake in the matter. Upon first settling in the valley, before donning badges for the town, the three had started their own small horse ranch—the Double M (for Mountain Men)—not too far to the south. Meaning they had stock of their own at risk to the marauder.

"Well, the cold night air and sleepin' on the uncomfortable ground is past us for now," said Firestick after pausing to blow a cooling breath across his coffee. "But we all know what *ain't* past us—and what we can't allow to get by whenever he decides he's ready to make his try. If we let him succeed, we'll be facin' more nights of the same."

Moosejaw made a sour face. "If he succeeds in gettin' past us, that could mean we won't be left in any shape to face more of anything."

"Throw that sort of talk out of here," responded Beartooth, scowling. "If Mr. Griz shows his face in the daylight where one of us can draw a clear bead on him, the only one endin' up in bad shape will be him."

"I like the sound of that," Firestick agreed. "But it all hinges on the little matter of when the griz decides to make his run. I figure it least likely for the middle of the day."

Beartooth nodded. "That leaves early or dusk . . . and we're already slippin' past what you could call early."

"I can't see him waitin' all the way till dusk," said Moosejaw. "There ain't no water back there in that thicket, and I don't reckon his belly is all the way satisfied, not after we chased him off in the middle of feedin' on that beef kill yesterday."

"I'm inclined to think the same." Over the brim of his upraised coffee cup, Firestick squinted in the direction of the deep thicket. "I expect our fires from last night and our palaverin' out here now in plain sight are holdin' the rascal back some. But at the same time his thirst or hunger or plain orneriness are likely workin' to prod him out of there."

"In that case," said Beartooth, "we're best off spreadin' back out and takin' up our night positions again. Even when our friend leaves the thicket, he'll have some cover in those patches of high grass pokin' up out there across the middle of the canyon. Bein' on the lookout from different angles will give us our best chance to spot him as soon as possible."

"The sooner the better," Moosejaw seconded. "The quicker we can turn that critter into a bearskin rug, the better it'll be for everybody."

"No argument on any of that out of me," said Firestick. "You fellas go ahead on back to your posts. I'll keep the coffeepot full and hot. In case we're wrong and Mr. Griz takes a notion to drag things out for a spell, you can always mosey back for a fresh cup of mud to keep from gettin' too bored."

Beartooth made a face. "I've never been a fan of bein' bored, and I sure as hell am all for gettin' this business over and done with. But you'll have to excuse me for sayin' that, on second thought, in this case findin' myself a mite bored if that dang bear turns out not to be in a hurry to come rushin' out at us . . . well, for a while anyway, that wouldn't be an altogether bad thing."

His two pals chuckled a bit at his admission before allowing as to how they understood exactly what he meant. Then, each of them taking a fresh-poured cup of coffee with them, Beartooth and Moosejaw went on back to the positions they'd maintained throughout the night, one toward either side of the canyon's mouth. At daybreak, with no bear activity having taken place to that point, they'd let their respective fires dwindle down and had converged on Firestick's center position, where they cooked coffee and palavered about how they were going to proceed.

Now, with that decided, they were extending the waiting game, leaving it for the griz to decide when he was ready to try his luck. Survival in the mountains had required many traits—skill, endurance, luck—but patience was always a key ingredient. Patience when setting out a trapline; patience when on the hunt; patience when stalking or being stalked by an enemy, man or beast. So the three former mountain men knew well how to play the waiting game. They might be a little rusty or soft, as Firestick had implied, but not so much that they didn't have another round left in them and one they damn sure reckoned to make end in their favor.

All up to the griz to make the next move, Firestick told himself as he refilled the coffeepot from a partially depleted water bag, set the makings, then placed the pot back on the coals to start brewing. He also fed a few sticks into the fire to keep it burning strong enough for the coffee to boil and stay hot. That done, he hoisted the water bag again and carried it over to where his horse was picketed. Removing his hat, he filled it with water and held it for the animal to drink, like his companions had done for their horses earlier. He noted that plenty of graze still remained within easy reach of the big gelding.

When the horse had slaked its thirst, Firestick shook out his hat and returned to the campfire. He put the water bag down, reached for the half-emptied cup of coffee he'd left sitting on the grass, then squatted on his heels beside his war bag. Tipping up the cup and swallowing some of its now tepid contents, his gaze again went to the heavy underbrush deep in the recess of the canyon. The sun was climbing higher in the sky, and the morning air was starting to warm, chasing away the last of the night's chill. It was early enough in the spring that the days were getting bright and warm, though the nights remained quite brisk.

The air was still, no hint of a breeze. Firestick found himself wishing for one, one that would carry the scent of the griz when he began to move around so that the picketed horses might pick it up and give warning. If the breeze was right, the horses would sense the bear's movement before any of the men had the chance to spot him.

As he continued to stare into the canyon, Firestick's right hand drifted down and brushed against one of the two rifles resting across his war bag. One of these was a Winchester repeater, the popular "Yellowboy" model that Firestick favored. The second weapon, the one his hand brushed against, was a single-shot Hawken muzzle-loader. Ol' Thunder. He had carried this rifle for most of his years up in the mountains—this very one, in fact, whose fine balance and accuracy and powerful .50-caliber punch had earned him the nickname he carried to this day.

From the standpoint of plain practicality, eventually Firestick had shifted more to the use of a repeater. Since taking on the job of town marshal, he'd also adapted to carrying a sidearm, namely the walnut-handled Frontier Colt .44 currently riding in the holster on his right hip.

Yet while his natural skill and keen eye served well in the use of any kind of firearm—up to and including the discovery he possessed uncommon speed when it came to drawing and firing the Colt—his Hawken continued to hold a special meaning for Firestick. These days, except for taking it down periodically to clean and fire a few target rounds, the finely crafted gun rested on hooks over the parlor doorway at the Double M ranch house. Upon preparing to head out for this bear hunt, however, Firestick had decided that the unmatched accuracy and added punch of his old friend might very well come in handy.

The right placement of a .50-caliber ball hurled from its precisely bored muzzle would bring a quick, clean end to the grizzly's reign of terror.

With this thought running through his head once again, Firestick's gaze narrowed into a glare and he muttered under his breath, "So show your shaggy ol' head, you stubborn cuss, and see what I got waitin' for you."

But the utterance met only silence. No sound, no movement from deep in the canyon. The only noise came from the nearby coffeepot as its contents started to bubble and boil. Catching scent of the aroma that accompanied this, Firestick tossed away what was left in his cup, figuring to replace it with hot, fresh brew in another few minutes. A glance toward the east caused him to wonder if, what with the sun continuing its steady climb and no sign of movement by the griz, he and his pals might not be in for a long day of nursing coffee.

Scarcely had this thought crossed his mind before something—an intangible sense, a prickling in the short hairs on the back of his neck—demanded his attention. His head snapped back around and he once more glared into the canyon, scouring the thick growth curving along its deepest recesses. Still no movement, no sound from there.

Yet something had triggered the instinctive warning in him, the kind of unsettled feeling he sometimes got when danger was close at hand. It wasn't something Firestick could define or describe, but times when he'd felt it in the past, it had proven right—and thereby saved his hide— too often to be ignored.

But what was it trying to tell him on this occasion? Something about the bear, most likely. But what? Where?

Firestick glanced over at Beartooth, about fifty yards to his right, and then toward Moosejaw an equal distance to his left. Neither of them seemed to have an awareness of anything amiss. Same for any of their horses.

What the hell? Was he losing his touch? Was his trusted warning instinct steering him wrong, letting him down?

And then, from deep in the bowels of the canyon—amplified and echoing off the surrounding cliff walls—came the thunderously fierce roar of the griz!

CHAPTER 2

"That's our boy! He's on the move!" shouted Beartooth.

"I damn well heard him, but I can't see anything yet," responded Moosejaw.

"Don't worry, you will soon enough," Firestick cautioned both of them. He was standing straight up now, feet planted wide and facing square into the canyon with the Hawken secure in his grip. A quick glance to either side showed Beartooth and Moosejaw poised similarly with their own rifles raised and ready. Back a ways, the horses were beginning to snort and skitter somewhat nervously.

Firestick swung his eyes back to the canyon, sweeping them in tight scrutiny for a sign of something to accompany the hackles-raising roar.

The beast sounded again, another powerful bellow followed by some short, choppy snarls and then the curious, almost goatlike bleating sound a bear will sometimes make when it is highly agitated. The roars had been a warning: *Here I come*. The snarls and bleats meant he was actually on the move, following through on the warning.

"There! On the left!" Moosejaw suddenly shouted. "He's coming through the high grass on my side."

Firestick saw it then, saw the tips of the tall grasses shivering and swaying as the bear made his way through them. The crafty devil was already well clear of the thicket, evidently having advanced stealthily out of the underbrush and along one side of the canyon's middle area.

"Make it hot for him!" Firestick called. "Even if you can't get a clear shot, see if you can drive him toward the center where the grass is shorter and me and Beartooth can throw in a little something to help make him feel welcome!"

"If you get a shot with that Hawken, make it count!" Moosejaw hollered back.

"That's the general idea," Firestick told him through clenched teeth.

A moment later Moosejaw began levering rapid-fire rounds with his Winchester, riddling the outside edge of the swaying high grass. The bear roared in protest but kept on the move. At first it didn't look like he was going to change course. But then, just as Firestick was getting ready to shift to his left in order to try and help Moosejaw intercept the charging beast, the bear veered toward the middle of the canyon.

For a fleeting second he was visible as he passed from the stand of tall grass and crossed a narrow, rocky-bottomed span where the grass grew much shorter. He was a huge brute, Firestick saw, with a head as big as a wagon wheel, probably weighing between eight and nine hundred pounds.

Unfortunately, the glimpse that showed Firestick this—because he'd been caught starting his turn to move toward Moosejaw—was too brief for him to get off a shot. By the time he'd wheeled back and again raised the Hawken, the bear had plunged into another patch of higher grass that made him invisible except for the shivering, swaying growth.

Now Beartooth opened up with his rifle, sending a rain of sizzling lead that sawed the grass and chewed the ground ahead of the griz's new direction. The quarry bellowed and bawled with increasing rage. The canyon mouth, so quiet only minutes earlier, was suddenly filled with a cacophony of noises—the crack of rifle fire, the increasingly louder protests of the bear accompanied by the crash and rustle of him stomping closer, all backgrounded by the snorts and shrill whinnies of the horses in their growing alarm.

Beartooth added to this, shouting between trigger pulls, "He's turnin' again! We got him zigzaggin' but there ain't no backup in him. He's gonna be bustin' out into the clear any second now—and it looks like he's gonna be headed straight for you, Firestick!"

With Ol' Thunder raised to his shoulder and the second trigger already set, Firestick sighted down the barrel and raked out, "Let him come—he'll find out there ain't no backup in me, neither."

The ground across the canyon mouth, sandier and more exposed to the elements, was covered with shorter, coarser grass than that farther into the canyon. When the bear emerged into this, charging suddenly out of the taller inner grass, he was once again fully in view. And this time it wasn't merely for a fleeting glimpse. He was *right there*, only fifty yards in front of Firestick's position, barreling full steam on all fours with furious intent to escape the canyon, and woe be to anything in his way. His fangs were bared and shiny with saliva, an ominous rumbling was issuing from his massive chest, and his blazing yellow eyes seemed locked fiercely on Firestick as he bounded directly toward him.

Even as he steadied his sights on a spot between those blazing eyes and just above that savagely gaping mouth, Firestick was aware of both Moosejaw and Beartooth converging on his position, meaning to try and help intercept the advancing beast. Because they were firing wildly as they ran, not taking time to aim carefully, Firestick saw a few of their bullets striking the shaggy body and giving off puffs of dust, but as many or more were sailing wide or gouging into the ground. None of the rounds that hit the griz seemed to slow him at all.

Which was why Firestick continued to take steady, careful aim—meaning to make sure he triggered a kill shot by penetrating the thick skull and planting a .50-caliber ball in the brain beneath.

But the same instant he stroked the Hawken's firing trigger, the griz stepped in a sharp rut with his right forepaw and lurched abruptly to one side. This staggered him momentarily but did little to slow him down. What it did do, unfortunately, was cause him to jerk his head far enough to the side so that Firestick's shot missed where it had been intended and instead clipped a large chunk off the bear's left ear and smashed into his shoulder. The impact was enough to stagger the beast harder, almost stopping him this time. But again, only momentarily. Then he was surging forward once more, emitting a roar of pain and rage as he came.

Realizing he didn't have time to reload the Hawken,

Firestick set aside the muzzle-loader and quickly snatched up his Yellowboy. Beartooth and Moosejaw had both skidded to a halt and were now bracing to take careful aim before doing any more shooting. With the lighter caliber guns it was going to for sure take a head shot, maybe more than one, to bring the beast down. And with him less than twenty yards from Firestick and building up speed, every trigger pull had to count.

Nobody was more keenly aware of this than Firestick. As he levered a round into the Yellowboy's chamber and slammed the butt to his shoulder, he calculated he might only have time for as few as two shots before the griz would be on him.

Once again, the bear jerked his head sharply to the side just as Firestick squeezed the trigger. Only this time it wasn't a wrong step by the animal that caused this. It was something far more violent. The griz's head was snapped viciously to its right, and in conjunction with the movement, a thick spray of blood, skull fragments, and brain tissue was slung through the air. An instant later, the dull, rolling boom of a heavy caliber rifle—quite different from the reports of the Winchesters going off—rolled across the mouth of the canyon.

Simultaneously riddled by Winchester bullets as well as the powerful slug striking the side of its head, the griz toppled in midstride, as if its legs had suddenly turned to mush, and crashed heavily to the ground. It skidded for a few feet on the stubbly grass and came to rest no more than a dozen feet short of Firestick.

CHAPTER 3

The mystery rifleman who delivered the head shot to the charging griz had fired from atop a high shoulder of brushy, tree-dotted ground off to the east, several hundred yards past the spot where Beartooth had stood his night post. This much was evident to the breathless trio now bunched in the canyon mouth as they turned their heads toward where the booming report seemed to have originated. The haze of powder smoke still hanging in the air where their gazes settled provided confirmation.

"I don't know who's up there," Beartooth muttered, "but he sure made one hell of a shot."

"You don't have to tell me," Firestick said. "But who he is and why he's up there to begin with still remains to be seen. So, until we know more about that, I think we'd best spread out some and stay on guard."

Moosejaw frowned. "That shot likely just saved your life. Why be suspicious about whoever was behind it? If he meant any harm, don't you reckon he would have just left it up to the bear?"

Firestick continued to stare up at the fading trace of powder smoke, saying, "Could be. Then again, could be it's somebody with a personal ax to grind and don't want anybody—or *anything*—else to handle it. Let's hold off judgment until we can be sure."

Bowing to Firestick's reasoning and the unspoken leadership role he had assumed among the three over the years, Moosejaw and Beartooth drifted a few feet off to either side. Each man then stood with his rifle balanced across the crook of one arm and held his gaze trained on the shoulder of high ground to see who was going to emerge.

In short order, a man on horseback came out of the brush near the base of the high ground. The horse picked its way sure-footedly down the last of the incline and the man leaned back easy in his saddle, giving the animal its head. A few feet behind came a modestly loaded pack mule on a tether line the rider gripped in one hand. When the stranger and his animals reached level ground, they continued unhurriedly toward the men who stood waiting.

As he drew nearer, the features of the horseman became clearer. He was a heavily bearded individual with quite a few years on him, judging by the streaks of gray in the beard and the kind of thickened torso that often comes with middle age. He appeared to be somewhat above average in height and build, clad in well-worn buckskins and a tobacco-colored slouch hat perched on an unruly thatch of hair much in need of barbering. The closer he got, though, what stood out more than anything was the wide, lopsided grin plastered on his face.

Then, on the heels of a deep, throaty chuckle, he called ahead, "What's the matter with you slack-jawed polecats? Ain't a one of you got no greetin' for an old friend from the high and lonely reaches?"

Three mouths dropped open as one.

"Cuthbert? Is that you?" said Moosejaw.

"Ripley, you doggone scalawag!" declared Beartooth.

Firestick's mouth stretched into a wide grin of its own. "I'll be damned! Rip Ripley, you old trapline pirate, it really is you!"

The buckskinned horseman let out a whoop. "Hallelujah! I was afraid maybe y'all's eyesight had gone bad or that the lot of you had turned too flatland stupid to recognize an old pal."

"The sight of you could sure enough rate as stupefyin', I'll admit that much," Firestick told him. "And speakin' of eyesight, that shot you just made showed plain enough there ain't nothing wrong with yours."

"You can say that again," said Beartooth. "That was a good five hundred yards if it was an inch. I never knew you to have such an eagle eye, Rip."

"That's because whenever Firestick was around he sucked all the air out of anybody else ever gettin' recognized for their shootin' skill," Rip replied. Then, arching one shaggy brow and aiming it directly at Firestick, he added, "Which makes me wonder . . . How did the great Firestick manage to miss that big ol' griz from such short range?"

The teasing remark brought a bit of a flush to Firestick's rugged features. But rather than let it rile him, he twisted his mouth wryly and responded, "I didn't miss that blamed critter. I just didn't hit him where I meant to."

"Yeah," said Rip with exaggerated seriousness, "sometimes the sun can get in the eyes of even the best shooter."

"Wasn't no danged sun involved, and you all know it," Firestick growled, fighting not to let the gentle ribbing get to him. "The bear stepped in a rut and jerked to one side just as I shot, causin' me to miss sinkin' a ball between his eyes. Wasn't no time for another try with the Hawken, so all that left was to try and finish the job with our Winchesters. Luckily, you *didn't* miss a head strike, Rip, and I'll be the first to say it was a helluva shot and one that most likely saved my bacon."

"Maybe *all* our bacon," Moosejaw said somberly.

Ripley scrunched up his face. "Aw hell, there ain't no fun in ribbin' y'all if you're gonna be so doggone agreeable. If I can't get a good rise out of any of you, what good is it? Ain't like I can go back up in the mountains and work up an argument with the old bunch tryin' to convince 'em I outshot Firestick, neither—on account of there's none of the old bunch left to listen."

Beartooth's forehead creased. "All of 'em are gone?"

"All of 'em who ever amounted to anything. A lot of 'em went under, permanent-like. A few others just wandered back on down to the flats, like you fellas done." Ripley sighed. "Oh, some fresh blood, some younger pups, show up from time to time. Lookin' for a piece of the old glory, hungry for an 'adventure' they can tell their grandbabies about somewhere down the road. Like the trails we blazed, the life we led was nothing but some kind of game!"

Rip paused, gazing off at something far away for a moment before continuing. "I wet-nursed a couple of those pups in order to keep their sorry asses from starvin' and dyin' without they ever made it through their first winter. But it didn't take long for that to get old and empty-feelin'." He sighed again. "So, I finally got around to comin' on down out of the high reaches myself."

"Is that what brought you to our neck of the woods?" Moosejaw wanted to know.

Ripley found his grin again. "In a roundabout way, yeah. Stories about you three settlin' here and pinnin' on badges, for cryin' out loud, spread all the way up to the high country there toward the end, when they was still a few who remembered you to pass word around. And I recalled how Firestick often talked about his hankerin' to see Texas someday . . . So, after knockin' around some and never really findin' a place to fit in, I figured what the hey. Decided I'd stick me a toe into this here Texas and see if it maybe suited me the way it seems to have you fellas."

"Well, I'm glad you came for a look-see, and I'm particularly glad for the timin' you picked to show up," Firestick said.

Ripley thumbed back the brim of his hat and leaned forward to rest a forearm across his saddle pommel. "Now that's real good to hear. Gotta admit, I was startin' to wonder just how welcome my showin' up truly was."

Beartooth frowned. "What makes you say that, Rip? What gives you any cause to think otherwise?"

Ripley lifted his brows innocently. "The thing is . . . and you gotta forgive me, seein's how I'm a stranger in these parts and maybe not understandin' the way things are rightly done hereabouts . . . but we been palaverin' a good long while now and I can't help noticin' how there ain't nobody yet offered to break out a jug and commence with the kind of proper howdy-do a body might expect for a pack of old friends meetin' up again after so long."

The three lawmen exchanged glances. Then, with a mildly sheepish grin, Firestick explained, "The long and short of it, I'm afraid, is that our purpose in bein' out here didn't seem to call for fetchin' along any kind of jug. However, I got a pot of fresh-brewed over here"—he gestured—"that the griz didn't quite make it far enough to wreck. We'd be mighty proud to share a cup of that with you."

"Ah, now there's a big step in the right direction," Ripley said. "After I saw your fires last night when it was too dark to make out who you was or figure what you was up to, I made me a cold camp. Then I rose with the sun and right off went on the skulk to satisfy my curiosity. In other words, I ain't had me no coffee in too dang long. What's more, it happens I got me a jug back on my pack mule that—less'n y'all have developed some kind of religion against it—could sweeten up a cup or two extra fine."

"Seems to me like your showin' up here keeps turnin' out better and better," said Beartooth. "So light down off that hayburner, fetch your jug, and let's have us some sweetened-up coffee."

For the next half hour, the four men sat or squatted around Firestick's campfire and swapped stories about the old days and then some of the more recent ones, filling one another in on happenings since they'd last been together. As they talked, they drank coffee laced with generous splashes from Ripley's jug of busthead.

Eventually, Ripley got around to giving more details about how he'd come to make his fateful appearance there that very morning. He'd been working his way down through the Viejas, he explained, aiming for the town of

Buffalo Peak, where he'd heard his old friends were keeping the peace these days. Night caught up with him before he made it out of the mountains, and since he'd spotted bear sign earlier in the day, he hadn't wanted to risk traipsing around too long after dark. It was as he was searching for a sheltered niche to make camp that he'd caught sight of the fires Firestick and the others had lighted across the mouth of the canyon.

"Reckon I've already told the rest of it from there," the newcomer concluded. "I found your fires mighty intriguin'. But even though I was curious, I figured I also needed to be cautious. And then, after I spied who you was come mornin', I still couldn't quite feature what in blazes you was up to . . . until I spotted that big ol' griz slippin' out of the thicket and makin' his way, crafty-like, through all that tall grass."

"So you must've saw the bear was on the move before we realized it," said Moosejaw.

Rip nodded. "'Spect so. I had the advantage of lookin' down. By then I'd also figured out what you three was set up for, layin' in wait for that critter to try and make his break. That's when I made up my mind to just sit tight, where I had elevation and a stout tree branch to steady my rifle gun on, and be ready to lend a hand if needed."

"Well, it turned out you sure were needed," declared Firestick. "You and that long-shootin' rifle gun of yours. What are you packin' there—that's a Sharps Big 50, ain't it?"

"Indeed so," confirmed Rip. "Fifty-*four* caliber, actually, in this case. Fires a prepacked, breech-loaded cartridge. Kicks like a mule with three hind legs but shoots straight and sweet, and as you saw, knocks down anything it hits. I traded an old buffalo hunter for it a couple years back. Swapped him a squaw I'd growed tired of and an Appaloosa stud I hated to part with." He paused for a swallow of his coffee and then, after gazing far off for another moment, added, "'Spect that buffalo hunter has growed tired of the squaw hisself by now. She had her uses on long, cold nights, but otherwise she had ways about her that could grind on a body something fierce." He sighed. "I still kinda miss that Appaloosa, though."

CHAPTER 4

It was noon by the time Firestick rode back into Buffalo Peak.

The way he'd left things at the canyon mouth was that Moosejaw and Ripley would remain there to field-dress and skin the bear. Since Ripley's shot had put the beast down, it was decided he'd earned the right to the pelt. It was further decided that Ripley would be staying as a guest at the Double M Ranch for a few days, and so—while Firestick returned to town to check on things there and start spreading the news about the killer grizzly being dispatched—Beartooth had ridden on to the Double M to arrange preparations on that front.

Victoria Kingsley, the cook and housekeeper at the ranch—who, just incidentally, also happened to be romantically involved with Beartooth—would need to know to set an added plate for supper and undoubtedly would want to fix something special. And since there were no spare rooms in the main house, Miguel Santros and his nephew Jesus Marquez, the two *vaqueros* hired to help work the horse herd at the ranch, needed to be advised they would be sharing space in the bunkhouse with Ripley.

As he trotted his horse down Trail Street, the main artery of Buffalo Peak, Firestick couldn't quite keep the hint of a smile off his lips. Seeing Ripley again, rehashing some of the old adventures and then thinking about even a few more as he'd been riding in, had that kind of effect.

Cuthbert "Rip" Ripley had always been a character, a wild man capable of saying and doing the kind of outlandish things that—though they sometimes came close to getting him killed—made for tales that could be told and retold to the lasting enjoyment of others. Some who actually knew him, some who only heard the tales. Either way, they were the kind of stories that helped make the hard, sometimes brutal life of a mountain man more bearable. As long as there was somebody like Rip Ripley out there, enduring the same sorts of things you were but doing it with such a rakehell flourish, then it somehow meant conditions couldn't be as bad as they otherwise might seem.

As he became aware of drawing attention from citizens lining the street on either side, Firestick put away his half smile and adopted an expression better suited for a lawman on duty. Most of the onlookers, he suspected, knew that he and his deputies had been out hunting the grizzly and were probably eager to hear how it had gone. The fact neither Beartooth nor Moosejaw were riding in with him likely only added to their curiosity. He'd see to it word got spread soon enough, but first things came first—and that meant a stop at the building that housed his office and the jail.

After climbing out of the saddle and hitching his horse

to the rail in front of the sturdy adobe-walled structure at the west end of Trail Street, Firestick strode inside, anticipating the coolness he knew would be waiting within the thick walls. At its midday peak in the sky, the sun had grown bright and hot, and the marshal was looking forward to getting out of it for a while.

"Ah, now. Welcome back. Since you're standing upright and appear not to have been mauled or chewed upon, am I to conclude the hunt was successful—or inconclusive?"

The greeting that met Firestick as he came through the door was voiced by an average-sized, elderly gent seated on a chair over by the side window. He had a neatly trimmed mustache and a few long, thin strands of hair combed straight back over the otherwise bald crown of his head. There was an open book on his lap, and on the floor at his feet lay a dog that lifted its head and regarded Firestick's entrance more or less indifferently.

The man's name was Sam Duvall; the dog was Shield. Duvall was a former New York City constable who suffered from bouts of tuberculosis. After the passing of his wife, he'd retired from the police force and moved to the drier climate of West Texas on the advice of a doctor who suggested it might be better for his health. During times when there was a prisoner in the lockup overnight or on occasions when Firestick, Beartooth, and Moosejaw all had to be absent from town for a spell, they'd come to rely on the former constable as a trusted someone to keep an eye on things. As long as Shield was allowed to accompany him and he was compensated in the form of meals from the nearby hotel dining room, he welcomed these breaks from the boredom of retirement.

"You can conclude a success," Firestick said in answer to Duvall's question. "One grizzly, now deceased, is bein' field-dressed and skinned even as we speak."

Duvall's brows pinched together. "There's a term I never quite understood. When you bag an animal in the wild, you say you 'dress' it. Yet part of that process involves removing its pelt or hide. Doesn't that amount to actually *un*-dressing it?"

Firestick gave him a look. "Boy, you big-city fellas think of the doggonedest things. You know that?"

"Matter of fact, that wasn't a big-city thought," Duvall countered. "It never crossed my mind until I moved out here and heard the term and had explained to me what it meant. In the city we got our meat from a butcher and anything pertaining to hides or whatnot were bought from stores. The kind of critters we hunted down and shot were the two-legged variety, and their lousy hides weren't worth a damn, dead or alive."

"Yeah, we got our share of that kind out in these parts, too," Firestick allowed as he moved over and leaned back to half sit on one end of his desk, facing out toward Duvall. "Speakin' of which, any sort of trouble along those lines crop up while me and the boys was away?"

"Nary a peep," Duvall replied. "No strangers arrived in town, and what with all the surrounding ranchers keeping their wranglers close in to ride watch over their herds on account of that grizzly, the saloons in town were practically empty all day yesterday and last night."

"Glad to hear things was quiet," Firestick said. Then, after considering a moment, he added, "But the bad news about the good news is—once word spreads that the griz has been bagged—there's a chance some might see it as a reason to celebrate. Especially some of the ranch hands who were bein' kept on a tight leash. Those quiet saloons could be due for a rowdy turnaround."

Duvall pursed his lips and tipped his head in a thoughtful nod. "Never really thought about it that way, but you raise a good point. And too much rowdy celebration, as we both know too well, could mean those empty cells back in the lockup are in for an increase in business, too."

"Afraid so."

"In that case," said Duvall, closing his book and rising to his feet, "I think Shield and I ought to mosey on home for a while . . . in case you find it necessary to invite in some overnight guests and need us back here later on."

"Let's hope it don't come to that. But I appreciate your willingness to sit in if it does," Firestick told him. "We ran into an old friend this morning who'll be joining us for supper out at the ranch come evening. I'll be back in town after that, though, in case things start bustin' loose."

Duvall cocked a bristly eyebrow. "You ran into an old friend while you were out grizzly bear hunting?"

"As a matter of fact, that's exactly how it happened. Trust me, if you knew this fella, that wouldn't sound nearly so strange. You'll get the chance to see for yourself since he sounded like he plans on stickin' around the area for a while." Firestick paused, forehead puckering. "Come to think on it, unless this pal of mine has tamed down considerable—which he didn't seem to show no signs of— if he makes it to town and starts hittin' the saloons, you might even get to know him in the line of duty."

CHAPTER 5

It didn't take long for Firestick's speculation to come true about the town saloons being due for a turn of rowdiness. It happened that very night, in fact, shortly after he returned to town following supper at the ranch.

The meal had gone extremely well. The gregarious, tale-spinning Ripley was an instant hit with Miguel and Jesus and even the usually rather reserved Victoria, who came from English aristocracy. She delighted in hearing stories about the mountain man days of Firestick, Moosejaw, and especially Beartooth. For his part, Ripley was on his best behavior when it came to keeping his language mostly sanitized and taming the yarns he spun somewhat so they weren't too graphic yet still plenty colorful. The meal Victoria prepared was delicious; the wine flowed freely afterward; laughter and camaraderie were abundant.

Firestick hated to leave the gathering, but it was something he felt committed to do. The way he worked it with Beartooth and Moosejaw was that—with very few exceptions—they always took supper together at the

Double M. This gave them the chance to simply visit as well as discuss events of the day related to their lawmen duties or the ranch operation. Then, following the meal, they traded off with one of them returning to town to make late rounds and see that things seemed relatively settled down before coming back home again. Tonight happened to be Firestick's turn for late town duty.

Once he'd put the continuing conversation and laughter behind him and was headed for the distant lights of Buffalo Peak, he remained in good spirits. He knew he'd hear about it tomorrow if Ripley came up with any particularly rousing tales in his absence. What was more, nights like this when he returned to town involved another arrangement quite apart from making rounds and rattling doors to make sure they were locked.

That arrangement involved one Kate Mallory, owner and proprietress of the Mallory House Hotel.

The relationship between Kate and Firestick was a lot more than just that of a marshal and a businesswoman who sat on the town council. Their feelings for one another were hardly a secret around town, but even so, they kept everything relatively discreet. Firestick made it a point to spend time with her during the course of most days, including frequently having lunch with her in the hotel dining room.

But it was on the nights when he returned for late duty that they had their most intimate moments. When he was done making his rounds, she would be waiting for him in her apartment at the rear of the hotel. Sometimes they'd make love, sometimes they'd just talk. Either way, this time together was always special. Though they'd never spoken about it at any length, they both sensed they were moving toward something lasting. But they felt no hurry, no pressure, and were giving it the time it needed to build and solidify.

Firestick reflected briefly on this again tonight as he reached the edge of town. He knew he was comfortable with the pace of how things were going between them, but he sometimes worried that Kate, despite what she said or maybe didn't say, might be less so. He didn't want to rush the matter but, above all else, he didn't want to risk losing her, either.

Quickly enough, however, Firestick put these concerns aside. What with the success of the bear hunt, meeting up again with Ripley and then having him turn out to be such an enjoyable supper guest, and now the imminent prospect of spending some private time with Kate, he was in too good a mood to dwell on anything even remotely negative.

Arriving at the west end of town, he passed the darkened, empty jail and rode on down Trail Street to the Mallory House Hotel. Here, he swung down from the saddle and tied his horse to the hitchrail in front of the building. This was his standard routine on nights when he had the late duty. Since he'd finish up back here at the hotel, it was where he began his rounds, eventually working his way down and then back up both sides of the street.

Moving around one end of the hitchrail and stepping up onto the boardwalk that ran in front of the hotel, Firestick paused when he noticed the bulky shape of a man seated in a chair tipped back against the outside of the structure.

"Evenin', Marshal. See you're back to make your night rounds," the chair's occupant greeted him in a deep Southern drawl. He was a black man of indeterminate age, maybe fifty, maybe six or eight years either side of that. His head was cleanly shaven. The sharply cut features of his dark face were lean and minus any facial hair or age lines. Even in his seated position it was clear he possessed a powerful build. Sloping shoulders, thick arms, shovel-sized hands. He was dressed in black trousers and a collarless white shirt with the sleeves rolled up at the forearms.

"Evenin', Big Thomas," Firestick responded. "You appear to be enjoyin' a nice, peaceful night."

"Yes, sir, I am. That's the way things are—peaceful and quiet, just the way they been for a couple nights now. And I ain't mindin' it a bit."

Firestick turned his head and swept his gaze along the opposite side of the street where Buffalo Peak's two main saloons were. The Silver Spur Saloon directly across the way, the Lone Star Palace Saloon catty-cornered up in the next block. Although both establishments were still open for business at this hour, not much activity appeared to be taking place at either one.

Turning back, Firestick said, "Reckon you got it pegged, alright. Peaceful and quiet indeed. Same in your place, too, eh?"

In addition to being Kate's right-hand man when it came to miscellaneous duties around the hotel, Big Thomas Rivers also worked behind the stick most nights in the small bar adjacent to the dining room. His plump, pretty wife, Marilu, was chief cook and boss of the kitchen.

Around the stem of the corncob pipe he was puffing on, Big Thomas said, "Our place ain't just quiet, it's plumb dead. Had me a customer an hour or so back who gulped down a couple of whiskeys. But then he went back up to his room and I ain't seen a soul since. So I came out to have me a smoke before the night air turns too chill."

Firestick glanced up at the clear, star-studded sky. "Yeah, it's got the feel of doin' that again tonight. Still too early in the season for the nights to hold much of the day's warmth. I can testify to that for certain, on account of havin' got a good taste of those conditions last night."

"Uh-huh. I heard about that," said Big Thomas. "Heard how you staked out that ol' grizzly who's been raisin' Cain on all the ranches and was able to finally bag him."

"Finally, yeah. It took all of us—me, Beartooth, Moose-jaw, and even an old friend from our mountain man days—but we got it done." Firestick had told the story often enough earlier in the day that he wasn't anxious to go through it all over again. Besides, he figured Big Thomas had already heard the details by now, probably with more embellishments than the marshal could supply anyway.

"However it went, it was good work by you fellas," Big Thomas said. "Lot of folks in the valley will be breathin' a lot easier tonight."

At that moment, as if in counterpoint to the big man's words, a voice wailed out in distress. The cry was so weak and faraway-sounding that if the street and the saloons on the other side had been typically busy, the two men might not have heard it.

But they did, and their heads snapped around accordingly. The voice came from down the street to the east. Firestick and Big Thomas peered in that direction, straining to see through the murky shadows that sliced across the street between the sporadically placed torch lanterns affixed to poles on either side. Firestick's hand drifted automatically down to the Colt riding on his hip.

As the men continued to stare, the voice sounded again, closer, and then a small, bouncing shape came into view hurrying down the middle of the street.

"Marshal! Marshal Firestick! Come *pronto*, there is big trouble!"

As the shape bounded closer, Firestick realized it was a young boy, not more than five or six. He was dressed in a baggy shirt and white pantaloons with rope sandals on his feet that slapped a rapid tattoo on the surface of the street as he ran. His breath could be heard chugging in frantic bursts.

Firestick stepped down off the boardwalk and extended his arms. The boy ran into his grasp. Momentum carried him forward as Firestick swept him up, feet off the ground, and recognized him.

"What is it, Pepito? What's wrong?" he asked as he set the youngster down.

"Mama sent me," the boy gasped. "She said for you to come *pronto* . . . There is trouble in the *cantina* . . . There are some mean, loud *Americanos* there and Mama is afraid they are going to hurt Papa . . . and maybe Consuela, too!"

Pepito was the son of Julio and Lucita Ramirez, who owned and ran the nameless little Mexican *cantina* at the east end of town. While most of the drinking in Buffalo Peak got done at either the Silver Spur or the Lone Star Palace Saloons—with the hotel bar drawing a smaller crowd of guests and other customers who sought quieter surroundings—the Ramirez place appealed almost exclusively to a Spanish-speaking clientele. With the border close by to the south and several of the surrounding ranches employing *vaqueros* such as Miguel and Jesus out at the Double M, the *cantina* did a modest but steady business. Julio and Lucita kept things controlled and tidy, and there was very seldom any trouble in their establishment. When there was, it usually came—such as sounded to be the case tonight—from liquored-up *Americanos* who went there expressly for that purpose.

"Please, Marshal. You must hurry," urged Pepito. "These are very nasty men!"

Firestick reached down and ruffled the boy's thick dark hair. "Don't worry, son. I'll go down there and take the nastiness out of 'em."

Pepito looked hopeful.

Big Thomas was up out of his chair. "Since Beartooth or Moosejaw ain't either one in town, you want me to come along in case you need a hand?"

"Thanks for the offer," Firestick said. Then, smiling and shaking his head, he added, "But this is what they pay me for. You stay here and keep Pepito with you, out of the way and safe. Bring him on down after I signal I've got things under control."

"But I should go back. Mama and Papa might need me," the boy protested.

As Firestick reached to untie the reins of his horse, Big Thomas stepped forward and put his massive hands on Pepito's shoulders. "You stay here with me, son. Let the marshal go do his job."

A moment later, Firestick was mounted and headed down the street at a hard gallop.

CHAPTER 6

Julio Ramirez stood four inches under six feet tall, with narrow shoulders, a potbelly, and a scraggly wisp of a mustache under a bulbous nose. In his early thirties, he was a kind, gentle man greatly devoted to his wife and son and wanting very badly to have an even larger family.

At the moment, however, Julio did not look like a gentle family man. He stood before the plank bar of his *cantina*, facing outward toward the middle of the room. To his left a table had been shoved back away, and one of its chairs was tipped over onto its side. Julio's usually neatly combed hair was spilling loose around the edges of a face flushed with anger, and a thin trickle of blood ran from one corner of his mouth. His feet were planted wide, and in his right hand he was brandishing a bung starter like a club.

Standing in front of Julio at a distance of about six feet, spread out so that they formed a loose semicircle, were three men. They were *Americanos* dressed in standard wrangler garb. Their unshaven faces all wore stern expressions anchored by sneering mouths and narrowed, menacing eyes. The man at the center of the trio had edged slightly closer to Julio than the other two, giving the impression he was the leader—or maybe just the most aggressive. He was tall and square shouldered with a *cigarillo* clamped between yellowed teeth and a spiral of greasy brown curls spilling down over his forehead from under the brim of a battered Stetson.

Off to one side of the smoky, murkily lighted room, two elderly Mexican men sat at a small, square-topped table arranged with domino pieces. They seemed frozen in place, gazing uneasily at what was occurring in the middle of the room.

This was the scene Firestick walked in on when he pushed his way through the front door. He took two heavy steps, then halted. His Winchester Yellowboy was gripped in his left hand, his right resting lightly on the grips of his Colt.

"Evenin', folks. How're things goin'?"

The man with the *cigarillo* did not turn. He stayed focused on Julio. His pals to either side, however, swiveled their heads and scowled at Firestick.

"Things are goin' just fine for all of us here," Cigarillo said over his shoulder. "We're what you might call real intent on keepin' it that way. So the best thing for you, whoever you are, is to drift on and find somewhere else to light."

Firestick's voice turned sandpapery. "Already been somewhere else," he said. "Now I got me a notion to be here."

The man to Cigarillo's right, a narrow-faced gent with a burn mark high on his left cheek that pinched the eyelid on that side permanently half-closed, said, "He looks to be some kind of law dog, Mort. He's wearin' a badge."

The man with the *cigarillo*, now identified as Mort, said, "I don't give a damn if he's wearing lace bloomers! I'm kinda busy here."

The *hombre* on the other side of Mort, a heavyset man with a tiny, thin-lipped mouth above a set of double chins, said to Firestick, "You heard the man, law dog. You got no business here. There ain't no trouble to be had unless you're itchin' to cause some."

Firestick's eyes went to Julio's face, narrowing for a second at the sight of the blood on his mouth. Then his gaze shifted past Julio to the two women huddled behind the plank bar. One of them was Lucita, Julio's wife, who was heavy with a child due in only another week or two. Clinging to her was a very pretty younger woman with long, lustrous hair falling to the small of her back. This was Consuela, a niece from south of the border who was staying with the Ramirezes for a few months to help around the *cantina* and assist Lucita in these last days of her pregnancy.

A little over a year earlier, Lucita had experienced the heartbreak of a stillborn baby. This time the Ramirezes were taking every precaution to make sure Lucita did not strain or exert herself in any way that might jeopardize a healthy birth. The fear that had been in her eyes when Firestick first walked in, however, definitely had to be causing some strain. But that fear was replaced by a wave of relief at the sight of him.

Firestick shifted his gaze again, now locking eyes with the man with the tiny mouth. "As a matter of fact, fatty," he said, "when I see my friend standin' there with a bloodied mouth and those two proud women cowerin' in fear behind the bar, all on account of you three foul-smellin' skunks . . . Yeah, that makes me itch real bad to cause some trouble."

At last, Mort turned around. Very slowly. When he was squared up with Firestick, the marshal saw he was wearing an ivory-handled Colt .45 holstered high on his left hip, tilted inward for the cross-draw. As if to emphasize the point, his right hand, hanging at his side, gave a little twitch.

"What the hell's wrong with you, man?" Mort said, *cigarillo* still clenched between his teeth. "I been in border towns from one end of the Rio Grande to the other and it's always the same. If they got any kind of law at all, the law dogs only worry about the citizens in the main part of town—the white folks, in other words—and let whatever happens in the Mexican part take care of itself. Don't you know how the game is played?"

Firestick had no *cigarillo* to clench, but his teeth were set on edge anyway. "Reckon nobody ever explained those rules to me before."

"Well, now they have. So I guess I done you a favor. And you can make it even by turnin' around, moseyin' on back to look after the white folks elsewhere in town, and leave us to our business here."

"I'm thinkin' I'd like to hear how my friend Julio feels about that," said Firestick.

Mort's eyes blazed. "Look. I told you—"

"And I told *you*," Firestick cut him off. "I want to hear what Julio has to say."

"It don't matter what he says," Mort insisted. "He's a damn pepper-belly! They'd sooner lie than tell the truth. They're as bad or worse than Injuns. Jesus, don't tell me you don't know about that part, neither?"

"These men are pigs," said Julio, speaking for the first time. "They barge in here, loud and already drunk, and pound the table, demanding tequila. When Consuela takes it to them, they try to grab her and make vulgar talk. They throw money on the table and ask her how many coins for her to lay with them in the back room!"

"By God, there's a first time for everything," exclaimed Mort. "That damn pepper-belly did it—he told the truth!"

"I don't know. I didn't care much for that callin' us pigs part," said Pinch Eye.

"Me neither," agreed Tiny Mouth. "We ain't pigs. What we are is curly wolves who ride the long coulees and anywhere else we by-damn feel like!"

"That sounds like a good idea," said Firestick. "Time for you three critters, whatever you want to call yourselves, to pack it out of here. Find yourselves a long coulee and keep on ridin'. Leave the money you got spread on the table there—we'll call that your fine for disturbin' the peace."

Mort bristled. "Like hell we will. We ain't ready to leave and we sure as hell ain't ready to pay no fine! We got business with that little *chica*, and we're willin' to pay a fair price. Where's the crime in that?"

"For starters, she ain't no workin' girl. She's barely seventeen years old," Firestick growled.

"Well, there you go. That's when they're at their ripest." Mort grinned lewdly. "From late teens to about thirty, ain't nothing sweeter to tumble with than a prime, pretty Mex gal. After thirty, they start runnin' to fat, and that's when they're only good for pumpin' out brats to their pepper-bellied menfolk. And as far as any of 'em not bein' workin' girls—hell, I ain't never seen one yet who wouldn't do the deal if the money was right. And their mamas and papas are only too happy to hold out their hands for the *pesos* that find their way home."

Julio could hold himself in check no longer. Purpling with rage, he shouted, "You filthy, lying scum!" At the same time, he swung the bung starter and slammed its flared end hard between Mort's shoulder blades.

Mort staggered forward a step, spitting a curse that sent the *cigarillo* flying from his mouth in a spray of sparks. The hat toppled from his head and his knees partially buckled. But he didn't go down. A look of fierce anger gripped his face as a second curse rumbled from deep in his chest. He started to spin back around to face Julio. At the same time his hand was reaching for the big Colt in the cross-draw rig.

"Hold it!" Firestick barked, swinging the Yellowboy up and around and levering a round into the chamber as he aimed from his hip.

But Mort was too furious to listen. He continued his spin and his hand continued reaching for the Colt.

Firestick didn't waste time with another warning. He triggered the Yellowboy and drilled a slug into the calf of Mort's right leg. With his leg knocked out from under him, Mort pitched to one side and crashed heavily to the floor on his right shoulder. The half-drawn Colt went skidding under the plank bar. This time the curse that came out of Mort was mixed with a howl of pain.

Instantly levering home a fresh round, Firestick swept the muzzle of his rifle in a flat arc covering both of Mort's companions.

Tiny Mouth was smart enough not to try anything except to ball his fists in futile frustration. Pinch Eye wasn't that bright, however. He made a grab for the hogleg holstered on his right hip.

The Yellowboy spoke again, and this time the result was a quarter-sized hole punched clean through the palm of Pinch Eye's hand before it could close on the hogleg. The wounded man sank to his knees, grabbing the damaged hand with the one that was still good as he issued a low, keening wail of agony.

Now Firestick's muzzle centered exclusively on Tiny Mouth. "You get the message? Or do you need a bullet of your own to drive the point home?"

Tiny Mouth's fists unclenched and he jerked his hands to shoulder height, palms outward. With both chins trembling, he said, "N-no. Not me! I ain't gonna try nothing."

CHAPTER 7

"It never occurred to you to allow their wounds to be treated by a doctor before you ran them out of town?"

Firestick didn't see the question as requiring a lot of contemplation. "Nope, can't say as it did," he replied. "I figured allowin' 'em not to have to be treated by the undertaker was reasonable enough."

The rather blunt response to his inquiry left Nelson Greaves at a momentary loss for words. Greaves was a trim, well-dressed man in his early thirties. He had handsomely chiseled facial features with clear, intelligent eyes under a sweep of straw-colored hair that seemed seldom willing to stay neatly combed. When he frequently reached to push it off his forehead and back into place, it was with long, delicately tapered fingers well suited to his profession as a doctor.

Regaining his composure somewhat, Greaves said, "I can appreciate how, from your standpoint, that might have seemed a prudent measure, Marshal. All I ask is that you, in turn, understand how someone in my line of work looks at things a little different. We're bound to offer whatever care and healing we can to *all* who are suffering.

That's why I came when I heard there'd been a shooting at this end of town."

"And I'm grateful you did, Doc. Everybody is," Firestick told him. "You're a good man, and our town is better off for you movin' in. But that don't change the way I was taught to handle a snake when I run across one—and that's to stomp the poison out of it thorough-like, not let it heal so it has venom left in its fangs for another try."

"But you *weren't* completely thorough in dealing with those three drifters," pointed out Greaves. "You only ran them out of town—wounded and humiliated. What if they heal up anyway, with renewed venom and drive to seek vengeance?"

Firestick's eyebrows lifted. "I'm surprised at you, Doc. You suggestin' I *should* have sent 'em to the undertaker as a way of makin' sure they never come around again?"

"No, that's not what I meant at all," Greaves said, frowning. "I was suggesting, rather, that if they'd been treated more civilly perhaps they would have left feeling properly chastised, possibly even inclined to consider the error of their ways, instead of merely burning with hate and wanting to get even."

Firestick's expression showed a tic of annoyance that he was trying to hold in check. "You're throwin' around a lot of fancy words, Doc, and you're entitled to the thinkin' behind 'em. Could be you're partly right and no doubt bein' kinda noble. But I handled this piece of trouble here tonight the way I thought best. Was a time, not so very long ago, I wouldn't've hesitated to simply kill all three of those *hombres*. Could be the sharpest point you made with all those fancy words is that it might've been a mistake to leave those varmints alive for a future try at revenge. But I'm more inclined to think they'll be damn sure to steer their paths plenty wide of mine from here on out. If not, I won't make the same mistake twice."

A corner of Greaves's mouth lifted in a thin, wry smile. "In which case, there likely still wouldn't be a call for my services."

"Not for those three, no. Not tonight, not if they ever come around again," Firestick confirmed. "But for the sake of you bein' here now not turnin' out to be a complete waste of your time, one of those skunks busted Julio in the mouth before I showed up. He says it ain't serious, but maybe you could take a look?"

"Of course," said Greaves, bending to pick up the medical bag that had been resting on the ground beside him.

Firestick, Greaves, and a gathering of twenty or so other townsfolk who'd been rousted by the gunfire were bunched in the street out front of the Ramirez *cantina*. A handful had arrived in time to see the marshal herd the three troublemaking drifters outside at gunpoint and then send them on their way after stripping them of their handguns and leaving each with only one pocketed cartridge for the rifles in their saddle scabbards. It was fifty miles to the nearest place where they could expect to find any medical attention; the cartridges were for minimal protection on the trail in between.

Greaves had shown up, as he'd explained, after someone thought to notify him of the shooting. Although he had a cramped office in one corner of a building that he shared with a boot and shoe repair business, the space wasn't big enough to provide living quarters. So the young doctor was temporarily occupying a room at the Mallory House Hotel. He'd only just settled in town late the previous year and was still getting established.

Among the first to reach the *cantina* once the shooting was over was Pepito in the company of Big Thomas. The boy was elated to see his parents were okay, and they in turn were relieved to see he was safe after carrying word of their plight. All—including the terrified barmaid Consuela—were immensely grateful to Firestick for his intervention on their behalf.

As Dr. Greaves urged Julio inside where the light was better for him to conduct an examination, the general uproar over the whole incident began to die down. Firestick turned to address those still milling around.

"It's all over with, folks," he announced. "The doc's just havin' a look at a cut to Julio's mouth, but it's nothing serious. He'll be fine. So y'all had best clear the street and go on home or about your business. Move along now."

The crowd dispersed without a fuss, one or two lingering a few steps behind the rest, craning their necks to look through the *cantina*'s open door in order to try and see what the doctor was doing. In a matter of minutes, everybody was gone except for two individuals who moved up to stand beside the marshal. One was Kate Mallory, Firestick's lady friend from the hotel. The other was Frank Moorehouse, the town barber, emergency dentist, and until the arrival of Greaves, the closest thing to a doctor the community previously had. He was a portly individual, older than Firestick by a handful of years, with a walrus mustache and bristly eyebrows that danced above and behind a pair of wire-rimmed glasses with lenses as thick as a man's thumb.

"You, my large friend," Moorehouse proclaimed now, "have had a busy day, even by your standards. Vanquishing a grizzly bear for breakfast and now overcoming a pack of villains at three-to-one odds for a nightcap."

"Not to mention," Kate added with a distinct edge to her tone, "having to listen to a mouthful of guff from the high-minded Dr. Greaves. For a minute there, if I hadn't known better, I might have thought I was listening to a preacher rather than a doctor."

Firestick smiled, both pleased and a bit amused by Kate getting her ire up in his defense. He never tired of looking at her under any circumstance or in any lighting, but right at that moment, the soft illumination from the pole torches serving as street lamps enhanced her sultry, dark-eyed beauty to an almost breathtaking degree.

"Aw, young Greaves isn't really a bad sort," Moorehouse said in response to her remarks. "He's from the Chicago area back in Illinois, remember. Idealistic and still getting his feet wet to the ways of the West."

"That may be," Kate said, though clearly not ready to give too much ground. "But I'll go back to my previous comparison. Idealism is like religion—it's all well and good for an individual to have, as long as they don't try too hard to cram it down somebody else's throat."

Firestick thumbed back the brim of his hat. "You two are throwin' around words almost as fancy as Greaves was. Idealism, comparison . . . But by and large, I gotta float my stick same as Frank. From what I've seen so far, I don't think Greaves is a bad sort. He seems to have his doctorin' skills honed pretty sharp. That's the main thing and—meanin' no offense to you, Frank—it's something our town has been needin'."

"None taken. I couldn't agree more," said Moorehouse. "I never claimed to be a *real* doctor, remember. Nor a dentist, either. But those were needs that folks around here had and—because of some skills forced upon me during the late war—I tried my best to fill them. I got pretty handy with bullet holes and broken bones. Beyond that, though, I did a lot more guessing than I ever let on. And every time I lost a patient or failed to properly diagnose an illness or infection . . . well, it was hard. Hard on me, harder still on those I let down."

"Nobody ever blamed you for your shortcomin's," Firestick told him. "You did the best you could, and you cured a helluva lot more folks than you let down."

"I hope folks remember it that way. Thanks for saying so." Moorehouse turned his head and looked through the open *cantina* door at where Greaves was ministering to Julio and Lucita stood looking on with concern. "Last year, when Lucita lost her baby—that was one of the ones that bothered me a lot. I just didn't know what to do to help her. As soon as I heard last fall that she was pregnant again, it worried me half-sick. But now, with Greaves here to see her through it . . . it's like a huge weight has been lifted off me."

Kate put her hand on his arm. Her tone softening, she said, "You shouldn't be so hard on yourself. Not in the past, and certainly not now. Like Firestick said, you helped scores of people, and our town was lucky you were here and willing to do as much as you did. And you can bet that's the way folks are going to remember it."

"Anybody recalls different, I'll arrest 'em," Firestick declared, aiming to lighten the mood a bit.

It worked. It got a smile out of Moorehouse. "Let's not get too carried away with legal recourse, Marshal. If we go too far down that road, it might lead to the day when some unfortunate suffers a slip of my barber shears and wants to bring charges against me for a bad haircut."

All three had a good chuckle over that and then Moorehouse announced it was time for him to head on home.

After he'd departed, Kate stepped closer to Firestick and slipped an arm through his. "How about you, mister? Don't you think you've had a busy enough day and evening? What say you walk me home and then come in for some brandy and relaxation?"

"I've still got rounds to finish. I never even got started before this ruckus broke out down here," Firestick reminded her.

With a gesture of her free hand, Kate said, "Look around. Apart from what took place here, things are especially quiet tonight. And now, with the smell of fresh gunsmoke in the air and word spreading that you're in town and how you were once again quick to quell trouble, what are the chances of anyone starting any new ruckus?"

"Never can tell. There are still locked doors to be checked and—"

"I don't see any doors hanging ajar," Kate interrupted. Leaning into him, the warmth and softness of her breast pressing against his arm, she added, "Besides, you know how I get sometimes after you've been in a shooting. The way I start to worry about something happening to you and how I want to hold you for reassurance and not let go . . . You wouldn't want me to cause a scene right here in the middle of the street, would you?"

"Ain't no place I'd mind bein' held by you, Katie girl," Firestick said, gazing deeply into the depths of her dark eyes. "Now that you mention it, though, I reckon those locked doors can wait awhile . . ."

CHAPTER 8

Technically speaking, Kate was right. There was no more trouble in town that night.

But within the first hour past midnight, which was officially the next day, it became a different story.

As luck would have it, the change coincided almost to the minute with Firestick's emergence from the Mallory House Hotel. He'd just stepped out onto the front boardwalk, after gliding quietly through the dimly lighted lobby, when he thought he heard voices floating on the still night air. He paused, listening, but heard nothing more.

Stepping off the boardwalk and reaching to untie his horse's reins from the hitchrail, he heard the voices again, this time sharper and louder. Men's voices, that much was certain—raised in anger, from the sound of it. Firestick paused and again pricked his ears, trying to make out the words and trying to determine where they were coming from.

Then a single statement rang out loud and clear: "I say the whole thing is a crock, and I'm callin' you on it—you're a damned liar! There, I said it. What are you gonna do about it?"

There immediately followed the sounds of a struggle. Bodies slamming together, fists thudding heavily off meat and bone. More curses.

Without conscious thought, Firestick was suddenly in motion. Since the sounds of the fight seemed to be coming from somewhere in back of the Silver Spur Saloon, that was the direction he headed, propelling himself across the empty street in long, hurried strides.

He plunged into a dark alley that ran along the west side of the building. The escalating sounds of cursing and scraping feet and pounding fists were directly ahead of him now. The meager illumination from the nearest torch lamp out on the street reached only a few feet into the alley; after that, everything was inky blackness. Firestick slowed his pace out of caution, yet still managed to bump hard against a big wooden rain barrel and stumble a couple of times over clumps of trash on the alley floor. The slice of sky overhead was clear and shot with glittering stars, but their brightness did little to penetrate this gap between structures.

Firestick neared the end of the alley. The fight sounds were closer and clearer now. There appeared to be a faint pool of light—dispersed to almost a flicker by the jerking, shifting shadows of the combatants—back where the battle was taking place.

Stepping to the edge of this intermittent light, Firestick called out in a loud, commanding voice, "Alright, that's enough! Whatever this is about, it's time to call it quits! This is Marsh—"

The marshal's attempt to announce himself and bring things under control was cut short by a heavy, gloved fist flying in out of nowhere and crashing against the left side of his face. The unexpected blow sent Firestick staggering to one side, nearly knocking him off his feet. He managed to maintain his balance, however, and retaliated instinctively by lashing out with a backhanded swipe of his left fist that collided with the face of, presumably, whoever had struck him.

Following the sweep of his arm, Firestick turned and caught a hurried but somewhat clearer glimpse of what he had barged in on. He was on the edge of an open area directly behind the rear of the Silver Spur Saloon. Wooden crates and empty beer kegs were neatly stacked to either side of the establishment's back door. At least they *had* been neatly stacked; at the moment, several were knocked over and scattered across the ground.

In the midst of this, half a dozen men were thrashing around, shoving and kicking and swinging fists. It appeared that one in particular was the target for all the rest, drawing blows and angry threats from the others while at the same time dishing out almost as good as he was receiving. Though faces were an indistinguishable blur of shadow and motion, Firestick was able to make out this much by virtue of a coal oil lantern perched on a beer keg that miraculously hadn't been tipped over yet.

The one holdout from the concentrated scuffle involving all the others seemed to be the varmint who had sucker-punched the marshal. But as he went flailing backward from Firestick's backhand, he slammed inadvertently into the pack and jarred loose one of the men involved in the attempted gang beating. Muttered words were exchanged between the two, and suddenly Firestick was faced by a pair of belligerents stepping away from the pack.

It crossed the marshal's mind to try calling out again and identifying himself in order to halt these violent proceedings, but a couple of things stopped him. The pair advancing to engage him weren't giving him much time, and the sight of so many ganging up on only one rankled him something fierce. Plus, he hated sucker punchers in general and the side of his face was still stinging from the cheap shot he'd taken there.

So the pair rushing him was met almost eagerly by a flurry of fists and feet that stopped them in their tracks and sent them reeling from the punishing blows. Teeth bared in a snarl, Firestick waded ahead. The murky lighting and fluttering shadows caused him to miss some of his punches, but enough landed solidly to keep him swinging. He took some hits in return, but none of any consequence. For him, the exercise quickly turned from a matter of trying to break up the fight to one of *winning* it—beating down the attackers who'd been ganging up on the lone figure and then had so quickly and indiscriminately turned on him as well. At the moment, whatever the fight was initially about or who had started it didn't really matter to the former mountain man. Five-to-one odds—now five-to-two—made it wrong, and that was all there was to it.

These thoughts ran through Firestick's mind in a rush, and then all that was left was to concentrate on the fight and make sure he found a way to come out on top. While his initial surge against the pair confronting him had sent them backpedaling—partly catching them by surprise and partly due to his aggression—they weren't showing any signs of taking flight. Instead, they were regrouping and getting braced to come at him again.

Out of the corner of his eye, Firestick gained a fleeting awareness that the man struggling against the remaining three attackers was still holding his own, though he appeared to be flagging somewhat. If he went down, Firestick realized, since he'd taken the man's side and dealt himself into the thick of this, he stood the risk of himself possibly ending up facing five-to-one odds. That meant he couldn't afford to waste any time trimming those lopsided numbers, and the best place to start was with the two shadowy forms right in front of him.

The pair confronting him, their faces still blurred by the flicker of shadow and light, both had some size to them and seemed to know how to handle themselves in a scuffle. They were spreading apart and starting to edge forward, apparently meaning to close in on him in a pincer-like maneuver. If Firestick allowed the men to pounce on him simultaneously, he'd be in trouble.

So he didn't wait.

He suddenly lunged forward and slightly past them. As they turned inward to make frantic grabs, thinking he was trying to get away, he stopped short and veered to his left, catching the man on that side as he was reaching forward. It was Firestick who did the grabbing, seizing the man's wrist in his left hand and gripping just above the elbow with his right, pressuring his captive's arm the way it wasn't meant to bend so that when he pulled, the man was unable to resist. As he continued to pull, Firestick pivoted sharply and whirled the man, accelerating the momentum he'd begun with his own move. Completing his pivot, Firestick let go and sent the man crashing head-long into his pal who was rushing in from the opposite side.

The pair collided with a satisfying thud and loud grunts of air being driven from their lungs. They struggled for a moment to stay on their feet but ended up hitting the ground in a tangled heap. When they did, Firestick was on them in an instant. He jerked away the one who happened to land on top and hauled him upright just long enough to make out the whitish smear of his face so he could drive his right fist into it. The impact was solid, snapping the man's head back and then leaving it to flop loosely when it fell forward again, indicating he was likely out cold. Just to make sure, though, Firestick rapped him again, meaning to make certain the varmint was out of it and the odds would be cut by one.

The thing he failed to make sure of, however—and *should* have, as things turned out—was that the *hombre* who'd been on the bottom of the pile was sufficiently stunned by the collision with his friend. When the marshal turned back to him after knocking the first man senseless, he quickly found out that wasn't the case. The remaining half of the pair was waiting with a vengeance. As soon as Firestick leaned over to yank him up off the ground, the second man uncoiled his legs and thrust upward hard and fast under his own power, ramming his shoulder so deep into Firestick's stomach it felt like he was aiming to shove all the way to the spine.

Now it was Firestick who expelled a great, whooshing gust of air as the breath was knocked out of him and he was driven backward and down. The second man stayed with him all the way to the ground, landing astraddle of him and then immediately beginning to hammer punches down at his face. Firestick turned his head from side to side, trying to avoid as many of the blows as he could. At the same time he twisted his upper body, enabling him to free his right arm. He raised it to block some of the punches. They kept pounding down relentlessly at such a frantic rate that enough were still slipping through to keep him rattled. And all the while he was desperately trying to suck some air back into his lungs.

Realizing he had to do something quick, before his situation worsened even more, Firestick straightened the arm he'd been using mainly to block and stabbed it upward, fingers curled clawlike. The claw closed around a tightly knotted neckerchief his opponent was wearing. This gained Firestick some much-needed leverage, and he didn't hesitate to use it. With all his might, he twisted his whole body, rolling to his left and simultaneously using his grip on the neckerchief to drag the man on top of him over in the same motion.

Now the two were lying face-to-face, locked together, pummeling, grappling for advantage. As he'd toppled to the side, the man in the neckerchief had stopped throwing punches and instead clamped Firestick's wrist with both hands, trying to break his hold.

But Firestick's grip hadn't loosened, nor did it now. So, changing tactics, Neckerchief let go. With his left hand he threw a couple of close-in, largely ineffective punches. With the right, he reached to gouge at Firestick's eyes. But the marshal was ready for that. Finally releasing his own hold, he swung his forearm upward to block the attempted eye gouge and then slammed down hard with the edge of his fist, flattening Neckerchief's nose. This caused Neckerchief to throw his head back wildly and roll out of the clinch, howling in pain as blood gushed down over his lips and chin.

Firestick rolled away, too, in the opposite direction. He came to his knees, pressing his palms flat on the ground, at first just to stabilize himself and then meaning to use them to help push back to a standing position. His legs felt unsteady, not to mention the ringing in his head from the punches he'd taken and the way he was still gulping to try and regain some breath. But he had to make it back to his feet. To stay down would be an invitation to get stomped.

Pausing a moment longer, steadying himself before making the push to try and stand, Firestick's eyes swept the shadowy scene, searching to see what his opponent might be getting ready to try next and at the same time checking on how things stood with the knot of other combatants. The latter appeared basically unchanged, remaining a shifting, swaying, multi-legged mass of flailing arms and fists—indicating, at least, that the embattled loner at its core was somehow still upright and still fighting back. Firestick saw this as something to be admired and something that gave him further motivation to climb back to his feet and forge on with his own portion of the fight.

What he saw next, however—when his sweeping gaze landed once more on Neckerchief—was a development that suddenly and dramatically altered everything.

In his frantic roll after getting his nose smashed,

Neckerchief had bumped hard against the beer keg upon which the coal oil lantern was perched. The impact rocked the keg sufficiently to tip over the lantern, causing it to roll off and fall directly down onto the man's back. Glass shattered, coal oil gushed freely from the reservoir at the base of the lantern, and in a fraction of a second it was ignited by the still-burning wick and turned into a flowing, spreading pattern of flames!

CHAPTER 9

Realizing he was on fire, Neckerchief sprang to his feet with a terrified scream. The movement scattered shards of broken glass and dollops of burning oil in all directions. Whirling around in panic, slapping first over one shoulder and then the other in a frantic attempt to beat down the flames climbing up his back, he screamed again. "Fire! I'm on fire!"

The desperate flailing caused him to stagger and fall to one knee, then leap up and race blindly ahead until he slammed into the knot of still-brawling men who weren't yet aware of his plight.

Meanwhile, in his wake, several splotches of the burning oil he'd shed off his back had landed on some half-trampled grass to one side of the well-worn path leading out of the saloon's back door. The result was the same as so much crumpled, dry tinder being touched off. Even worse, some of the flames that burst to life began immediately licking at the toppled wooden crates bordering that side of the pathway.

Witnessing this, a rush of adrenaline coursed through Firestick and instantly made him forget about his unsteady legs and achingly emptied lungs. He shoved to his feet, yanking off his jacket as he did so, and rushed toward the man who was becoming more and more engulfed in fire. His screams began taking on the more strident edge of pain as well as panic.

Finally realizing what was going on, the pack of brawlers Neckerchief had run into splintered apart and stopped fighting with each other. A couple of them began slapping at their own smoldering clothing, the result of the flaming man bumping up against them.

"Fire! Fire! For God's sake, he's burning up!" somebody shouted.

"There's grass and crates on fire, too! Watch out or we'll all end up roasted!"

Making a flying leap, with his jacket extended before him in both hands, Firestick tackled the flaming man and rode him to the ground. Landing on top of him, he shoved down with the jacket in an attempt to smother the fire while at the same time jerking Neckerchief first to one side and then the other, rolling him in the dirt to try and grind out still more flames.

In the midst of this, he shouted blindly over his shoulder to the other men, "Beat down the rest of those fires! Use your jackets, throw dirt—don't let those flames spread!"

As if bewildered and frozen by fear, the former brawlers hesitated momentarily. But then, casting their differences aside, they broke into motion as one and attacked the burning grass and crates in the ways Firestick had ordered.

While they were doing this, Firestick succeeded in extinguishing the last of Neckerchief's burning clothes.

He pushed back and dropped onto his rump, pulling the smoldering, smoking ruins of his jacket off the man and casting them to one side. He coughed against the curls of smoke that wrapped around him. Neckerchief, lying very still on his stomach, with an even thicker layer of smoke hugging the length of him, alternately coughed and groaned.

Looking around, Firestick was relieved to see that the former brawlers were doing a good job of beating down the rest of the fire. And then, off to one side of the group, something else caught his eye. Craning his neck to look closer, he saw the thick-bodied shape of a man hurrying down the alley, brandishing one of the street lamp torches high above his head.

A moment later, the newcomer was close enough for Firestick to see—by the flickering light of the torch he held high—that it was none other than Moosejaw.

"What the hell's goin' on back here!?"

Firestick raised one hand to draw attention to himself. When he was sure Moosejaw recognized who it was, he said wearily, "You're just in time, Deputy. Swing up that street sweeper you got in your other paw"—he gestured toward the shotgun Moosejaw was carrying in addition to the torch—"and keep it aimed at this bunch of squirrel-brained rowdies who, among other things, made a stab at burnin' down our town. When they get done stompin' out the last of the fire, we're arrestin' the whole lot for disturbin' the peace, bein' drunk and disorderly, arson, resistin' an officer of the law, and bein' too damned dumb to go out in public . . . Maybe a few more things when I've had a little extra time to think on it."

"Is that you, Marshal? Marshal Firestick?" asked one

of the former brawlers, shown now in the illumination thrown by Moosejaw's torch to be a lean young wrangler barely into his twenties.

"You're damn right it is," growled Firestick.

"Shucks, Marshal, we never woulda carried on this way if we'd'a known you was back here tryin' to put a stop to it," the young man said earnestly. "And we sure never meant to do no harm by startin' no fire."

"Save your breath, Smitty," said one of the other men as he leaned over in order to kick some more dirt onto a still-smoldering patch of grass. "He's got his mind made up, no sense wheedlin' and whinin' about it."

Smitty protested, saying, "But we was stickin' up for him. That's what started—"

The other man cut him off. "I said to save your breath. Let it drop."

Firestick frowned. "Wait a minute. What do you mean, Smitty, by sayin' you were stickin' up for me?"

Before Smitty could answer, another man, still off on the edge of the shadows, spoke up. "He means me, Firestick." The man stepped closer into the light and revealed himself to be a bloodied, bedraggled Rip Ripley.

Firestick's eyebrows pinched together. "Rip? What the hell are you doin' here?"

"That's why I showed up," Moosejaw said. "After Miguel and Jesus reported he had wandered away from the bunkhouse instead of turnin' in for the night, I came lookin' for him . . . hopin' I could make it before something like this happened."

Ripley sighed. "This whole thing is my doin', Firestick. After you left and everybody turned in back at the ranch, I got me a cravin' for some store-bought whiskey.

That wine Miss Victoria served with her meal was real fine, but it just didn't do the trick. You understand. It just woke the wolf in me wantin' something meaner.

"So I found my way to town and this here saloon and took to feedin' the wolf. Feedin' it copious-like, if you know what I mean. These fellas was in there shootin' dice and they was kind enough to let me join in. When the bartender said he had to close up, we all came out back here and spread out a blanket on the ground to shoot some more. That's when the wolf in me took to feelin' kinda snarly. You know how I get sometimes. So I started layin' it on a mite thick with the tales I was spinnin'. I could see I was ranklin' these boys, and that inclined me to lay it on even thicker. I told 'em how I shot that griz out from under you this mornin' and how I could outshoot you any day of the week and twice on Sunday, if I was a mind to.

"There was some exception took to that. Oughta please you to know that folks around these parts—includin' these lads—think right kindly of you. Long story short, my layin' it on so thick and pokin' at you in the process finally resulted in the word 'liar' gettin' tossed out. Naturally, I couldn't let that go, even though I'd been a-purpose eggin' it on. So one thing quick-like led to another and the next thing you know . . . well, I guess you can take it from there."

When the old rascal finished talking, all eyes swung to Firestick for his reaction. By that point, voices were also drifting back to the alley from out in the street, indicating that all the shouting and smoke and fire from back here had rightfully succeeded in rousting some other townsfolk.

"Well?" said Moosejaw. "We still haulin' this whole bunch to the hoosegow?"

Firestick's gaze hung on Ripley for a moment before dropping down to where Neckerchief still lay moaning and then moving over to the scorched, smoking grass and busted-up wooden crates. When his eyes returned to his old friend from the high places, his expression and tone were equally flat as he said, "Nothing's changed. We're takin' 'em in just like I said, and on all the charges I said."

CHAPTER 10

"The one whose clothes caught on fire came out of it far luckier than he probably should have." Dr. Greaves's expression was very solemn as he made this announcement. "Thanks to your quick actions, Marshal," he continued, "he suffered only relatively minor burns to the back of his neck and to his hands. The shirt and undershirt he had on kept the heat from penetrating through to his back and torso before you smothered his flaming outer jacket."

"Which cost me a damn good jacket of my own," Firestick muttered sourly.

"If it's any consolation," Greaves said with a rueful smile, "one of the blows to his face—which also came courtesy of you, I understand—did a pretty thorough job of breaking his nose."

Firestick grunted. "That's something, I guess."

This exchange was taking place in the front office of the jail building, where Greaves had been summoned after the six brawlers were taken at the point of Moosejaw's shotgun and placed behind bars in the cell block at the rear. Greaves had only just emerged from back there, having provided necessary medical treatment to injuries resulting from the brawl.

"What about the others?" Firestick asked from where he sat on the edge of his desk. "Any of the rest of 'em come out with any serious damage?"

Greaves gave a faint shake of his head. "Nothing I'd call serious. Nothing you wouldn't expect from a violent confrontation like that. Some loosened teeth, a couple of split lips, plenty of facial and body bruises, maybe a cracked rib or two. Like I said, nothing serious. The one with the burns will require some additional treatment— further application of salve, dressing changes to keep the burn areas clean and make sure no infection sets in, et cetera. Oh, and a couple of the others will need to have some stitches removed in a few days. Otherwise, they should all heal up satisfactorily on their own."

Firestick grunted again. "They're all cowboys who wrangle for some honest, hardworkin' ranchers in the valley. For the sake of those ranchers, it's good none of the fools are gonna be laid up for the upcomin' spring roundup. Far as the squirrel-brained rowdies themselves, I for one can't say I'd mind if they was stove up a mite worse. Teach 'em a stronger lesson."

"They ain't all wranglers," spoke up Moosejaw, who was leaning against a post over near where a large coffee-pot gurgled on top of the office stove. "What about the older gent? The one in buckskins I stuck in a separate cell from the rest?"

He was referring, of course, to Ripley.

"Him," Greaves said, his eyebrows lifting. "Just a cursory check of that old rascal revealed to me that he's suffered numerous injuries in his time—everything from bullet and arrow wounds, to knife lacerations, to broken bones and Lord knows what else."

"Yeah. That ain't exactly news to some of us," Moosejaw allowed.

Greaves's eyebrows stayed elevated. "I understand that the brawl involved those other men, the cowboys, basically ganging up on this older gentleman. Is that correct?"

"All except for callin' the old cuss a 'gentleman,'" Firestick growled. "So how bad is he hurt?"

"That's the rather amazing thing," Greaves replied. "Other than those past injuries I mentioned, this fellow—whatever you want to call him—came out of tonight's incident the most unscathed of any of them. A few very minor nicks and bruises, a split knuckle . . . Hardly anything worth mentioning."

Moosejaw's mouth curved into a lopsided grin. Firestick almost followed suit, but then caught himself and adopted a frown instead. "Be that as it may, he was in the thick of it with the rest of 'em, and by his own admission, he's the one who set the pot of trouble to brewin'."

Also present in the room, seated in a chair hitched up in front of the marshal's desk, was Dan Coswick, owner proprietor of the Silver Spur Saloon. He'd been notified of the trouble that had taken place behind his establishment and subsequently found his way to the jail after learning those responsible had been brought here.

Coswick was a gruff-voiced man of proud Irish heritage—often called "Irish Dan" as a result, though in truth he'd never actually set foot on the emerald sod—who ran a clean, no-nonsense place. He was in his late forties, huskily built, with a lantern jaw and deep-set eyes that always seemed to have a hint of sadness about them. Atop his craggily handsome face sat an unruly thatch of hair, once fiery red but nowadays shot with a nearly equal amount of gray.

"Didn't I hear that *hombre* is an old friend from your mountain man days, Marshal?" Coswick asked.

"True enough. But that don't figure nohow into this," Firestick answered rather stiffly.

"His name's Ripley. He's an old friend of mine, too. And Beartooth's. Just for the record," said Moosejaw, glaring at Coswick.

The Irishman didn't miss that glare. "Hey, I wasn't implying anything. I was just saying, that's all."

"Well, while you ain't implyin' nothing," said Firestick, "keep in mind we know *all* those fellas back there behind bars. Some better than others, but they've all been around for a spell. I can't recall none of 'em causin' any trouble in town before but, like I already said, it don't make no difference. This time around they did what they done, and they got to make right by it. That means they'll stay behind bars until their fines are met . . . which'll probably fall to their ranch bosses until they can work out a payback to them."

"I'll send word out in the mornin' so somebody can come in to square things for them," said Moosejaw.

"That means you need to tally up any damage to your property, Irish, so I can figure that into the fines and get you squared away, too," Firestick told the saloon owner.

"I'll double-check in the morning when I can see better, but I already had a look before I came here," Coswick replied. "Luckily, it don't look like much harm was done. Only to those crates that caught fire and then got smashed in order to put them out. I trade them back to the freight company for a few cents each, so I don't think it's too big a deal."

Firestick shrugged. "Just let me know. Keep it fair and reasonable, but don't short yourself, neither."

Coswick rose from his chair. "I'll let you know in the morning." He started for the door, then paused and looked back. "I'm sure glad you showed up when you did, Marshal. If that fire had gotten out of control, I could be standing here a ruined man right now. And when I asked before about that old mountain man being a friend of yours, I wasn't meaning anything. Honest."

Firestick waved a hand dismissively. "Go on home and get some sleep. Don't worry about it."

When Coswick was gone, Firestick turned to Greaves and said, "Same goes for you, Doc. This makes twice you got called out after you tried to settle in for the evenin'. Sorry about that, but I appreciate you comin'."

Greaves shrugged. "Goes with the territory. Which you obviously know something about as well. You've had not only a very full evening but, from all reports, an entire day." He glanced at Moosejaw, adding, "Both of you."

"Like you said—goes with the territory," Firestick responded. "And, speakin' of fines and money and such, you need to figure up your bill for treatin' that bunch back in the cells. I'll turn it in to the town council and see to it you get paid in short order."

"I'd appreciate that. But," Greaves said, raising the medical bag he'd been holding and plopping it on the marshal's desk, "I can't complete figuring up my bill until I've finished providing my services. Meaning, I still haven't examined you. And from the reports of how you waded into that melee and by the look of you—no offense—you appear a little worse for wear."

"Aw, hell. It ain't necessary to go pokin' around on me," protested Firestick. "I just need some soap and water, a few hours' sleep, and a clean shirt when I wake up. I'll be fine as frog hair."

"Don't listen to him, Doc," said Moosejaw, stepping forward. "He's been mostly avoidin' usin' that left hand of his. I think it probably got burned some. And he's also favorin' his right side a bit, like his ribs are maybe stove in."

Firestick scowled fiercely at his big friend. "Who's the doctor around here? It sure ain't you! My ribs ain't stove in and my hand is maybe singed a little, but that's all. It's nothing, I tell you."

"Don't pay no attention to him, Doc," Moosejaw insisted. "He's ornery as a catamount with its tail caught in a trap and more stubborn than a whole herd of jackasses, but that don't make me wrong about what I saw. It'd be great if, while you're at it, you had a cure in that bag of yours for one or both of those other conditions I mentioned. But, even if you don't, don't let it keep you from checkin' out his ribs and that sore paw . . ."

Chapter 11

"Doggone you. You should have come back over to my place the first chance you got last night—we could have taken care of this right then."

Kate Mallory was administering this scolding while at the same time doing some additional ministering to Firestick. The latter was seated on a straight-back chair in the far corner of the jail office, where a washstand had been set up behind the stove and off one end of the cot that served as a bed for anyone acting as overnight jailer when there were prisoners in the cell block. Firestick was shirtless, his middle bound by a thick wrap applied by Dr. Greaves to secure the cracked rib the marshal had received when Neckerchief plowed into him the previous night. A burn on the palm of his left hand was also bandaged in gauze.

"Wasn't no sense botherin' more people than had already been rousted by those fools and their shenanigans," Firestick argued, his mouth twisted to one side as Kate leaned over him to sponge warm, sudsy water on the opposite side of his face, cleaning away streaks of soot and grime. "Ain't even no sense in you botherin' yourself this mornin' to come and fuss over me like this. I may be a little battered, but it don't mean I can't wash myself."

"Then why didn't you?" Kate countered. "You should have cleaned yourself up last night after rolling around in that alley and throwing yourself on top of a fire."

"Because I was too blamed tired. As soon as everybody cleared out and left me alone, I sacked out on that cot over there and slept just fine, dirt and all," Firestick said. "Besides, the doc cleaned all the important parts before he bandaged me up and lathered my paw with that stinkin' awful salve of his. Almost as much as bein' plumb tuckered out, I wanted to go to sleep to get away from the smell of that stuff."

"Well, it must have worn off. I don't smell anything now," said Kate.

"No, I don't, either. Thank God." Firestick gazed up at her as she continued to sponge him. He smiled. "But I can sure smell you. And it's a pure delight. How do you wake up and smell so fine right off first thing in the mornin'?"

"Maybe you should stick around sometime and find out," Kate said, a bit tartly.

Firestick's smile faltered. "Aw, come on, Katie gal. You know I'd like nothing better than that. But what would folks think if they saw me paradin' out of your rooms bright and early some mornin'?"

"They'd think—no, they'd *know*—the same damn thing they already know, Elwood. That we're two adults who have feelings for one another and sometimes those feelings mean we spend time together doing what other adults all over the world, including in this town, also do. I doubt they'd find it all that shocking, and even if they did, that would be too damn bad."

Firestick's smile returned. "Wow. First you called me Elwood and then you swore, twice, all in one roll. I'm glad you're about done scrubbin' me—you get any more worked up, you might start takin' the hide off."

"I *am* done scrubbing your ungrateful hide," Kate announced, unable to hold back a small smile of her own. She flipped the sponge into the washbasin, sloshing water on Firestick. "You can dry yourself. When you're done, I borrowed a clean shirt from Big Thomas you can put on. I suspected—and saw I was correct as soon as I got here—that your own clothes would be in pretty sorry shape."

"Appreciate the thought. Moosejaw is bringin' me some of my own clean duds when he comes in from the ranch this mornin'. Tell Thomas I'll bring his shirt back then."

"You can tell him yourself. Or are you in a hurry to get rid of me?"

Firestick shook his head. "Not at all. You got a hotel to run . . . I figured you'd need to get back to it."

"Thomas and Marilu know where I am, and they're perfectly capable of looking after things while I'm away. After they woke to the news of what happened last night," Kate explained, "it was Marilu who got me up to tell me about it and how you were still over here, that you'd stayed overnight with the prisoners."

"You know I don't leave men in the cell block without somebody servin' as jailer," Firestick said as he continued to towel himself dry. "I decided it was too late to roust Sam Duvall again, and besides, like I already said, I was bushed and didn't feel like ridin' all the way home to the ranch anyway."

Without putting it into words again, Kate gave him a look that was another reminder of what she'd said earlier about how he could have gone to her place. Firestick dodged the look by turning to put aside the towel and then picking up the clean shirt, courtesy of Thomas, that Kate had provided. As he was putting on the shirt, Kate reached for a coffee cup after checking to make sure there was still something in the pot on the stove.

Watching her pour some of the steaming black liquid into her cup, Firestick said, "You might want to be careful with that. It's been steepin' there all night; it's bound to be pretty stout."

"That's all right," Kate assured him. "I like good strong coffee in the morning, and I haven't had any yet." A moment later, after she'd blown a couple of cooling breaths across the top of the cup and then took a sip, her eyes bugged huge as she rolled them back in Firestick's direction. "Good Lord! This is far beyond merely 'stout' or 'strong'! You could scour the rust off iron with this stuff. It's a wonder it didn't eat through the bottom of the pot."

Firestick laughed. "I tried to warn you. Moosejaw made that last night. He piles on the coffee beans pretty generous to begin with and then, after settin' for as long as it did . . ."

Kate lifted the coffeepot lid and poured the contents of her cup back in, saying, "When is the doctor due back to

check on your hand and the condition of your prisoners?
I may need some sort of medicine to counter that sip I
took."

"He'll probably be around before too long, if you think
you can last for a while," Firestick said, still grinning. "In
the meantime, we've got a spare pot over here in a cabinet
somewhere. I'll let you make a fresh batch to suit your
tastes."

"Why bother with a second pot?" Kate asked. "Why
not just rinse this one out and reuse it?"

"Because it's still more than half full, and I don't want
to waste what's left," Firestick told her. "We'll have to
fetch those prisoners some breakfast when Moosejaw
gets here . . . I can serve 'em that coffee along with it."

"You'll do no such thing. It would be kinder just to
shoot them."

"Aw, come on. The coffee ain't *that* bad."

"Well, it's certainly not that good. Besides, I already
told Marilu to prepare some breakfasts for you and the
prisoners and have them sent over when they're ready. It
would be a shame to ruin good food by serving it with
this vile concoction. So take that pot and dump it somewhere, then refill it with fresh water and show me where
you keep your coffee beans so I can get a new pot going
and brewed in time for when the food arrives."

Seeing that Kate had her mind firmly made up—not
to mention also having the promise of breakfast on the
line—Firestick did as instructed. A short time later, with
a new pot of coffee starting to fill the office with its rich
aroma, he was settled behind his desk and Kate was
seated in a chair before him.

"So what kind of charges are you bringing against those men you've got in custody?" Kate asked, making conversation.

Firestick screwed his mouth up thoughtfully for a moment. Then: "Nothing too terrible serious, I don't reckon. Last night, when I was prime pissed off due to the fire and all, I threatened some pretty harsh stuff—to throw the book at 'em and then add on a few frills to boot. But now that I've cooled down some, I figure I ought to hold it to just disorderly conduct or some such. Time served, and a fine."

"They're all just working cowboys, right?"

"All but one. Three of 'em ride for Mick Plummer's Bar Six, two of 'em for Clint Harvey over at the High Point. Moosejaw's gonna send word out to the ranches for somebody to come in and go good for their bail. I expect they'll all be released by sundown."

Kate arched a pretty brow. "But what about the one who isn't a wrangler? I heard he's your old mountain man friend—the one you were telling me about last evening. Is that right?"

Firestick sighed. "Yeah, unfortunately, it is. Ain't that a fine howdy-do? One minute the old scoundrel is a guest out at our ranch, next minute he's a guest in my jail."

"But you aren't going to keep him locked up, are you?"

"I am unless he can make bail. And the chances of him being able to do that—especially after he's been shootin' dice—are about as slim as whiskers on an egg." Firestick's expression became tortured. "What choice do I have? I can't have one set of rules for other folks and a different set for somebody just because he happens to be a friend of mine, can I? Especially after he admitted in front of everybody how he stirred up the whole ruckus to start with. How would that look?"

Kate's brow furrowed in sympathy. "Well, if he's short of money to make his bail, could you maybe loan him some?"

"Now you sound like Moosejaw," Firestick said sourly. "That's all I heard from him last night—moanin' and groanin' about how lowdown it was for us to slap an old friend behind bars and then carryin' on about finaglin' the quickest way to get him out. When he shows up this mornin', I expect to hear more of the same. And if Beartooth didn't have to stay behind at the ranch waitin' for those horse buyers due in from over Marfa way, I'm pure certain he'd be comin' around to give me an earful, too."

Kate could see that the decision to keep an old friend in jail was deeply troubling to her man, but didn't quite know what to say to ease his anguish.

A moment later the issue was put aside by the arrival of two strangers who opened the office's front door and strode in.

One of the men was tall and lean, with a narrow face, high cheekbones, and squinty eyes. His companion was an inch or so shorter, stockier in build, with a round, rather plump-looking face and deceptively mild eyes. Both appeared to be around thirty and were dressed in rugged, top-quality trail clothes that had seen more than a few miles. Each man also wore the distinctive star-within-a-circle badge of a Texas Ranger.

"Pardon us for intruding," said the round-faced ranger. "But we're looking for a Marshal McQueen."

Firestick stood up behind his desk. "That would be me."

The taller ranger nodded. "My name's Arbry. Roy Arbry. My partner's Gene Rodgers. If you can spare us a few minutes, Marshal, we'd like to talk to you about a matter of some importance."

CHAPTER 12

Kate excused herself so the business with the two rangers could be discussed. As she was exiting, she told Firestick she would hold delivery of the breakfasts until their meeting was over.

After she was gone, Firestick motioned for his visitors to hitch up a couple of chairs and take seats in front of his desk. "You gents care for some fresh-made coffee before we get down to business?" he asked.

When both men answered in the affirmative, he poured each of them a cup and also one for himself. Then, settling once more behind his desk, he said, "I gotta tell you, it ain't every day our little town of Buffalo Peak rates a visit from the Texas Rangers. Reckon that's a good thing in some ways, but it's an honor to have you here anyway. Now, what's on your mind?"

"That's a mighty kind greeting," said Rodgers, "especially seeing how we intruded on your time with such a pretty lady, and from the sound of it, are also delaying your breakfast."

"Expect I don't have to tell either of you that law business don't always crop up at convenient times."

"Especially not law business related to murder," said Arbry, evidently the more direct and serious of the pair.

"Murder?" echoed Firestick, his eyebrows climbing several notches.

"That's the ugly word for it," said Arbry. "One of the worst kinds, too—the killing of a beautiful, innocent young woman."

Firestick planted his elbows on his desk and leaned forward. "Where and when did this happen? And what does it have to do with anybody in Buffalo Peak?"

"Katy Carruthers, that's the victim's name," said Rodgers, "was killed late last fall up in Pecos. Smack in the heart of Judge Walter Buchanon's territory."

"You know who Judge Buchanon is, don't you?" prodded Arbry.

"Reckon anybody who's spent more than a handful of minutes in West Texas has heard of Judge Buchanon," said Firestick.

"Yeah. Well, it happens that the judge has taken a special interest—a sort of personal one, you might even say—in this case," explained Arbry. "He wants the killer damn well caught, and he's made it known it will give him considerable delight to sentence the varmint to a speedy hanging."

"If there's any truth to his reputation, he ain't ever exactly reluctant to see a man dance at the end of a rope," Firestick remarked.

"He certainly won't be in this case," said Rodgers.

"Which puts a lot of pressure on Roy and me to get the culprit hauled before him."

"I can appreciate that," allowed Firestick. "But it comes back around to my question—how does you two showing up in Buffalo Peak figure into any of this?"

"Because only about a week ago," Arbry said, "the judge got a new lead. A tip that provided a name and description for the killer—along with information that he could be found here in your town."

Firestick scowled. "If that's the case, I want to know it as bad as anybody. We ain't hardly in the habit of harborin' murderers in these parts. What's the name?"

"Skinner. Malachi Skinner," said Arbry.

The words hit Firestick like a punch to the gut.

Malachi Skinner . . . *Beartooth!* What the hell!? How could such a thing be possible?

It *couldn't* be! That was the answer that rocketed back through Firestick's mind. Whatever these rangers knew— or thought they knew, because of something told to them—it was a terrible mistake. Firestick knew for a fact that Beartooth had killed in his time. Indians, to be sure, and white men, too. All varmints who'd had it coming. But he wasn't a murderer, and certainly not of an innocent young woman.

Firestick's mind continued to race. Calculating. Weighing options on how to handle this, what to say and not say. He couldn't outright lie, couldn't deny knowing Beartooth. Everybody in the valley knew otherwise. Five minutes of the rangers asking questions anywhere else would reveal that much.

Rodgers joined in, repeating the words. "Malachi Skinner. The name familiar to you, Marshal?"

"Yeah, I know it well," Firestick said, fighting to hold his voice steady. "Matter of fact, Skinner is a close personal friend of mine. Also happens to be one of the deputies workin' under me."

Rodgers and Arbry looked a little startled and then exchanged uncertain glances. Firestick didn't know what showed on his own face. None of the turmoil that was raging inside of him, he hoped.

He spoke again, still striving to keep his voice level. "As you can imagine, what you're claimin' comes as a surprise and quite a shock. I'll work with you to get this straightened out, but I can tell you right now you're barkin' up the wrong tree. There's been some kind of mistake. A bad one. Ain't no way Beartooth murdered a young woman or anybody else."

"Beartooth?" said Arbry.

"It's the name he more commonly goes by. Most folks know him as that, not so much by Skinner."

"So it's an alias, in other words."

Firestick was feeling frustrated and confused and very aware that it wouldn't take much for his temper to flare. Something, he cautioned himself, that wouldn't help the situation at all. Through gritted teeth, he said, "It's not the way you make it sound. It's a nickname, nothing more. For what it's worth, I got one, too. And so does my other deputy. Reasons why go back a ways. But last I knew, there's nothing illegal about such a thing."

"No, of course not," said Rodgers. "Look, Marshal, based on what you've told us, I can understand how unsettling this must be for you. But we're just here to do a job. Serve a warrant on a wanted man. If he's truly innocent, if it's all some kind of mistake like you believe, then the truth will all come out in a court of law."

"The court of Judge Walter Buchanon," Firestick grated. "Everybody's heard the stories about some of the rulings he's handed down, and in this case, you've as much as said he's already got his mind made up."

"In the first place," Rodgers replied, his own voice tightening, "you ought to know better than to believe everything you hear. In the second place, even if Judge Buchanon's rulings sometimes seem harsh or unorthodox, he's never been known to railroad an innocent man."

"And in the third place," Arbry added, "none of that makes a damn bit of difference to the here and now. Like my partner already explained, McQueen, we're here to serve a warrant on a wanted man and take him back to Pecos to face charges and a trial. That's the long and the short of it. So the only thing you need to concern yourself with is doing what you said you'd do—and that's to co-operate by telling us where we can find this Skinner or Beartooth or whatever the hell he's calling himself . . ."

CHAPTER 13

"So where are they now?" Moosejaw wanted to know.

"Over at the hotel, havin' some breakfast," Firestick answered. "They camped somewhere out of town overnight . . . rode in first thing this mornin'."

"They gonna be stayin' at the hotel?"

"They didn't say and I didn't ask. How long they stick around—if at all—I expect will depend on how they decide to proceed with what they came for. Way I see it, they only got two or three ways to go."

"And that would be?"

"If they buy the line I fed 'em about Beartooth bein' off on a horse-buyin' trip, they could either wait around for him to return or head out to try and catch up with him. Or they could split up, with one goin' after him and one stayin' behind in case he gives the first one the slip and returns here. Either way, once they've got some grub in 'em I don't figure on 'em doin' much of anything until they've asked some more questions around town to check out what I already told 'em."

Rodgers and Arbry, the two Texas Rangers, had left the jail about half an hour earlier. Once they were gone,

one of the waitresses from the hotel dining room had made good on Kate's promise to deliver breakfasts. Moosejaw had shown up shortly after that and Firestick had wasted no time filling him in on the visit by the rangers and their shocking allegations concerning Beartooth.

"That's why," he continued now, "I was careful not to tell 'em anything somebody could directly contradict me on. I didn't like lyin' to a couple of rangers at all, but I had to buy some time to think. To warn Beartooth and talk to him—see what he's got to say for himself."

Moosejaw frowned. "Say for himself? You don't mean you—"

"Hell no. Not for a minute," Firestick growled. "But stop and think . . . That gal got murdered last fall, up in Pecos. Well, it so happens Beartooth was up that way last fall, on a horse-buyin' trip. Remember? When he came back, he even said somethin' about some gal bein' murdered in town while he was there."

"That's right . . ." Moosejaw's voice was hushed, like he hated making the admission out loud.

"What I'm wonderin', what I want to run by Beartooth," Firestick said, "is if he maybe tangled with somebody over something while he was up that way. Don't matter what necessarily, just something that might have left the other party holdin' a grudge—a big enough one to possibly make 'em want to try and get even by throwin' Beartooth's name into the middle of a murder investigation."

Moosejaw's expression brightened some. "Hey. Yeah. Something like that could explain it, couldn't it?"

"It *could*. But all it is right now is a possibility, a straw I'm grabbin' at to try and come up with some kind of answer to this craziness. That's why I need to talk to Beartooth, to see if he's got any other ideas to offer, and in the meantime, to make sure he stays out at the ranch and out of sight while these rangers are sniffin' around."

"You goin' out to the ranch to see him then?"

"First chance I get, yeah. But I don't want to make it too sudden, so it might look suspicious to the rangers. They might decide to try and tag along."

"Don't you reckon they'll be makin' their way out to the ranch anyway? Rangers are like that—when they dig into a thing, they tend to dig in mighty thorough."

Firestick nodded. "I know. That's why I want to get to Beartooth first and then see to it he makes himself scarce until we have a chance to get something better figured out."

"You can't afford to hold off goin' out to the ranch for very long," Moosejaw said. "As soon as he gets done with those horse buyers that are due in, Beartooth will be high-tailin' it this way. He's plenty sore about us throwin' Rip in jail and is set on havin' words with you about it."

Firestick rolled his eyes. "Oh, that's just great. Any other time I'd be glad to butt heads with him over it. I was already expectin' it. But maybe—just maybe—he'll see that Rip bein' behind bars is a little less important right at the moment than his stubborn, sorry ass facin' a hang rope!"

"That's plain enough," said Moosejaw. Then, choosing his words cautiously, he added, "So what *are* you gonna do with Rip?"

Firestick gave him a look. "You ain't gonna start in again, are you?"

"No. But you can't just leave him behind bars to rot."

"He's only been in a handful of hours, for Crissakes. That's a far cry from rottin' away, and in case you forgot, those other fellas are right in there with him. You still expect me to show Rip special treatment, even before the rest of 'em are released?"

"No, I understand that much. Those others should be makin' bail before too long, by the way. I sent Jesus out early this mornin' to carry word to the High Point and Bar Six Ranches, lettin' 'em know where their missin' wranglers are. I expect somebody with money to pay the fines will be showin' up pretty soon."

"Good. I'd like to get at least that much cleared up. The sooner the better." Firestick made a sour face. "That still won't account for Rip, though. When I took breakfast back to all of 'em a little while ago, I asked him if he happened to have any money for bail. Not surprisin', he ain't got but a handful of coins he won throwin' dice last night. Wouldn't pay for the coal oil was spilled out of that lantern that got tipped over."

The office door opened at that point and Daisy Rawling came marching in. Daisy, unlikely though it seemed to some, was the town's blacksmith. Standing only five-two, she more than made up for her lack of height in spunk and outspokenness. She was chunky, not fat, and as strong as most men due to the work required by her trade. Nevertheless, a pug nose and luminous brown eyes that flashed beneath a cap of butter yellow curls worn functionally short made her quite pretty. This was certainly true in the eyes of Moosejaw, for she had become the love of the towering deputy's life.

"There you are, you big lug!" she announced, pinning

him with those big brown eyes. "How the hell much longer do you figure on avoidin' me, I'd like to know?"

Moosejaw appeared taken aback. "What are you talkin' about? I ain't been avoidin' you."

"What would you call it?" Daisy demanded. "I haven't seen you in three whole days and now here you are, finally back in town, and you still ain't come around."

"I was fixin' to, just as soon as I got the chance. Honest I was," Moosejaw told her. "Jeez, you think I ain't been missin' you, too? But things been poppin' all around and keepin' me awful busy. You know we was out on that griz hunt. And no sooner was that critter handled than we had to haul in a handful of rowdies and slap 'em behind bars, and if that wasn't enough, this mornin' we just got word—"

He stopped himself short and immediately cast a glance over at Firestick.

But Daisy was focused on something else he'd said. "Did you really? Did you really miss me, too?"

"Of course I did. Something fierce," Moosejaw assured her.

Firestick spoke up. "You bet he did, gal. It was practically all he talked about the night we had to camp out in order to keep that griz cornered. Like to drove me and Beartooth loco, the way he was pinin' for you . . . Didn't I mention that to you yesterday?"

When Firestick had come into town alone the previous day to check on things and report the success of the bear hunt, he'd spoken with Daisy to assure her that Moosejaw was okay but wasn't able to make it in because he'd stayed behind to field-dress and skin the grizzly they'd killed.

"No, you never," Daisy replied in a half-dreamy voice.

The words were spoken to Firestick but her gaze was locked on Moosejaw. "But it's grand to hear it now—to hear how my man pined so bad for me while he was away." She came forward and put her hands on Moosejaw's chest. He placed his hands gently over hers.

Looking on, Firestick weighed the wisdom of telling Daisy about the plight facing Beartooth—the thing Moosejaw had restrained himself from blurting out a minute ago. The thing was, Daisy was a talker who came in contact with a lot of people in the course of a given day, and her words and opinions tended to be rather blunt and not always filtered very carefully through any hint of discretion. It was this habit Firestick was weighing, same as what had caused Moosejaw to hold back on what he said. But after considering it, Firestick decided what the hell. She was bound to hear the news anyway, might as well get it over with and save Moosejaw an ear-chewing for not having told her when he had the chance.

"Go ahead and tell her the rest of it," he said to his big deputy. "Tell her about the latest tangle of trouble that just landed in our laps."

CHAPTER 14

At eleven o'clock, Firestick was ready to ride out to the Double M. By then, a number of things had taken place. For one, he calculated enough time had passed since the rangers' visit to his office so that his departure shouldn't look suspicious. For another, representatives from both the Bar 6 and the High Point Ranches had shown up to pay the fines necessary to get their wranglers released from jail. That continued to leave Ripley behind bars, but Moosejaw would still be in town to look after him while the marshal was away.

With the wranglers gone from the cell block, Firestick had taken the opportunity before leaving to sit and talk privately with Ripley for a spell. Despite holding a hard line in front of everybody else, keeping his old friend locked up had been weighing heavy on Firestick's conscience all along.

When he explained this to Ripley, how he was wrestling with the dilemma of having to stick to the rules and laws that were in place even though he personally wanted to give a pal a break, the old mountain man was wholly understanding.

"Hell's bells, ol' hoss, I see how it has to work. You got a standin' in this town that you and the boys have well earned. You can't piss it away just 'cause an old rapscallion like me comes along and spits tobaccy juice in the buttermilk. I wouldn't want you to do no different— I wouldn't *let* you treat me favorite-like."

Ripley paused to lean back against the cell wall and lace his fingers over his belly. His mouth twisting ruefully, he went on, "Truth to tell—though I ain't necessarily proud to say it—I been spendin' more than my share of time in jails, ever since I came down out of the mountains. Seems I'm havin' a hard time fittin' back in to so-called civilization. I try, I really do. I go along for a spell and I do pretty good. But then it seems like just a matter of time before I find myself in some situation or other where that ol' wolf gets to snarlin' inside of me and all of a sudden there's a ruckus busted out and I'm smack in the middle of it."

"Yeah, life down in the flatlands is a heap different than up in the mountain camps and at Rendezvous gatherings," Firestick conceded. "I guess me, Moosejaw, and Beartooth had it some easier with each other to sort of lean on to help keep ourselves in check when one of us felt the wolf snarlin'. It helped, too, to settle in this valley when it was still young and boisterous and our own rugged ways could be put to use tamin' owlhoots who'd got in the habit of runnin' roughshod through these parts . . . Which don't mean our bark is all the way rubbed smooth, but like you said a minute ago, I guess we've mostly got a pretty good standin' around here."

"Indeed you do, and I credit y'all for it," said Ripley. Then, eyeing Firestick through the bars, he added, "Come to think on it, maybe, once I get out of this pickle I wasted no time plunkin' myself in, I could stick around for a spell and maybe you fellas could tolerate me sort of leanin' on you until I get some of my own bark smoothed a mite."

"We'd be more than willin'," Firestick told him. "Now that those other fellas are took care of, give me a chance to come up with some reasonable way for you to earn your bail and then we'll talk more about it. In the meantime, though, I got another matter—what you'd call a real pressin' one—I've got to look into first."

And then, after a slight hesitation, Firestick had gone ahead and told him about the situation concerning the two Texas Rangers and the warrant they had for taking Beartooth into custody.

"Thunderation!" Ripley had exclaimed. "You damn betcha you got a more pressin' matter to look to. So get after it! No hurry about me, I got no big discomfort here. I've surely endured worse conditions and can make it just fine here until you get something figured out. But look after gettin' things squared away for Beartooth before anything else."

That was how Firestick had left things when he rode out of town. Weather-wise, the day was shaping up to be another fine one, spring coming on strong. The sky was clear and the grasses on the rolling hills were greening up nicely under a high, bright sun.

At first, Firestick didn't ride directly toward the Double M. He aimed due west for a ways, checking his back trail to make sure neither the rangers nor anyone else was following him. Only when he was satisfied nobody was taking any interest in him or the way he was headed did he angle his route to the north toward home.

Before leaving town, Firestick had loosely monitored the activity of the rangers after they left the hotel dining room. As he'd suspected, they made their way around to various establishments. The saloons, the livery, the barber. Exactly what their line of questioning was, he didn't know. He doubted they told the people they talked to that they were looking for Beartooth in connection with a murder. If that had been their approach, Firestick was pretty certain it would have generated enough excitement for word to have circled back to him almost immediately.

More likely, the marshal guessed, they were saying something along the lines of looking to talk with Beartooth as part of an unspecified matter, and while Beartooth had gotten crossways with a few people in the valley over the years, Firestick couldn't think of any with sufficient grounds to bad-mouth him to any serious degree. Certainly nothing near as serious as the accusations the rangers already had against him.

As he rode, Firestick again thought how much he regretted misleading Arbry and Rodgers. But at least until he had a chance to talk to Beartooth, he didn't see how he could have done any different. A murder charge carried a lot of impact. Especially when it had strings reaching clear the hell up to Pecos and fell under the jurisdiction of the infamously unpredictable Judge Walter Buchanon.

Firestick also had some reservations about how many people he'd let in on his subterfuge. Moosejaw, of course, but that was no problem. Nor was Kate, whom he had briefed the first chance he got. Daisy was of a bit more concern, but there was greater risk of her letting something slip inadvertently if she *didn't* know the full story than if she did. Besides, she was Moosejaw's lady and part of their inner circle; she deserved to be in the know.

In telling Ripley about the charges against Beartooth, however, Firestick hadn't revealed how he'd played false with the rangers. In fact, he'd made the same claim to the old mountain man—that something had come up suddenly and Beartooth would be gone for a few days on a horse-buying trip. He wasn't exactly sure why he'd felt ill at ease saying anything more. But quite a few years had passed since Ripley's path and theirs had crossed. A man, even a onetime solid friend, can change during a long absence.

So, with Ripley's reappearance being too recent for Firestick to have gotten a good feel for any changes that might have occurred with him, it simply hadn't seemed like a necessary risk to take. What was more, when Ripley had been talking about how hard he was finding it to fit back into "civilization," something had flicked across a corner of Firestick's mind—something trying to trigger a memory that seemed like it was somehow connected. But then it flicked elusively away again and was gone, though still factoring in to the mildly ill-at-ease feeling that kept him from speaking too freely to his old friend.

CHAPTER 15

Beartooth scowled fiercely above a pair of balled fists planted on the tabletop before him. "You really expect me to just lay low and go into hidin'? To stay penned up in my own house like a . . . a turkey waitin' its turn to be plucked and carved for Thanksgiving dinner?"

"It's not like it'd be forever," Firestick told him. "Only till those rangers quit sniffin' around here close-like. Time enough to give me a chance to try and maybe find some other angle on this whole murder business."

"What angle are you likely to find from the outside lookin' in?" Beartooth protested. "Why wouldn't it be better for me to face up to these rangers and go straight at 'em with the truth? Tell 'em they got the wrong man. Try to convince 'em—"

Firestick cut him off. "That's the whole problem. These rangers ain't interested in hearin' the truth or bein' convinced of nothing. That ain't their job. The only thing they're here to do is haul you back up to Pecos and plop you in front of that wild-assed Judge Walter Buchanon. The fella who, by their own words, is takin' this whole thing mighty personal and sounds already strong inclined toward you as the guilty culprit."

"Well, he's inclined damned wrong then."

"You know that, and I know that," agreed Firestick. "But it seems to me our best chance to get him *un*-inclined is to not plant you in front of him until we've got something that'll give him cause to lean in another direction. He gets a crack at you before then, he's liable to do something sudden and rash that could go so far as to leave you dancin' at the end of a rope."

"That cannot be! It is unthinkable," exclaimed Victoria Kingsley.

The three of them were seated at the dining room table in the main house at the Double M Ranch. Firestick had arrived just as the horse buyers from Marfa were riding off, leading the string of six fine geldings they had just purchased. At the sight of Firestick—with his morning's business now completed and the buyers departing—Beartooth had wasted no time cutting loose with his angry complaints about the treatment of Rip Ripley. Firestick had let him unload his first salvo of cussing and snorting, allowing him to get some of it off his chest, then had backed him down by announcing he had something a hell of a lot more important to discuss and leading the way into the house to get to it. He'd summoned Victoria to sit with them in order for her to also hear what needed to be said.

There was no way to ease into it, especially not with Beartooth fuming about the Ripley matter, so Firestick had laid it out quick and direct. After the initial reaction of stunned silence brought on by relating what the rangers were in town for, he'd gone on to reveal how he'd misled them and his subsequent idea for Beartooth to lay low until they could figure out some way to counter the warrant and allegations against him.

Victoria had sat quietly, listening, showing little reaction except for an understandably anxious expression, until the mention of a hang rope.

"Surely," she said now, on the heels of her sudden outburst, "a barrister—what you call an attorney or lawyer here in the States—has to be considered. A professional representative to stand before this judge you find so worrisome in order to ensure a fair and proper hearing is conducted. Doesn't that sound preferable to lying and dodging the authorities and thereby piling unquestionably illegal acts on top of those that are so far only outrageous accusations?"

Victoria was a chestnut-haired, blue-eyed beauty just past the thirty mark, full-figured and normally soft-spoken. Born to modest wealth and privilege in England, an independent streak and the urgings of an adventurous female cousin had brought her to America and specifically the American West in her early twenties. When the cousin had subsequently died of a sudden illness, Victoria was left on her own. Her pride and her desire to remain in America—knowing that any request for aid from back home would include a requirement for her to return there—had forced her to survive by taking various clerical and cleaning jobs until she'd applied for the cook and housekeeper duties at the Double M.

Somewhat surprisingly, she and her more refined ways had blended quite well with the household of rugged former mountain men, and before long the big, rambling house had taken on the added warmth of a real home. The attraction between her and Beartooth had evolved slowly but steadily until finally blossoming into the acknowledged romance that others had seen building right along. Though she continued to cook and clean for all, it seemed just a matter of time before she and Beartooth would branch off as a couple on their own.

At the moment, her half-admonishing statement on how she felt the problem facing Beartooth should be handled left the two men seated at the table with her a bit lost for words. They exchanged uncertain glances, as if silently questioning who should respond.

Finally, after clearing his throat in order to gain an added second to gather his thoughts, it was Firestick who spoke.

"That's some real fine thinkin', Miss Victoria," he said. "And I hope you believe that my skirtin' around the truth with those rangers and recommendin' we do some more of the same—dodgin' 'em, as you put it—ain't a choice that comes easy for me. I ain't comfortable with it at all."

"Then why pursue it further? What about my idea of hiring a lawyer?" Victoria asked.

Firestick's forehead puckered deeply. "See, now there's the thing. I ain't very comfortable with that notion, neither. Under different circumstances and if the *right* lawyer was somewhere to be had, that could be a good way to go. But you know right well we don't have no lawyers in Buffalo Peak. And if we was to hire one from up Pecos way . . . Well, I'm afraid we'd only find one who was used to operatin' under the heavy thumb of Judge Buchanon, and that would make him about as good as nothing. Maybe less."

"What about hiring one from somewhere else? Presidio, or Fort Davis—somebody outside the influence of this judge?"

"That might work if we had more time. But the only way I know to gain time would mean keepin' Beartooth out of the reach of those rangers, just like I been sayin'." Firestick shook his head. "We drop this dodgin' and misleadin' business and let them take him into custody, they'll ride him up to Pecos pronto-like. And one of the things Buchanon is best known for is holdin' particularly speedy trials. He'd have Beartooth tried and sentenced before a lawyer from Presidio ever got halfway there."

Victoria's nostrils flared. "Who is this bloody judge? You make him sound more like some medieval tyrant than a duly appointed law official."

"The way I heard it," Beartooth said, "Buchanon was appointed justice of the peace—duly or otherwise—back when Pecos was a wide-open hellhole. His rulings were hard and sudden, not always popular and not always by the book. Other than his interpretation of it, that is. He works out of a single lawbook, they say, a twenty-year-old copy of Texas statutes. Story goes that whenever they revise those statutes and send him a new copy from Austin, he uses it for kindlin' in his fireplace."

"You almost sound like you have a certain amount of admiration for the man," Victoria noted.

"Long as I ain't on the receivin' end of his rulings," Beartooth said with a crooked grin, "I guess I sort of am. He's an original. Independent. You can't help but sort of admire that in a fella. And from most reports, since he started layin' down the law in Pecos it's turned into a fairly decent place. You got to give him credit for that, too. The Texas Rangers—and I'm talkin' more than just the two now on my tail—seem to be okay with him. They keep haulin' in fugitives to stand trial before him. In addition, he keeps an enforcer of his own close at hand—a bailiff he calls him, though most would say just a hired gun—to guard him and keep order in his court. Even with that, under his robe, when he bothers to wear one, he packs a brace of Colt .45s that he's been known more than once to draw and start blastin' with on his own."

Victoria sighed and gave a weary shake of her head. "I don't understand how that kind of behavior can be acceptable for a man in his position."

"Like I said, most folks see Pecos as bein' a lot better off since he's settled in." Beartooth spread his hands. "That goes a long way toward puttin' up with the rougher side of him."

"Another thing you might want to remember," spoke up Firestick, "is how it wasn't that long ago that Buffalo Peak was a mighty rowdy place, too. Then the townsfolk decided to rope in three old mountain men—who were about as far from bona fide lawmen as you can get—and convince 'em to slap on badges and set to reinin' in some of that rowdiness. We don't always toe the line real tight, either, when it comes to followin' the letter of the law. Hell, we don't have even a twenty-year-old lawbook to go by . . . But sort of like up in Pecos, I'd still like to think we've managed to make things considerable better around here."

Victoria flushed. "Of course you have. That's a fact no one could dispute, and I never meant to imply otherwise." She paused, her flush fading and then her pretty face taking on a dubious expression. "Although habits like running the Texas Rangers in circles, not to mention aiding and abetting a wanted fugitive, *might* rate as cause for concern in the eyes of those less discerning."

CHAPTER 16

Long shadows of late afternoon were starting to be cast by the buildings lining Trail Street when Firestick rode back into town. He reined his horse to a stop in front of the jail building and paused to scan down the length of the street, the way he always did when first arriving in town.

Everything looked quiet, which was to be expected for this time of day. Most customers had already completed their shopping or other business and would probably be at home, planning supper. Most of the stores and shops, except for the saloons and the livery and a couple others, would be closing up before too much longer.

In addition to the standard things he looked for on such occasions, Firestick was also searching for some sign of the two rangers, wondering if they were still roaming around and asking questions. He wondered, too, if they had gone ahead and checked into the hotel, indicating that they were going to hang around awhile longer. Before he left town again, he'd do some closer checking on what they'd been up to while he'd been away. But as of right now he saw no indication of them.

That stopped being the case less than a minute later, as soon as he'd tied his horse at the hitchrail and stepped into the jail office. Moosejaw was seated behind the marshal's desk, looking decidedly uncomfortable. Occupying straight-back chairs hitched up before him were Arbry and Rodgers. Each held a cup of coffee in one hand, their hats removed and balanced on a knee.

All eyes turned to Firestick as he came through the door.

"Evening, Marshal," said Rodgers with an amiable smile. "We were hoping you'd show up before too long."

Moosejaw started to rise but Firestick motioned for him to stay put. He walked to the end of the desk and then turned so he was facing all three men.

"I believe I explained earlier," he said to the rangers, "that my friends and I have a small horse ranch not too far outside of town. We split our time between that and our peacekeepin' duties here in town, almost always with at least one of us at one place or the other. Since my other deputy is away on business, there were some matters out at the ranch I needed to attend to this afternoon."

Rodgers nodded. "Understood. Since we're going to be staying in town for another day or so, we could have caught up with you in the morning. But in the meantime, Deputy Hendricks . . . or Moosejaw, as he says he prefers . . . has been very considerate and cooperative."

"No reason not to be," Moosejaw said.

"As a matter of fact," spoke up Arbry, "all the folks around town have been considerate and cooperative. Speaks well of the little community you run here."

Firestick rocked his head back. "Can't say I ever looked

at it that way—that me and my deputies 'run' anything around here. Exceptin' for our ranch, that is."

"Boils down to the same thing. The point being, everybody we've talked to has been real obliging." Arbry's gaze became very direct. "One thing that seemed a little curious, though, was the fact that, to a person, not one of them knew anything about Deputy Skinner being away from town on a horse-buying trip."

"Don't see where that's so surprisin'," Firestick replied calmly. "For starters, we discuss ranch business mainly amongst those of us involved with the Double M. We don't go out of our way to announce it all over town. And since Beartooth only left such a short time ago—at first light this morning—there simply hasn't been much time for word to spread about it."

Arbry stiffened in his chair. Frowning, he said, "Wait a minute. Are you saying Skinner rode out just a few hours before we showed up earlier? Why didn't you tell us that to begin with?"

Firestick blinked innocently. "I guess I never thought of it that way. Time-wise, I mean. You sort of walloped me with your news about wantin' him for murder. And then, when you asked where to find him, well, sayin' he was on his way to Sierra Blanca and nowhere around seemed like the main thing you needed to know."

"Damn it, man," Arbry seethed. "Don't you see that if he was so close—gone for such a short amount of time—we'd have had the chance to take out after him right then and there and likely have him in custody this very minute?"

"I'll allow I could have been more clear on the time factor," Firestick said. "But even if I had, I'm thinkin' you catchin' up with Beartooth and takin' him into custody could've proven to be two different matters. Might be I did you a big favor, mister, by not bein' as clear as you're wishin'."

Arbry glared and looked ready to fire back with a heated response, but Rodgers stopped him. "Alright, everybody just take it easy. What's done is done."

"What's done is that we missed a helluva good chance to have ridden out and nabbed our man practically as soon as we got here," Arbry insisted. "And I'm not convinced it was a simple oversight."

Now heat flared in Firestick's eyes. "You're entitled to think what you want, mister. But you make any more noise that sounds like you might be callin' me a liar, this cooperatin' business is gonna sail out the window in a damn big hurry."

"Knock it off, the both of you!" Rodgers said, his voice sharper this time. "Going at each other's throats isn't going to gain anybody anything."

There followed several seconds of tense quiet.

Until Rodgers spoke again, saying, "We had two reasons for stopping by to talk with you again, Marshal. First off, during none of our inquiries today regarding your Mr. Beartooth did we reveal to anyone outside of you that a charge of murder was involved."

"I appreciate that," said Firestick. "I figured as much, otherwise I would have been hearin' the buzz it was bound to stir up."

"However, we have now decided against continuing down that path." Rodgers reached into a vest pocket and withdrew a folded sheet of paper, which he held out to Firestick. "First thing in the morning, we aim to start posting these around town."

Firestick shook open the paper and studied it intently. His expression tightened, grew even more somber. In the center of the page was a clear and reasonably accurate drawing of Beartooth. Bold lettering above the image read: **WANTED FOR MURDER: MALACHI SKINNER.** Below, in equally bold though somewhat smaller print was: **REWARD AVAILABLE FOR INFORMATION LEADING TO CAPTURE. CONTACT NEAREST TEXAS RANGER HEADQUARTERS OR WIRE JUDGE WALTER BUCHANON—PECOS, TEXAS.**

Firestick lowered the paper and silently handed it to Moosejaw.

"All our talking today failed to gain us much," said Arbry. "Sometimes a little added jolt is needed to jog folks' memories or loosen their tongues."

Firestick said, "I can't say I like the idea of this, but I reckon it's your call. What I will say, though, is that I think it's kinda shortsighted."

"How so?" Rodgers asked.

"Seems to me that stickin' with showin' some patience would be a sight smarter. The way it stands now, there's every reason for Beartooth to come back here after he's finished his horse dealin'. Then you might have a chance to take him into custody and get this mess ironed out proper. You circulate those dodgers, though, word of it is bound to reach him and he'll damn certain steer clear of here—leastways clear enough so's you'll never know it if he does come around."

"The Texas Rangers have a pretty good record of nabbing *hombres* who think they're smart enough to steer clear of us," said Arbry.

Firestick's broad shoulders rose and fell in a shrug. "Like I said, it's your call to make."

"Besides, starting tomorrow, that wanted dodger"—Rodgers jabbed a finger, indicating the paper Moosejaw now held—"is being circulated all through West Texas. Even if we held off putting it up here in Buffalo Peak, Skinner will soon be finding out wherever he goes that he's a wanted man. If he knows what's best for him, he'd be better off just turning himself in."

"Good luck with that," Moosejaw grunted.

Seeing that any further discussion of the wanted dodgers was destined to only go in circles, Firestick said, "You said you came by for two reasons. So what else is on your mind?"

Rodgers leaned back in his chair. "We'd like to come out to your spread tomorrow and have a look around."

This didn't come as a surprise to Firestick; he'd been expecting it and would have only been surprised if the rangers *hadn't* taken that measure. But he was feeling just ornery enough not to agree too easily.

"You're not convinced he ain't there?"

"Oh no, we fully expect not to find him there," said Arbry, the half smirk on his face driving home the double meaning to his words—"not to find him there" as opposed to "he ain't there."

Not wanting to let his partner and the marshal start in on another pissing contest, Rodgers said, "What we want to do is have a look at his room, check through his clothes and personal items, see if we might be able to spot something in the way of evidence that might tie him in to the incident up in Pecos."

"Hell no! That's goin' too far," Moosejaw declared, slamming the broad, beefy palm of one hand down on the desktop. "I don't care if you *are* Texas Rangers, you don't have the right to root through a man's stuff that way."

Rodgers looked over at Firestick. "I thought we were promised cooperation at the start of this."

"You're not bound by that, Firestick," Moosejaw protested. "It ain't a right thing to allow, and you know it."

Meeting his big pal's half-pained, half-angry look was hard for Firestick to do. "Unfortunately," he said in a tight voice, "they have the means to go past what we're in favor of allowin' . . . Not much doubt that a wire to Judge Buchanon up in Pecos would result in a court-ordered search warrant bein' sent back pronto-like." He turned his eyes to Rodgers. "Ain't that about how it'd work?"

"If you force the matter, yeah, that's how we'd have to do it."

Moosejaw muttered a curse under his breath.

Firestick sighed. "Alright. Come ahead, then. Ain't a demand I probably can hold you to, but I'd be obliged if I could be present while you're doin' your search."

"We'd have no problem with that," said Rodgers. He stood up; Arbry followed suit. Both men reached to set their emptied coffee cups on the desk, then placed their hats on their heads and turned toward the door. "We'll be out there first thing in the morning."

CHAPTER 17

"I used to like Texas Rangers. Had a ton of respect for 'em." Moosejaw had vacated the desk and was pacing back and forth in front of the stove, his balled fists shoved straight down at his sides. "But these two are quick makin' me think otherwise."

"Aw, you can't hardly condemn the whole outfit. Hell, even the pair we're dealin' with—though I'll admit that squint-eyed Arbry has a way of purely gettin' under my skin—probably ain't all bad. If we wasn't so tight with Beartooth, none of this would be rubbin' against our grain so hard." Firestick paused with the cup of coffee he'd just poured raised partway to his mouth, and scowled through the steam rising up from it. "It's that blasted judge up in Pecos worryin' me the most. Arbry and Rodgers are just doin' a job, lookin' to haul in a wanted man they got papers on. But Buchanon, he's showin' every sign of bein' almighty eager to take it from there. He hurries through the rest of it and is too quick to slam down a guilty verdict, Beartooth could be lookin' at some mighty serious consequences."

Moosejaw stopped pacing and regarded Firestick closely. "But we ain't gonna let that happen—are we?"

Firestick carried his coffee over behind his desk and sank down in the chair. "We're damn sure gonna do everything we can to stand in the way."

"But how, exactly? You got something in mind besides just keepin' Beartooth hid out?"

"That's an important step for gainin' us time so's we *can* get something more figured out. Beartooth ain't likin' the part about stayin' cooped up and out of sight very much, but I finally got him talked into it. At least for the time being."

"What did he say about havin' tangled with somebody up in Pecos when he was there—somebody who might be holdin' enough of a grudge to make trouble for him by claimin' he's the murderer?"

Firestick took a drink of his coffee. "Matter of a fact, he did get in a bit of a tussle while he was up there. Don't really sound like nothing too serious, but you never can tell about something like that. He got into a card game one night and hit a sweet winnin' streak. Some pipsqueak on the losin' end started makin' noises, hintin' that Beartooth was pullin' something shady. When Beartooth told him to trot out some proof or shut his piehole, the joint's bouncer stuck his nose in and Beartooth ended up flattenin' him."

"That's all?" Moosejaw made a face.

"Well, there was a little more to it. The bouncer, it turned out, was a pretty rugged character and something of a bully who had a reputation for bein' one of the toughest *hombres* in town. When Beartooth left him layin' on the floor in the sawdust, there were those in the saloon who made a pretty big deal out of it. Wantin' to buy Beartooth drinks and such for showin' the bully up."

"So it would have been a pretty hard bruise to the bouncer's pride. That what you're thinkin'?"

Firestick shrugged. "It's a possibility. Maybe just a slim one, but it ain't like we got a lot of fatter ones to sort through. Then there's the pipsqueak, too—the fella who lost money and thought he'd been cheated. Maybe one of 'em or maybe the two of 'em together, each feelin' put out in his own way, decided on a way to get some pay-back."

"I guess you're right—it's a possibility. But it's kind of a stretch and still don't sound like much. Beartooth couldn't think of nothing else?"

"Nope. Nothing along the lines of what I was lookin' for, anyway. I did find out a little more, though—not that it means much one way or the other—as far as what Beartooth remembers about that gal who got murdered. She was a showgirl, a dancer, in town as part of a big travelin' show that played in Pecos for a three-day engagement. The Orleans Queen Travelin' Extravaganza, it was, starrin' Miss Della Devane."

Moosejaw perked up. "Hey. I've heard of her."

"Ain't likely to find too many red-blooded fellas out here in the West who haven't. And that includes Judge Walter Buchanon," said Firestick. "Beartooth remembers how the whole town was in a tizzy not only about the show comin' in the first place but about how the judge had written letters and hounded and wheedled to make it happen. He bragged about bein' a close personal friend of Miss Devane's, knowin' her somehow from back in the past. His claims had a fair amount of doubters until she actually showed up."

A thoughtful frown gripped Moosejaw's face. "And then havin' one of the girls from her show get killed while in the judge's town . . . Reckon that explains why he's so intent on runnin' the culprit down."

"Might explain it," Firestick allowed. "But it don't make it right. Not if he's more intent on runnin' down *a* culprit than he is in makin' sure he's got the right one."

"Which brings us right back around to how we can make sure Beartooth don't get roped in for something he didn't do."

Firestick said, "I've got a couple of ideas about that. One of 'em is a notion that came from Miss Victoria—to hire a lawyer to defend Beartooth in case he does end up in court. A lawyer who ain't gonna shrivel up if he has to go before Judge Buchanon."

"Where you gonna find somebody like that?"

"Ain't sure yet. I'm gonna talk to Kate about it when I go see her in a little while. Her, Frank Moorehouse, maybe Jason Trugood . . . they've all dealt with lawyers, at least for business matters. I'm hopin' one of them can recommend somebody we can get in touch with."

"You realize it would still be best to keep Beartooth *out* of court. Right?"

"Of course I do. If Buchanon already has his mind made up and takes a notion to start throwin' his weight around from the bench, I don't know if the slickest lawyer anywhere could have any luck holdin' him in check. But it's a plan worth havin' in our pocket, anyway. When those damn wanted dodgers start makin' the rounds, it's gonna be harder and harder to keep Beartooth from gettin' nabbed by somebody."

Moosejaw didn't look ready to pin much hope on a lawyer. He said, "You mentioned a couple ideas—what else you got in mind?"

"I'm thinkin' it's comin' time for me to take a ride up Pecos way," Firestick said. "For starters, even though it don't sound like it amounted to much, I want to have a talk with that bouncer Beartooth tangled with. Hardy is his name. And the pipsqueak sore loser, too, if I can find him. Beartooth don't recall hearin' a name for him."

"You figure you can go up there and start nosin' around without drawin' the attention of the judge?"

"Nope. I'd welcome the chance to have a chin-wag with that old rascal and try to get my own idea of what he's up to. And I'd damn sure like to find out more about whoever it was who stepped forward after all this time and named Beartooth as that gal's murderer."

Moosejaw gave a low whistle. "Whew. Sounds like a mighty ambitious undertakin'."

"Don't see where it can hurt," Firestick said firmly. "Even if I don't do nothing more than stir up a hornet's nest, sometimes it can be mighty interestin' to see which hornet comes lookin' to sting first and hardest."

"Interestin' . . . Yeah, that's sure to be one word for it."

"With Kate scoutin' a lawyer for us, you lookin' after things around town, and Beartooth layin' low out at the ranch, I ought to have the time I need to ride up and see if I can have any luck."

"What kind of luck, though? That's the risk I'm worried about."

"You got any better ideas? We can't just sit back and

wait for the real murderer to all of a sudden step forward and clear up the whole mess."

Moosejaw sighed. "No, I reckon not. You know what you're doin'. And you know you can count on me to hold up my end, whatever it is you need me to do."

"Remember," Firestick told him, "you can bring in Sam Duvall to help keep watch over the jail as long as we've got Rip in here, or in case you have to put anybody else behind bars."

"Hey, that reminds me!" Moosejaw's expression suddenly brightened. "I think I came up with an acceptable way for Rip to make bail so we can release him."

"Let's hear it."

"Actually, it was Daisy who set things rollin'," Moosejaw explained. "She was disappointed to hear I had no claim on that griz we killed. She's always wanted a bearskin rug, she said, and was hopin' I'd be able to present her with one. So that's when it hit me. Since we let Rip lay claim to that griz hide, I wondered what it would take for him to part with it? When I asked him, he grinned and said the cost of his fine. Which ain't unreasonable, by the way. And when I ran that by Daisy, she jumped at it and said she'd be glad to pay the price."

Moosejaw paused and spread his hands. "So what do you think? Is it okay to arrange it that way? Rip's gettin' no special treatment, nobody's doin' him no improper favors . . . all he's doin' is sellin' something and usin' the money to cover his fine and make bail. You see any problem with that?"

"Not a one," Firestick said. "Go right ahead with it. It may not measure up to clearin' Beartooth of murder, but it's still a concern it'd be a relief to get out of the way."

"I'll have Daisy bring the money over first thing in the mornin', and we can take care of everything then."

Firestick waved a hand. "I think we can trust Daisy without waitin'. Might as well go ahead and release Rip right now. Turn him loose and get the jail cell stink scrubbed off him while I'm over at Kate's. Then we'll haul him back out to the ranch and see if we can't do a better job of keepin' him corralled there this time, at least until we get an idea that wolf inside him ain't ready to start snarlin' again . . . Be good for Beartooth to see him turned loose, too—give him one less thing to bellyache about."

CHAPTER 18

Darkness was settling over the land as Firestick and Ripley rode back to the Double M.

Moosejaw remained in town, planning to take supper at Daisy's and then spend the evening with her in order to soothe her feelings about them being apart too much of the time lately. He had said he also would stick around to cover making late rounds before calling it a night.

Firestick rode quietly for much of the way to the ranch, but thoughts were grinding steadily in his mind. One of the things he thought about and needed to address was setting the record straight with Ripley as far as Beartooth *not* being away on a horse-buying trip.

"I fed that line to the rangers in order to buy some time for tryin' to get to the truth of this cockeyed murder accusation," he explained. "I figured the more folks I left out of the lie, the better off it would be for 'em in case the whole thing blew up in my face. But now—since you're gonna be runnin' smack into Beartooth as soon as we get to the ranch—you're gonna be sucked into it regardless."

"Hell's fire, ol' hoss, that don't concern me none,"

Ripley replied. "Comes to dealin' with law dogs on the hunt—'ceptin' for you fellas, now that you're badge toters—I've found it works out best to know nothin' about nothin'. So if it should come to pass that one of those rangers tries to pump something outta me, that's all he's gonna get—nothin'."

At the main house, everybody was surprised and delighted to see Ripley back again. Especially Beartooth, who managed to get in a few choice words about "stubborn, wrong-headed cusses puttin' old friends behind bars" before finally dropping the matter for good. The unexpected presence of Ripley was offset by the equally unexpected absence of Moosejaw, so the meal Victoria had planned was plenty sufficient to feed everyone and typically delicious to boot.

When supper was done, Miguel and Jesus—who always took their breakfast and evening meals in the main house—excused themselves to go finish some final chores before retiring to their bunkhouse for the night. While Victoria was clearing the table, Firestick, Beartooth, and Ripley repaired to the den, where they sank back in overstuffed cowhide easy chairs and broke out cigars to go with their post-meal brandy. Like in the dining room and indeed through the rest of the house, the curtains were drawn tightly closed over the windows to make sure no one on the outside could look in and spot Beartooth's presence.

"I got to hand it to you, fellas," said Ripley, lounging back in his chair with flames crackling softly in the huge stone fireplace just past his shoulder, "it's heartenin' the way y'all have made such a fine life for yourselves here. Downright inspirin' is what it is, showin' an old mountain goat like me how a body can come down to the flatlands and change their ways to fit in and make a go of it."

"You can't hardly say that about me and my present circumstances," replied Beartooth. "Not unless you're inspired to have one of these damn things"—he pulled from his shirt pocket the wanted dodger Firestick had brought from town and gave it a frustrated shake—"issued against you."

"That's a rough spot in the road, sure enough," Ripley allowed. "But it ain't like you did anything to earn the dad-blasted thing."

"It's for sure he didn't do anything to earn that drawin' they slapped under his name," Firestick said, aiming to lighten the mood a bit at the end of a long, frustrating day. "It's way too handsome to be an accurate match."

"I'll go along with it not bein' all the way accurate," Beartooth conceded. Then added, "In order for it to be a better match, it'd have to be a lot *more* handsome."

Firestick smiled faintly, glad to see his old friend was still able to maintain some of his sense of humor.

But Ripley, of all people, seemed more deeply troubled by the situation than was his typical nature. Even through supper, though he'd been pleasant and participated in the exchanges of conversation, he'd been far from his usual gregarious self.

"Ain't nothing funny about a wanted dodger," he said now, somberly. "It's the kind of thing sticks with a body for a long time and can keep croppin' up and causin' trouble even when you figure it's long forgot."

Beartooth tossed back a swallow of his brandy. "Well, I ain't gonna have no trouble forgettin' this rascal, I'll guarantee you that—just as soon as Firestick and that lawyer fella Kate is gettin' hold of have convinced crazy old Judge Buchanon he's barkin' up the wrong tree." He turned his head to regard Firestick. "Kate was pretty sure she'd be able to hire that dude from Presidio, right?"

Firestick nodded. "She'll get a wire off first thing in the mornin'. Hopes to hear something back before the end of the day."

"I reckon puttin' your trust in one of these lawyer fellas is another part of this so-called civilization I don't yet understand," Ripley said, frowning. "I guess you gotta play all the angles. But me, I'll be puttin' more faith in Firestick doin' some good up in Pecos."

"I got hope for that, too," Beartooth admitted. He paused, a corner of his mouth quirking upward before adding, "Long as he don't piss off that judge so bad he ends up with his own ugly mug on a wanted dodger."

They talked awhile longer, until Ripley drained the last of his brandy and announced that he was ready to head out to the bunkhouse.

"No complaints on my former accommodations, mind you," he said, "but the pure fact is that jail cell cot was only a mite softer than a slab of Rocky Mountain granite. And it's important I catch a good night's sleep tonight on account of I gotta get to work early in the mornin' on finishin' up that bearskin for Miss Daisy. I don't want to disappoint her, because, if I did, then I might have to answer to that big ol' Moosejaw."

Firestick chuckled. "If you disappoint Daisy, she won't be slow to let you know it her ownself. And in that case, I think you'd find dealin' with her enough of a handful without worryin' about Moosejaw."

"Good to know. I appreciate the warnin'," Ripley said with a wry grin.

After they showed their guest out, Firestick and Beartooth stood for a moment in the parlor, Beartooth having stayed well back from the doorway while it was open. Once it was closed behind Ripley, he glanced at Firestick and said, "You think the ol' scoundrel will stay put for the night? Or do we have to worry about his wolf startin' to snarl again?"

"I think he'll behave for at least tonight," Firestick answered. "But, just in case, I told Miguel to sleep light and let me know if there's any sign of him actin' restless."

Beartooth nodded. "Sounds good. Reckon what I'll do now is mosey into the kitchen and help Victoria finish cleanin' and puttin' away the supper dishes. Since I'm sentenced to be housebound for a while and can't do any good on the outside, the least I can do is pitch in and help a little around here."

"Just don't get to likin' it so much I find you wearin' an apron when I get back from Pecos," Firestick advised.

"I'll try to hold myself back." Beartooth started toward the kitchen but then paused after a step and a half and turned to look back at Firestick. "About that trip to Pecos . . . and the way you're stickin' your neck out with those Texas Rangers . . . Reckon I don't have to say it, but I hope you know how obliged I—"

"Save it," Firestick cut him off. "You, me, and Moosejaw have stuck our necks out for one another too many times and over too many years to start worryin' about keepin' track of who's obliged to who. What you're better off worryin' about right now is gettin' into that kitchen in time to give Miss Victoria a reason to be obliged for the helpin' hand."

Once he was alone, Firestick returned to the den where he'd left a half-smoked cigar burning in a stone ashtray and an inch or so of brandy still in the glass he'd been drinking from. He picked up both and strolled slowly around the big room, the thoughts starting to grind inside his head again.

Damn, what a mess this was turning into. What—and who—could be behind it? There wasn't a morsel of doubt in Firestick's mind that Beartooth was innocent of murdering a young woman. Even if, through some tangled series of events, he'd been present or somehow involved in such a killing, he wouldn't be lying about it now—not to Firestick and Moosejaw. So why and how did someone seize on his name and description to shove in front of Judge Buchanon, and why was the judge so willing to completely accept the accusation?

The answers, Firestick was convinced, lay up in Pecos. But what, realistically, were his chances of uncovering them when he went up there? Especially with the clock ticking and the odds growing steadily more unfavorable against Beartooth being able to stay out of the clutches of the Texas Rangers?

Not that any of that affected to any degree the amount of effort Firestick would put into working on the problem, but the weight of it pressing down on him sure as hell wasn't getting any lighter.

And then there was that elusively nagging feeling that kept poking at him—a side matter it seemed, though perhaps somehow connected—regarding Rip Ripley. The sense of something that put him ever so slightly on edge, ill at ease. What the hell was that all about? He'd felt it again tonight when Ripley had commented so sternly and unnecessarily on there being "nothing funny" about a wanted dodger and how one could "stick with a body for a long time." He hadn't elaborated, and it would have been rude to press, but the message seemed to be that Ripley had had some past experience with wanted dodgers . . . Possibly one with his *own* picture on it? If so—

Firestick's thoughts were suddenly interrupted by a loud pounding on the front door from out in the other room. Tossing down what was left of his drink and flipping the stub of the cigar into the fireplace, he strode out to see what sounded so urgent.

When he pulled open the door, Ripley and Miguel were standing there, crowded up close. Both wore anxious expressions.

"Begging your pardon, *patrón*," said Miguel. "But there is something going on you must know."

"What do you mean? Something like what?" asked Firestick.

"Gunshots, for one," Ripley answered. "Quite a ways in the distance, back toward town. A body can just barely make out hearin' 'em—but they're there, and whoever it is is blazin' away mighty serious-like."

CHAPTER 19

Beartooth appeared, hurrying from the direction of the kitchen. A dish towel was slung over one shoulder. Victoria followed behind him, drying her hands on her apron and wearing a curious, mildly concerned expression.

"What's all the dang commotion?" Beartooth said.

"Ain't sure yet. Trouble maybe—gunshots soundin' off toward town," Firestick replied as he passed between Miguel and Ripley and stepped outside.

Beartooth followed him out and the four men stood still and quiet for a moment, listening. Sure enough, the distant, unmistakable crackle of gunfire floated on the night air.

"I heard 'em when I was headed for the bunkhouse," Ripley reported. "I called Miguel out to make sure my ears wasn't playin' tricks."

"Ain't a trick. Those are gunshots, sure enough," said Firestick.

"Something more, *patrón*," Miguel said. "When Jesus and I left the house after supper, the moon was just rising and up on that first big hill to the west I saw it catch the glint of something. When I looked closer, I saw it no more so I did not think to worry . . . But now I am wondering if maybe someone was up there."

Firestick frowned. "Someone watching the house, you mean?"

"Those damn rangers!" Beartooth was quick to say. "That glint of light Miguel saw could have been a reflection off a spyglass or maybe even a gun barrel."

"Could have been a lot of things. Or nothing. Let's not be too hasty to jump to conclusions," Firestick cautioned. "I hardly think the rangers were up there drawin' a bead on you or anybody else down here. And as far as those shots we're hearin' now havin' anything to do with them . . ."

"Whatever they got to do with," Ripley said, "we oughta check 'em out, oughtn't we?"

"Of course," said Firestick. "Miguel, start saddlin' some horses while I get my guns."

"Jesus is already doing that, *patrón*."

"Saddle one for me, too," said Beartooth.

Headed back into the house, Firestick paused just long enough to shoot him a look over his shoulder. "I don't think that's a good idea. On the chance this *does* have something to do with those rangers, it could be a trick to draw you out where they can catch sight of you. We've got enough—Rip, Miguel, and me—to handle this without you takin' the chance."

"The hell with that!" Beartooth exclaimed. "I'll go along with stayin' hid away durin' the day, even though I don't like it. But it's nighttime and dark now. Ain't nobody gonna see me unless I damn well want 'em to."

"I don't have time to argue with you," said Firestick, reaching for his gunbelt hanging on a peg beside the door. "Even if you want to risk your own neck, there's also Victoria to think of. Could be this is some kind of diversion to draw all of us away from the house and corrals . . . But you go right ahead and do whatever your bullheaded ass insists on!"

A handful of minutes later, Firestick, Ripley, and Miguel were mounted and riding hard toward the west, the direction of the shooting.

A nearly full moon had risen high in a cloudless sky also filled with a heavy sprinkling of stars. Once their eyes had adjusted away from the lantern light spilling out of the house and other buildings back at the ranch, the riders found their way illuminated well enough by the silver-blue glow from on high.

Firestick set an aggressive pace, urging his horse full out over the rolling, mostly treeless grassland that surrounded the Double M. At first, the pounding of the horses' hooves drowned out the distant sound of the gunfire up ahead. But then, as they drew closer, the reports grew louder and more jarring.

At the base of a long, gradual slope, with the crack of guns seeming to come from just beyond the crest, Firestick reined up and signaled Ripley and Miguel to do the same. They drew up even with him on either side. The horses were breathing heavily, their exhalations creating clouds of fine mist in the cooling night air.

On the other side of the rise, the gunfire continued in somewhat sporadic bursts. The reports indicated both rifles and handguns at work. Some curses were also being hurled, but the exact words were indistinct.

"We'll dismount and walk our horses up to near the

top. Then I'll belly the rest of the way to where I can get a look at what the situation is," Firestick said in a whisper. "We don't want to expose ourselves until we got some idea what's what."

"Whoever's over there," said Ripley as he swung down from his saddle, "I make it two handguns and three or four rifles they're poppin' away with. You be mighty careful pokin' your head up for a look-see."

"Don't worry. I didn't come out here to get a fresh part in my hair."

The three men started up the incline, leading their horses. When they were within a few yards of the top, Firestick stopped again. He removed his hat and hung it on the saddle horn, and handed his horse's reins to Miguel. Then he continued on, dropping into a crouch for a short ways, then to his knees, and then onto his belly.

He'd left his rifle in its saddle scabbard, but now he drew the Colt .44 from the holster on his hip and held it gripped in his right hand as he pulled himself forward on his elbows. On the crest of the hill, he pushed in behind a cluster of foot-high prairie grass and used the barrel of the Colt to spread apart the tough, stubborn growth so he could peer through the gap and down the hill.

It didn't take long to appraise the situation.

Five men were involved. Two were in the middle of a broad, shallow draw. They were hunkered in tight against the belly of a fallen horse—evidently shot out from under one of them. Pinning them there were three riflemen positioned at higher points on spurs of rocky ground to either side of the trapped pair. The apparent ambushers were using Winchester or Henry repeaters, and the men down low were returning fire with only pistols.

Considering heights and angles, Firestick judged the handgunners were positioned to hold out for a while. The dead horse provided adequate cover as long as they didn't foolishly expose themselves. What it likely would come down to, the marshal reckoned, was a matter of ammunition. Assuming there had been a saddle rifle on the horse, the animal appeared to have fallen in such a way that the long gun was now pinned underneath its carcass. The pistols had sufficient range for the exchange currently taking place, but depending on how many cartridges the two men were carrying in their shell belts or maybe in a saddlebag they could get to, that would determine how long they could keep their attackers at bay.

There was also the possibility that one or more of the ambushers might move to a new position so they'd be able to fire down on the pair from an angle where the dead horse wouldn't provide enough cover.

However, scanning the high ground that bracketed the draw, Firestick couldn't see any other spots with a concentration of sawtooth rock fringe like that which was now shielding the riflemen. Otherwise, the crests of the slopes close by were merely rounded and grassy, with a few stands of coarse brush.

So yeah, somebody could move and gain a better angle on the targets, Firestick thought, but doing so would mean a considerably greater degree of exposure. A little more patience would be the smarter play, he told himself . . . even though the notion of attributing smarts to a pack of stinkin' lowdown ambushers tended to stick in his craw.

So that left only two questions: Was he assessing the situation correctly? And how should he and the others go about breaking it up?

As far as the accuracy of his assessment, Firestick didn't see how it could be any other way. The men in the high rocks obviously had been lying in wait and then opened up on the two below. No matter who the targets were or what they might have done, Firestick couldn't think of any acceptable reason for trying to cut a man down that way. He had a particular dislike for back shooters and ambushers.

How he, Ripley, and Miguel should—

Firestick had been ready to push away from the grassy clump and slide back down to the two companions waiting for him when one of the riflemen suddenly called out during a lull in the gunfire, "Arbry, you stubborn son of a bitch, you just couldn't leave it be, could you? You had to keep rootin' us out and closin' in on us wherever we tried to go. No matter it's been three damn years since we caused anybody any trouble! Well, now you've rooted one time too many and I hope you're happy to know that all it's gonna get you and your partner is bein' left for buzzard bait out here in the middle of nowhere!"

Firestick didn't recognize the voice of the man calling out. But he certainly had no trouble recognizing the name of who he was addressing—Roy Arbry, one of the Texas Rangers. That still left plenty of unanswered questions, but it removed any doubt about who was on the right side of things down there.

"Nobody's buzzard bait yet, you pack of yellow bushwhackers," Arbry shouted back. "But step out and show yourselves like men—then we'll damn well see who ends up getting their bones picked clean!"

The response to the ranger's challenge was a new flurry of rifle fire pouring down at the trapped men. While this lead-storm was being unleashed, Firestick shoved away from the clump of high grass and scrambled back down the way he'd come.

Reaching out to help stop the marshal's downward slide, Ripley said in a harsh whisper, "Did I hear right? Ain't Arbry the name of one of them rangers who's makin' it hot for Beartooth?"

"It is for a fact," Firestick confirmed. "Him and his partner Rodgers are pinned down in a draw on the other side of this hill. Three ambushers were layin' for 'em from high up on either side. So far they only got a horse for their trouble. That's what the rangers are usin' for cover, and it's doin' 'em okay for right now, but they still ain't in good shape."

"To hell with 'em, then," growled Ripley. "Leave 'em to deal with their own trouble. Maybe whoever's layin' for 'em will finish the job and take care of gettin' 'em off Beartooth's back."

Firestick scowled at him. "You know I can't do that. Apart from sidin' with a pack of stinkin' ambushers, I got a badge of my own to think of. Besides, gettin' rid of these two rangers wouldn't end Beartooth's problem. Not by a long shot. It would just cause more of 'em to come swarmin' with Judge Buchanon proddin' 'em on all the harder."

The gunfire from the other side of the hill tapered off again but still kept popping sporadically.

Ripley heaved a sigh. "Alright. How do you want to play this then?"

Firestick regarded him for a long moment, looking him hard in the eyes, like he was trying to make up his mind about something. Then: "We leave the horses here. You and Miguel circle wide on foot and come up behind the ambushers on either side. There's two to the left—you take them, Rip. That leaves one on the right for you, Miguel . . . I'll give you time to get in place. Then I'm goin' back up and over this rise. I'll holler down on 'em, makin' sure to identify myself so the rangers will know not to fire on me. Doubt it'll matter much to the others, though." Firestick paused, cutting his gaze back and forth between Ripley and Miguel. "Means I'll be lookin' to you two to stop 'em from plantin' any lead in me. Take 'em alive if you can—but do what you have to."

Chapter 20

The waiting while he gave Ripley and Miguel the chance to get in position didn't come easy for Firestick. He had too much time to think, to wonder about his choice to freeze Beartooth out of this, knowing how it had to be eating his old friend up inside to be left behind.

But finding out Arbry and Rodgers were in the thick of this ambush, whatever the exact circumstances, meant it had been the right thing to do—the right thing as far as keeping Beartooth away from the rangers. Still, he knew that wouldn't necessarily make being left out any easier for Beartooth to swallow.

And something more to wonder about was Ripley's suggestion to simply turn their backs on whatever fate Arbry and Rodgers would meet at the hands of the riflemen pouring lead at them. Life in the mountains could be brutal at times and force a cold-blooded practicality on certain choices.

But this didn't come anywhere close to that. Arbry and Rodgers might be an unwelcome intrusion, but the fact remained they were just two men trying to enforce the law, doing their jobs as assigned. Leaving somebody in their position to the mercy of night-skulking ambushers was simply not in Firestick's makeup, even if he'd never pinned on a badge of his own. And to hear an old pal like Ripley suggest something so contrary was unsettling, to say the least.

Ripley and Miguel ought to be in place by now, Firestick decided as he put aside his brooding. No time for any more wondering or fretting. Only time for going ahead with the plan, setting it in motion.

Pulling his Yellowboy from its saddle scabbard, he jacked a round into the chamber, then turned and once more clambered the remaining yards to the top of the slope. He paused there a moment, standing this time near the same clump of high grass. Everything below also looked the same, still clear, still bathed in moon- and starlight.

Again, the shooting had gone into a lull. Taking advantage of this, Firestick stepped forward to announce himself. Thrusting the Yellowboy skyward and triggering a round to make sure he drew plenty of attention, he called down, "Everybody hold your fire! This is Marshal McQueen from the town of Buffalo Peak! You're on my land and you're surrounded by half a dozen of my men deputized to take action against anybody who continues shootin'!"

The scene froze for a long, tense moment. Firestick kept his eyes on the two rangers because he could see them more plainly. The ambushers up behind the fringes of rock were only visible when they leaned out to shoot.

But they were up there alright . . . he could *feel* their gazes and gun muzzles swinging in his direction, locking on the skylined target he made.

"You're a liar and a fool, mister," replied the same voice that had called out to Arbry a few minutes ago. "And you just stuck your stupid damn nose in somebody else's business for the last time!"

Firestick tensed, flexing his knees slightly, getting ready to dive and roll in the event any lead got sent his way. Judging by the tone of the man who'd called out, he expected just such an attempt. The tone was that of someone who'd come primed for killing and was hell-bent on settling for nothing less—and so, too, would likely be the attitude of his companions.

Despite that, Firestick gave it one more try. "It'd be a bad mistake on your part to think I'm bluffin'! Throw down your guns and—"

His words were cut short by the crack of rifle fire coming at the same time muzzle flashes appeared amid the rock fringes flanking the draw. Firestick threw himself to the ground and rolled back away from the grassy crest. Bullets whined through the air above him, and a burst of dirt and dust kicked up mere inches from where his feet had been planted only a second earlier.

Firestick dug in his heels to stop his downward slide and then immediately scrambled several feet to one side of where he'd vacated the top of the rise. Dropping once more onto his belly, with the Yellowboy cradled across his forearms, he squirmed upward again, aiming to take up a new position.

All the while, the gunfire from down in the draw was raging furiously again, initiated by the shots that had driven him back and then intensified by more guns joining in. At one point he heard someone—he thought it sounded like Ripley—holler, "Give up your guns, you ain't got no chance!" But that didn't cause the shooting to slow down one bit.

Only as Firestick cautiously poked his head above the rim of his hill did the gunfire abruptly sputter and start to come to a halt. As his gaze scanned the scene below one more time, he saw that the two rangers still appeared okay, still hunkered tight against the dead horse, guns raised so that one was aiming to each side, covering the rock fringes where the ambushers had been firing from. Sweeping his gaze to those higher places, the marshal saw no signs of movement or activity and indeed all of the shooting seemed to have ceased.

To the left, from Firestick's viewpoint, where two of the ambushers had been grouped close together, a weak, quavering voice called out, "No more . . . please . . . ! Don't shoot no more. I'm hit bad, I'm out of it . . ."

From somewhere above that wail, the booming voice of Ripley responded, "What about your partner?"

"He's dead," came the answer.

"Alright. Throw your rifles out over the edge of those rocks—both of 'em," Ripley ordered. "Then ease yourself into sight with both hands raised high."

The rifles were heaved out and sent clattering down from the rocks. After that came the weak voice again. "I . . . I don't think I can move . . . I told you I'm hit bad."

"Well, you better figure out a way to move to some kind of position where I can see you with your hands held wide away from your body," Ripley said. "Elsewise you'll lay there and bleed out a-fore I stick my neck into what might be some kind of trap."

"No trap, mister . . . Honest. Please . . . I'm in a bad way here."

Firestick raised himself a little higher and called over to the other side of the draw. "Miguel! Are you alright? What's your situation there?"

"I am fine, *patrón*," came the answer. "The *hombre* in the rocks below me—he is no longer a threat to anyone."

Firestick stood up. "You heard that, Rip. You stay put, keep your man covered. I'm comin' over."

On the floor of the draw, Arbry and Rodgers also shoved to their feet.

"We're coming up, too," Arbry said. "If at all possible, we need to keep that polecat alive long enough to answer some questions."

Just under fifteen minutes later, the wounded man—who had been identified as one Merle Eckert—opened and closed his mouth in an effort to say something more but only managed to emit a soft, gurgling gasp before his mouth sagged open permanently and he was dead.

"Yup. He's done for," announced Ripley in a dispassionate tone as he rocked back on his heels beside the body.

Firestick, Arbry, Rodgers, and Miguel were also gathered close around the dead man. They were still up on a flat, gravelly patch of ground behind the fringe of sawtooth rocks on the slope to one side of the draw.

After converging cautiously on Eckert, they'd found he was up to no tricks but they also discovered he was too badly hurt to try and move. A .54-caliber punch from Ripley's Sharps had torn a hole as big as a fist through his torso.

They'd hurriedly built a small fire for better lighting

and for an attempted cauterization and had worked to save him where he lay. In the short time this bought them, they'd learned the bare bones of what was behind the ambush attempt by him and his companions, but that was all.

"What a waste," said Roy Arbry bitterly. "Him and his brother were wanted for only one lousy bank robbery. They got less than five hundred dollars and no one was harmed in the act. That was nearly three years ago. If they'd been caught—or, better yet, turned themselves in—they likely would have been sentenced to just a handful of years. All this time on the run, thanks mostly to Jackson, when instead they could have been on the brink of being free men with a clean slate."

The background on the three ambushers, as told partly by Eckert and then filled in the rest of the way by Arbry, went like this: Three years prior, down near Galveston, Merle and Clell Eckert had partnered with Hal "Pig Nose" Jackson to rob a small bank. The Eckert brothers hadn't been in any serious trouble with the law before that. But the aptly though cruelly named Pig Nose was already wanted for a range of crimes, including murder. When all three were accurately identified as a result of the bank robbery, they went on the run and had been running together ever since.

Twice before—once on his own and once with a different partner—Arbry had cut their sign and nearly nabbed them. That was why, when they heard his name mentioned as being in the Buffalo Peak area on some kind of investigation, they jumped to the conclusion he must be after them. Eckert claimed the trio had recently made a vow to go straight, and toward that end, had signed on to the nearby Box T spread for spring roundup work with the intent of using their pay as a grubstake to start fresh. But Pig Nose convinced the brothers they could never get in the clear with Arbry dogging them. So they set out to get rid of him—and Rodgers, too, since he was now Arbry's partner—once and for all.

Their original plan had been to break into the rangers' hotel room in the wee hours and blast them in their beds. But then, when they saw their intended targets riding out of town earlier in the evening, they decided the chance to kill them and bury them out in the middle of nowhere was a better idea. After trailing Arbry and Rodgers to their surveillance of the Double M, the fugitives knew what route the rangers would be taking when they returned to town. Based on that, they'd retreated and selected the outlying draw to set up their ambush.

"If they'd have been better shots, good enough to either cut us down with their opening volley or finish us off before you were able to hear the shooting that followed," Rodgers pointed out, "they likely would have gotten away clean. Our disappearance wouldn't have gone unnoticed, certainly, and there would have been more rangers following up pronto. But their focus would have been all the more intense on your pal Skinner, and there's a good chance nobody would have been the wiser about Pig Nose and the Eckert brothers even being in the area."

Firestick looked somewhat bemused. "So you're sayin' that, by savin' your hides, in a roundabout way we also saved Beartooth's."

"I can't say that yet. Not completely," Rodgers replied. "But you surely helped avoid the added pressure that would have been put on him if we'd gone down to these other guns. No matter what else, there's little doubt you and your men saved *our* hides. And we're mighty grateful."

"I'll second that," said Arbry. He fixed his gaze on Firestick. "I want to say, too, that I've been less than respectful to you, Marshal, in the course of our time here. When all you were doing was speaking up in defense of a friend. I hope you'll accept my gratitude along with my regrets for the way I've acted."

Firestick gave a dismissive shrug. "You're just a fella doin' a job got handed him. I can allow for that."

"If I'd done *my* job and taken these varmints out of circulation when I tangled with them in the past," said Arbry, "we'd all be standing here under better circumstances now. Including them, possibly."

"They done reaped what they sowed. Right up to the end," Ripley stated somberly. "Me and Miguel both hollered down to 'em in addition to Firestick's callout. Let 'em know we had 'em cold and gave 'em the chance to give it up and live . . . They wasn't smart enough to make the right choice."

"Some men start making wrong choices and they just can't seem to stop. I guess that sort of sums it up for these three," said Rodgers.

Arbry's expression suddenly changed and he swung his gaze first to Miguel and then to Ripley. "Hold on a minute, though. What you said a minute ago about reaping what you sow . . . It occurs to me there are wanted papers on these three. They were issued quite a while back, though the marshal may still have some copies in his older files. The reward isn't all that big, as I recall, but it's a few hundred dollars all the same. Because we're law officers, neither me nor my partner nor Marshal

McQueen can claim it. But for the way you pitched in here tonight, you two men"—he indicated each with a thrust of his finger—"certainly are entitled. I'll send some wires out first thing in the morning and get it set in motion."

Both Ripley and Miguel looked a little stunned. Ripley opened his mouth to say something but for one of the few times in his life appeared speechless. It didn't last long, however.

"Hell's bells!" he finally exclaimed. "Why wait all the way till mornin'—don't those there telygraph lines also sing at night?"

CHAPTER 21

The Mallory House dining room had only been open for a few minutes when Firestick came in and quietly took a seat at a table near the back. He was the day's first—and so far, only—customer.

"My goodness, Marshal, you're up and about mighty early this morning," greeted the pretty red-haired waitress who promptly appeared with a pot of coffee held at the ready. "I'm guessing you'd like some coffee?"

"You're guessin' absolutely right," Firestick replied, turning up his cup and pushing it forward for her to fill. "And you can just go ahead and leave the pot."

"Will someone be joining you?"

"Not necessarily." A corner of Firestick's mouth quirked upward. "But like you said—it's mighty early in the mornin'."

"Yeah. Don't I know that," said the waitress, whose name was Cleo. After filling the marshal's cup and then placing the pot down on a folded napkin, she said, "Are you going to be having breakfast?"

"You bet. Tell Marilu to cut me a thick slice of ham

and then dress it up with three over-easy eggs and a pile of butter-fried potatoes."

After Cleo departed, Firestick hitched forward in his chair, rested his elbows on the table, and took a thoughtful sip of coffee. He was glad the dining room was empty, absent of any background chatter and especially grateful there were no citizens present who might feel the need to come over and say hello or, worse yet, register some kind of complaint. Even after a fitful night's sleep and plenty of time to think, he still had plenty churning inside his head to reflect on.

Following the dispatch of the ambushers, Firestick had returned to the Double M with Ripley and Miguel. There, he'd hitched up a buckboard and gone back to where Arbry and Rodgers were waiting with the bodies of Jackson and the Eckert brothers, standing guard over them in order to keep any nocturnal scavengers away from the remains.

Moosejaw, following his pleasant evening in town with Daisy, had arrived before Firestick left the ranch again and he, as well as Ripley and Miguel, all offered to go with him. But he'd told them to remain behind and go on to bed . . . there was no sense in everybody coming up short of sleep.

In the draw, Firestick and the rangers had loaded the dead men into the buckboard, gathered up the stray horses along with the saddle and gear from the slain animal, and hauled the whole works back to town, where Clem Worden, the undertaker, was wakened to take delivery of the bodies.

After parting company with the rangers, Firestick had opted, because it was so late, to sleep in his office at the jail building rather than return to the ranch. When sleep didn't come easily, he'd gotten up and done some prowling. Reminded of Arbry's comment about possibly having some old wanted posters on Jackson and the Eckerts in his files, he'd pulled out a stack of dodgers that had been stuffed in a desk drawer to see if that might be the case.

Firestick would be the first to admit that neither he nor his deputies spent a lot of time poring over wanted dodgers that showed up in a steady trickle. Often as not, the one soon to be circulated on Beartooth being an exception, the likenesses provided were not particularly good matches—seldom strong enough to look at a given individual and instantly make the association. And though the descriptions given tended to be a bit better, any fugitive with half a brain and lacking some distinct physical deformity was likely to do something to alter his or her appearance.

As it turned out, the dodgers on Jackson and the Eckerts—which Firestick *did* unearth from the stack— turned out to be examples both ways. The drawings and descriptions on the Eckerts were so ordinary as to be practically meaningless, while Jackson's "pig nose" feature surely would have worked to his disadvantage.

But it was the *other* dodger Firestick had run across in his search that was really adding to his tangle of thoughts this morning. It was right there on paper, plenty damn plain when it came to the drawing, the description, and even the name: WANTED—CUTHBERT "RIP" RIPLEY. CHARGE—DISTURBING THE PEACE. REWARD—$1.00.

The warrant was issued by a Marshal Cotton Bailey from a town called Alsup's Crossing and was dated two years earlier. When Firestick had first turned the sheet of paper over and found Rip's features staring back up at him from the desk, it had been like a slap to the face that jarred him out of his bleary-eyed grogginess.

What the hell was going on with old friends turning up on wanted posters? And then, after the initial jolt, the rest of it had hit him—a *one-dollar* reward!? What would make a lawman go to all the trouble of issuing a wanted poster but offer such a meager enticement for anybody to act on it? It had to be some kind of joke . . . didn't it?

Yet it remained a legitimate warrant. Ripley was a wanted fugitive until or unless Marshal Bailey called in that dodger.

"I'd offer a penny for your thoughts, but you look so stern and gloomy I'm afraid it might not be a very pleasant purchase."

The soft voice pulled Firestick from his reverie. He looked up to see Kate standing beside his table. Even this early in the morning she looked fresh and lovely, and the subtle scent of her perfume was distinctively her and something he wanted to drink in and be willingly intoxicated by.

"Nothing unpleasant about the sight of you, pretty lady," he said. "I didn't know if you'd be out minglin' so early, but I'm mighty glad you are."

"Is that an invitation to join you?"

Without words, Firestick stood and pulled out a chair for her. As he settled back onto his own chair, Kate turned up another cup and poured herself some of the coffee.

"Me being out mingling this early isn't really uncommon," she said. "You, on the other hand, hardly make a habit of showing up in town at this hour. I don't suppose it's good news that brings you around?"

In response, Firestick gave her a quick rundown of last night's events. He stopped short of telling her about the wanted poster he'd found for Ripley.

When he'd finished, Kate said, "Did those rangers actually admit to spying on your house?"

"They didn't have much choice after what that Eckert fella spilled before he died. They owned up to followin' me and Rip out from town and then keepin' watch all through supper. With all the shades drawn, they weren't able to spot anything. When they saw the *vaqueros* headin' back to the bunkhouse after the meal, they took it as a sign to call it quits. By the time Rip followed suit, they'd reached the draw where the ambush was waitin'. That's how he was able to pick up the sound of the gunfire."

Kate gave a disdainful sniff. "A part of me wants to say it almost serves them right for sneaking around like they did. But I can't hardly hold with an ambush intended to leave them dead."

"No. Much as I don't like the notion of bein' spied on," Firestick allowed, "I wouldn't have wanted it to turn out that way, either."

Cleo returned with a plate heaped with food that she sat in front of the marshal. Kate declined when asked if she wanted anything, and Cleo moved on to some other customers who were entering up near the front of the dining room.

"I feel kinda awkward chowin' down in front of you," said Firestick. "Sure you don't want something?"

"I'm fine. I like to watch a hungry man eat," she told him. "Besides, it's not like I'm having nothing. I've got coffee."

Firestick was too hungry to argue the point any further.

As he forked in a big bite of ham and followed it with a scoop of potatoes, Kate went on. "So does that change anything as far as the situation goes with the rangers? I mean, you and the others basically saved their lives."

"They're grateful. They said as much and I believe they're sincere," replied Firestick as he chewed. "But that's really about as far as they can take it. They've still got the wanted paper on Beartooth that they have to act on. Only Judge Buchanon can do anything to pull in the reins on that."

Kate frowned. "I'll be sending that wire off to Lawyer Taggert as soon as the telegraph office opens. But, in the meantime, you're still bound to make that trip to Pecos, aren't you?"

"Don't see where I've got much choice. The roots to this whole thing are up there. If I'm gonna find some way to rip 'em out and clear the charges against Beartooth, I figure goin' to Pecos will give me my best chance."

"And what about Judge Buchanon?" Kate said. "You figure he's going to stand quietly by while you start tearing up roots right there in his town?"

"We'll have to see. I'll deal with that when the time comes," Firestick answered tersely.

Kate drank some of her coffee. "When will you be leaving?"

"Soon as I can. Probably early this afternoon. There's some things here I've got to get out of the way first."

Kate said nothing but was clearly waiting for him to elaborate.

"For starters," said Firestick, "I figure it's best I stick around until the rangers start puttin' up those dodgers on Beartooth. You can bet—and understandably, I suppose—

that'll whip up a flurry of excitement in a lot of folks. Wouldn't be fair to leave Moosejaw facin' all of that on his own, so I'll hang around long enough to help weather at least the first wave of it with him.

"After that, there'll still be the matter of the rangers comin' out and searchin' the ranch. After last night, I'm hopin' they might call that off. But if they still aim to go through with it, I want to be on hand." Firestick paused, made a sour face. "As much as anything, I've got to make sure Beartooth don't decide to do something stupid while they're there. Hidin' away and bein' cooped up ain't sittin' well with him at all. And Moosejaw ain't exactly takin' a shine to these rangers bein' in our hair, neither. It's a chore all its own sometimes havin' to remind 'em both we ain't livin' the rough-and-tumble mountain ways no more."

"They're good men. They won't let you down," Kate told him.

"I know." Firestick sighed somewhat wearily and pushed his emptied plate away. He almost reached for the wanted dodger on Ripley that was folded inside his shirt pocket, not liking the idea of keeping secrets from Kate. But then he decided against it. He hadn't yet made up his mind what he was going to do about the damn thing. He sighed again and repeated, "I know."

CHAPTER 22

As expected, when the *Wanted for Murder* dodgers on Beartooth started going up around town they got a lot of attention. Once shops all up and down Trail Street opened for the morning's business, people—clerks, customers, deliverymen—quickly began gathering in tongue-wagging clusters either inside the stores or on the boardwalks out front.

Rangers Arbry and Rodgers had appeared in the hotel dining room just before Firestick was getting ready to leave. They'd come over to the table where the marshal sat with Kate, and the lawmen had engaged in a brief conversation. Almost sheepishly, the rangers stated their intent to begin posting the dodgers on Beartooth as soon as they'd finished their breakfasts.

Firestick had told them he expected nothing less. He'd then produced the wanted papers he'd found on Pig Nose Jackson and the Eckerts, reminding them of their promise to arrange reward payment to Ripley and Miguel.

Before the rangers left to go sit at their own table, Firestick asked about their plan to come and search the Double M, only to be informed that had been called off.

His mouth curling into a wry smile, Arbry had explained, "We decided a search of the ranch would end up revealing just about as much as we were able to see last night through all those closed curtains and shades."

Firestick left the Mallory House and got back to the jail just as Moosejaw was arriving from the ranch. Inside, over cups of coffee, Firestick provided an update on his restless night and on events of the morning so far, including the news of the rangers having abandoned their plan to come search the ranch.

"That's a relief," Moosejaw exclaimed. "Beartooth is gettin' so ornery and restless about stayin' hid all the time—especially after bein' froze out of that action last night—it's hard to tell what he'll do. If those rangers had come snoopin' around like they'd planned, I don't know if we'd have been able to hold him back from rushin' out and confrontin' 'em."

"Yeah, I had some worries about that, too," Firestick admitted. "I know bein' bottled up is hard on him, but damn it, he's got to give us some time before his sorry butt gets hauled in front of Judge Buchanon. Take that business last night. See what a pickle that would've turned out to be if I'd let him come along and he'd've found himself smack in the middle of those rangers?"

"I know, I know," said Moosejaw. "But I also know that, in his place, same conditions, I'd be havin' a hard time of it, too—and so would you."

Firestick didn't bother to try and deny it. "It still comes down to keepin' him out of the hands of those rangers—or anybody else, as far as that goes, who might come lookin' once those dodgers go into circulation—until we've got some kind of solid defense built up for him. In the meantime, we'll take that blasted search bein' called off as a good break."

"Yeah." Moosejaw grunted. "Unfortunately, it comes mostly swallowed up by the bad news of those damn wanted dodgers goin' up all over creation."

"Speakin' of wanted dodgers," Firestick said, "I found some on those polecats from last night when I did some diggin' through my drawerful of old papers. Turned 'em over to the rangers this mornin', so that should help hurry along the rewards Rip and Miguel stand to get."

"Good for them. I guess that's another good break of sorts, though it don't do nothing to help Beartooth."

Firestick considered a minute, then heaved a sigh and said, "Yeah, and my diggin' also turned up something more that don't do Beartooth no good, either. Nor is it a good break for somebody else." He pulled from his pocket the folded wanted dodger on Ripley and handed it to his big deputy.

Moosejaw took the paper, looking puzzled, unfolded it, and read it. His expression shifted from puzzlement to surprise to anguish. Lifting his gaze back to Firestick, he said, "What the hell? What does this mean?"

"You can read the words and see the picture same as me. Rip is a wanted man—a fugitive."

"For a *one-dollar* reward? That don't seem worth the bother of even puttin' out a paper on him!"

"I can't argue with that. But it don't change the facts none. Until he's called to account for the charges shown there, he's a wanted man."

Moosejaw tossed the paper onto Firestick's desk, as if he could make it go away by getting it out of his hands. "So what are you gonna do? Arrest him again?"

"Hell, I don't know," Firestick growled. "With those rangers already prowlin' around . . . if the wrong person ran across that dodger . . . I'm damn well gonna talk to him about it, see what he's got to say for himself. Past that, I ain't sure. I got a few more pressin' things on my mind, in case you don't know."

After finishing their coffee, knowing that by then the posters would have begun going up around town, the two lawmen decided it was time to go out and face whatever got stirred up as a result. They took two straight-backed chairs out of the office, planted them on the strip of board-walk that ran in front of the jail building, sat down, and leaned back to wait.

It didn't take long before folks began coming around.

The overriding reaction, not unexpected, was surprise and shock. In addition, a welcome swelling of support for Beartooth and earnest declarations of "preposterous!" and "outrageous!" as far as the abundant charges against him were concerned.

Of course, no one with any suspicions or disparaging remarks about Beartooth was likely to step forward and voice them to Firestick or Moosejaw. That didn't mean the pair weren't bombarded with plenty of questions, however.

Where did such ridiculous charges come from? What does Beartooth have to say in defense of himself? When will he be taken into custody?

In answer to these, Firestick and Moosejaw stated their stalwart belief in their friend's innocence and stuck to the claim of Beartooth being gone on a horse-buying trip and therefore unable to respond, so far, for himself. Standard procedure, barring any new developments, would be for him to be taken into custody by the rangers as soon as he was located and transported to Pecos to stand trial. Yes, his friends would certainly be on hand to stand by him. As far as the basis for the charges and what the rangers might additionally know, that needed to be addressed directly by them.

After a couple of hours, the initial furor began to die down, and Firestick and Moosejaw found themselves sitting alone for increasing gaps of time. Sam Duvall, Frank Moorehouse, and a handful of others who rated as more than just citizens but also good friends, lingered awhile longer, but then they, too, drifted away. The sun climbed high and warm in a clear sky, and activity up and down the street settled into a normal flow.

"Well, that wasn't so bad," Firestick summed up. "You can bet it'll keep poppin' up in discussions for some time to come, though. Goin' into the afternoon and evenin', when liquor starts figurin' into some of the opinions that get spouted in the saloons, I expect a touch of rowdiness is bound to result sooner or later. And likely more than just tonight."

"Like you said—pretty much bound to happen," Moosejaw agreed.

"I don't like leavin' you to handle that all on your own, what with Beartooth layin' low and me headin' off to Pecos," said Firestick. "But I don't see a way around it, not believin' the way I do that I got the chance to do some good by travelin' up there."

"I understand. That's the way it has to be. Don't fret about it; I can handle things here. And I expect you'll have your own hands full once you hit Pecos and announce what you're there for."

"If need be, don't forget you can call on Sam Duvall or Frank Moorehouse, even Pete Roeback, if you need a hand . . . and those Texas Rangers, too, if they continue to hang around."

Moosejaw huffed. "Ain't much chance I'd call on the likes of them for any help."

Firestick's brows pinched together. "I'd like to say you could call on Rip as well. But all things considered, countin' on him to break up a fracas, rather than addin' to it, probably wouldn't be the smartest thing."

"Speakin' of him," said Moosejaw, "did you notice him ridin' into town a little bit ago when we had a gaggle of citizens around us?"

"Yeah, I did. But now that you mention it, I ain't seen hide nor hair of him since. Any idea what he's up to?"

"Said he had to come in for some supplies—salt and alum, mainly—for tannin' that bearskin he's workin' on for Daisy. But it shouldn't have taken him this long to find what he needed at Greeble's. Most likely he got to jawin' with somebody somewhere along the way."

"Yeah, most likely . . . But why is it that don't give me a particularly easy feelin'?"

"You still aimin' to palaver with him about that wanted dodger?"

"Gonna have to, sooner or later. But for right now—"

The rest of what Firestick was going to say got cut short by a sudden crash of noise and a burst of activity from a block and a half down the street. As the two lawmen's eyes were drawn to this, they saw a man come hurtling out the batwing doors of the Lone Star Palace Saloon. He was staggering backward, arms windmilling wildly, feet digging frantically to find purchase on the boardwalk before the planks were no longer underneath him and he was dumped unceremoniously onto his butt in the dust of the street.

Moments later, the front window of the Lone Star shattered outward, spraying pieces of glass all over the boardwalk, and a second man came sailing through, crashing down amid a shower of broken shards.

Firestick and Moosejaw exchanged quick glances before shoving up to their feet.

"Aw, shoot," muttered Moosejaw as they broke into a run toward the Lone Star Palace, "I got a hunch I know where Rip disappeared to."

CHAPTER 23

"What in blazes did you expect me to do?" Ripley fumed from where he sat on a jail cell cot. "Those two varmints were runnin' their mouths, talkin' down Beartooth. Sayin' how it was just a matter of time before a half-assed wild man from out of the mountains was bound to show he was unfit to mingle amongst respectable folks and be around any woman who wasn't some passed-around squaw! You think for a minute I was gonna stand by and listen to crap like that? Would *you* have?"

Firestick stood in the doorway of the cell, the door not yet closed and locked. "In the first place," he replied, "it ain't likely they would have spouted stuff like that in front of me. If they had, there ain't no doubt I'd've given 'em some argument. But that don't mean I would have waded in and started breakin' bones and knockin' out teeth . . . Damn it, Rip, you can't keep *doin'* stuff like that! Not if you ever want to fit in anywhere down here on the flats and especially in the towns. It ain't like a mountain man camp where differences are settled with fists or knives. You ain't in that world no more."

"And more's the shame I ain't," Ripley muttered, hanging his head.

"You said yourself that world is all but faded away," Firestick reminded him. "You've got to find a way to fit in somewhere else."

Ripley lifted his head and peered up at Firestick with a look of genuine bewilderment. "Why? Why ain't there no places suited to men like me—and you and Beartooth and Moosejaw and others like us? Progress . . . Civilization, everybody calls it." The disgust was obvious in his voice. "Seems to me like things was a helluva lot more civil up in the high places, livin' the lives we used to. You spoke straight and showed respect to those who earned it. And everybody understood there was quick, hard consequences if you didn't measure up. Down here you got connivin' bastards and double-dealers and liars who smile to your face and then spit on your tracks walkin' off. And they know they can get away with rude behavior and worse because there's all these nicey-nice rules and laws they can hide behind and twist and wiggle in and out of so's the weaselly sonsabitches get protected instead of knocked into line like they oughta."

"I don't have the answers to that kind of thinkin'. Fact is, I've felt like that myself at times." Firestick heaved a sigh. "But havin' rules and laws for everybody to follow— applied fairly, needless to say—ain't all bad, neither. It can't always be left to just the toughest or strongest to decide what's right and what's wrong."

Ripley rested his elbows on the tops of his knees and said nothing for several seconds. Then: "So what now?

Seems you're fixin' to lock me in here for another stretch. What about those two loudmouths I laid into?"

"Right now they're still bein' treated by the doc. Moose-jaw's with 'em. From what I saw, you busted 'em up pretty good." Firestick grimaced. "Accordin' to everybody else in the saloon—most of 'em who I know to be truthful and decent sorts—you tore into those two with no warnin' when they weren't even talkin' to you. And what they was sayin' wasn't necessarily to the likin' of those others, either, but it still didn't warrant what you did. Like it or not, folks *do* have a right to state their mind on things without gettin' thrashed for it."

"If they're gonna pop off at the mouth, then they oughta be ready to defend their words, says I." Ripley squinted up at Firestick. "But what you're fixin' to tell me is that they ain't lookin' at no jail time even though I am."

"That's the way it shakes out. I got nothing to charge 'em on. Like I already said, they got every right to—"

Ripley cut off the rest of it with a dismissive wave of his hand. "Good. I wouldn't want 'em in here, close-like, stinkin' up the joint anyway."

Firestick's patience with this belligerent side of his old friend was starting to wear thin. "What I do or don't do around here ain't aimed a damn bit at suitin' what *you* want. I've got a helluva lot more important stuff to worry about than tryin' to keep you on a leash because you can't control your own self. If you're pinin' so bad for the mountain ways, go back and live 'em. But, in the mean-time, nowhere else is gonna put up with how you see fit to handle things. The sooner you get that through your thick skull, the better off you and everybody around you is gonna be!"

Ripley's shoulders sagged. "Hell's bells, ol' hoss . . . You're right. You know it, I know it. I even *asked* you to help me get better squared away and then I go right ahead and . . . Worst of all, if that business with Beartooth wasn't bad enough, I haul off and give you more grief with my temper and shenanigans at a time when I know you're needin' to be off to Pecos. Damn it, Firestick, I'm sorry. I know that's pitiful, but I really mean it. Lockin' me up for a while, at least while you're away, is probably the best thing. Even *I* can't manage to get in more trouble when I'm already behind bars."

"I wish that was so. But you ain't even right about that," Firestick grated.

"What's that supposed to mean?"

Firestick took the wanted dodger from his pocket, shook it open, and dangled it at arm's length in front of Ripley's nose. "It means *this*, you ornery old cuss. You ain't just in trouble here in Buffalo Peak, you're a wanted man all over the whole doggone state!"

Ripley took the paper and studied it, scowling fiercely. Then, lifting his face and handing it back, he said, "See? Now right there's a prime example of the kind of thing I'm talkin' about. Cotton Bailey"—he spat the name—"he's about the sorriest two-legged critter you'd ever want to meet. Shifty-eyed and spineless and about as worthless as an acorn nub, if you know what I mean. Yet somehow those lamebrained folks back in Alsup's Crossin' saw fit to pin a badge on him. Didn't change a thing as to what a sorry specimen he really is, except it made *him* think he actually amounts to something.

"But one of the main things it didn't change or help any—and one of the closest to home, you might say— was in his own bedroom. By some cockeyed stroke of luck that nobody will ever understand, he nabbed himself a pretty young wife. Trouble was, the truth soon came to show that he couldn't satisfy her. Not nohow. And so it wasn't long before she began droppin' her bloomers for other fellas."

Firestick groaned. "Let me guess . . . one of 'em bein' you."

"No," Ripley said firmly. "That's the double-damned shame of it. I surely would have accommodated the gal, don't ever think I wouldn't. But I never got the honor. I never even got close enough to her for a good whiff of her perfume. No matter, though, 'cause ol' Cotton got it firm in his head that I was dallyin' with her. Nothing I said could convince him otherwise. That's when I shoulda lit out, right then and there. If you ever saw Alsup's Crossin' you'd see mighty quick-like that there wasn't no good reason for stickin' around. Well, less'n maybe you *was* lucky enough to be dallyin' with Cotton's missus.

"But I weren't, I swear. Still, you know me and my cussed stubbornness. I wasn't gonna skedaddle and take the blame for something I never did. Not, that is, until I got a little more persuadin' from the good sheriff and some of his helpers. Cotton hired a couple of saloon toughs to crowd me into a fight one night and then threw me in the clink over it. Said he'd leave me there to rot less'n I took the hint and put some dust behind me. So

I did. But then, after I was gone, just to embarrass me and make me look all the more lowdown, the dirty skunk put out that dodger on me with only a one-dollar reward."

In spite of himself, Firestick found the tale convincing, largely due to Ripley making no excuses and not embellishing things the way he usually did with a yarn. If he'd included a claim that he *was* dallying with the young wife and proved to be the answer to all her passionate dreams, then it would have been more typically Rip and therefore less believable.

But none of it really mattered, because the overriding truth was that the dodger was real and its existence made Ripley a wanted man, regardless.

"I'm backed into a corner," Firestick explained. "I'm already stickin' my neck out a mile with Beartooth, but at least I got some things in motion to try and get a handle on that. If I stick it out even farther with you and you go on drawin' attention to yourself with these scrapes you keep gettin' in, then what? What if the wrong person— like maybe one of those rangers who are already prowlin' around—turns up another copy of that dodger? You might get your fool self shot over it and I'd be left lookin' and feelin' like a boob for not takin' care of it when I had the chance."

"How do you figure you can take care of it?"

"By gettin' hold of that marshal, that Cotton fella. Try to work out something to get him to call in the dodger. Tell him you saw God and took up preachin' or fell down an outhouse hole and drowned or . . . or whatever. Hell, I don't know. But it'd take time to trade wires with him and figure something out. And time ain't something I got a lot extra of right now."

"Then don't waste no more of it on me. Leastways not in the short term," Ripley told him. "Leave me here, like I said, so I can stay out of the way and out of trouble. You hightail it up to Pecos and do what you can for Beartooth. Then worry about clearin' things up for me when you get back."

Firestick sighed. He didn't see that he had any other option but to do what Rip suggested. The only sure way to keep the old rapscallion out of trouble was to leave him behind bars.

And Firestick wasn't a hundred percent convinced even *that* would work!

CHAPTER 24

Normally it was a two-and-a-half-day ride to Pecos. By pushing hard and steady until after the sun was down the first day, and then heading out again before it poked above the horizon in the morning, Firestick cut it to less than two, arriving early in the afternoon of the second day.

Before leaving Buffalo Peak, he was somewhat surprised to find that both Moosejaw and Beartooth were grudgingly agreeable to the notion of Ripley remaining behind bars for a while. In the first place, until the reward money due him and Miguel came through, Ripley had no way to come close to paying any fines or damages that resulted from his latest escapade: the Lone Star Palace's destroyed plate glass window and two chairs and a table broken, not to mention the dislocated shoulder and cracked jaw suffered by the men he'd attacked.

Plus, he still owed Daisy a tanned and treated bearskin rug to cover the first fine she had paid off. He could complete that in his jail cell once the bear pelt was brought in to him.

All of this was geared toward keeping the rascally Rip

out of more trouble, making it one less thing Moosejaw might have to deal with and freeing Firestick from worrying about it while he concentrated on trying to turn up something to help Beartooth.

Another piece of business that Firestick saw fit to take care of before departing—apart from supplying himself for the trip and saying good-bye to Kate—was to meet with Arbry and Rodgers in order to inform them that he'd be out of town for a few days and the reason behind it.

"We're obliged to you for letting us know," Arbry had told him. "Not sure what you think you're going to be able to accomplish up there in Pecos, though, except maybe stir up Judge Buchanon even more . . . but if you got your mind made up, I reckon you've got to give it a try."

"Got to hand it to you," Rodgers added, "for your loyalty and all your effort on behalf of your friend. I hope he's deserving of it."

"He is," Firestick had assured them. "That's the one thing out of all this I'm certain of."

"One more thing you can be pretty sure on," Arbry said, "is that if and when Skinner turns up, we still mean to arrest him."

To which Firestick had replied, with a thin smile, "Like you said a minute ago . . . if you got your mind made up, I reckon you've got to give it a try."

He reflected about that exchange now, as he steered the horse he was riding onto the main drag of Pecos. What *would* Beartooth's reaction be if, in spite of the measures being taken to avoid such a thing, he was faced with an attempt to try and arrest him?

Firestick knew his old friend well enough to know that

the restless, trapped feeling Beartooth was struggling with after laying low at the ranch for only a relatively short time was no act. For him, the prospect of being truly trapped, put behind bars, would be close to unbearable. He didn't have it in him, like Ripley did, to stand being caged, not even for a little while to give things a chance to work out. Firestick didn't want to think about how far Beartooth would go not to be put in that position. He just knew he had to find some way to prevent things from reaching that point.

"Howdy there, stranger. Got a couple horses you want to put up for a while?"

The question was posed by a portly, middle-aged man wearing bib overalls. He had a fringe beard that did a halfway decent job of hiding the rolls of fat under his chin and a wide, friendly grin that did nothing to hide the fact he was missing his two front teeth. He stood in the open doorway of a barnlike structure Firestick had reined up in front of. Bright yellow lettering on the weathered wooden slats over the doorway read: LIVERY.

Firestick tipped his head to indicate the lettering. "That's the business you're in, right?"

"Indeed it is. Stuart Strousel's my name. Comes to tendin' horses, you ain't gonna find better care nor more reasonable prices anywhere in town. And I can see right off you got a pair of fine-lookin' animals who deserve the best."

"That they do," agreed Firestick as he swung down from his saddle. "I've put some long, hard miles on 'em over the past couple days. Like for you to give 'em the works—rub 'em down, water 'em, feed 'em plenty of good-quality hay and grain."

Firestick had brought two mounts for his trip, each a sturdy young mare from the best of the Double M stock. Two horses allowed him to push them hard and frequently change which one he rode in order to keep them fresh and not overworked.

Taking the reins, Strousel said, "Will you be stablin' 'em overnight?"

"Expect so," replied Firestick, pulling down his saddle-bags, war bag, and Yellowboy rifle. "Maybe some longer. Not sure about that yet."

"Not a problem at all. I've got plenty of stalls and I'm happy to care for 'em."

"How about overnight lodgings for me? Any hotels in town you'd recommend?" asked Firestick.

"Oh, yeah. We got plenty of hotels. They're all good, just depends on how fancy you want things."

Firestick smiled and said, "I don't require much in the way of fanciness."

Strousel pointed. "Just up the street in the next block, then. The Traveler's Rest. Nice German couple runs it. Clean and quiet and fair prices. They make up your bed fresh every day and keep a pot of hot coffee in the lobby—that's about as fancy as they get."

"Sounds like it oughta suit me just fine. Take good care of my horses and gear. I'll check back later."

As he strode away from the livery and headed up the street in the direction Strousel had pointed, Firestick took time for a slower, more thorough gander at the town of Pecos. It had some size to it: three, maybe four times bigger than Buffalo Peak. There was a main drag inter-sected by two cross streets, with residential areas sprinkled to either side. The businesses lining the heart of town were mostly wood-framed structures that appeared sturdy and well maintained and seemed to offer a full range of goods and services, including no shortage of saloons. These drinking establishments as well as the other stores and shops all appeared to be seeing a brisk amount of activity in the middle of this fine, clear day.

Firestick hadn't gone far, however, before his gaze fell on something that gave him a bit of a start in the midst of all this peaceful, busy activity. Nailed to a street lamppost he was passing, along with several other papers and notices, was a crisp new wanted dodger with Beartooth's face and name on it.

He'd been warned they were going into wide circulation, of course, and he'd already seen the ones that had been put up in Buffalo Peak before he left. But he'd been on the trail, away from any other town ever since then, making the sight of this poster a stark and sudden reminder of the seriousness behind him being here at all. After he'd walked a ways farther, he saw more of the Beartooth dodgers on other posts and even a few buildings. He had to fight the urge not to tear down each one he passed.

Entering the lobby of the Traveler's Rest, Firestick found himself in quiet, cool surroundings filled with a faint pine scent that made him think of the mountains. There was a tall desk made of dark, highly polished wood straight ahead, and to one side, before the wide front window, were situated a pair of well-padded chairs framed in the same dark wood. A cast-iron stove with a huge copper coffeepot sitting on top stood over by the side wall.

A short, thick-bodied man with bushy white eyebrows and a shiny bald head appeared behind the desk. His chin jutted out only a couple of inches higher than the desk's surface.

"Is it a room you wish, sir?" he asked with more than a trace of an accent that testified to his German heritage.

Firestick affirmed that it was and in quick order, with no wasted words, he paid for a night's stay, was given a key, and was shown to a room just down the hall. "To your satisfaction, is it?"

Again Firestick assured the gnome-like proprietor that it was.

"Very good," his host declared. "My name is Rudy. My wife is Anna. Should anything further you need, one of us you will find at the front desk or there is a bell you can ring. Always available is hot coffee in the lobby."

"Okay. I'll keep all of that in mind. Thanks."

Rudy left and closed the door behind him.

The room had a straight-backed chair with a padded seat located beside a washbasin and pitcher of water on a stand. Firestick draped his saddlebags over the back of the chair, placed his war bag on the seat, and leaned the Yellowboy against the chair. At the washbasin, after removing his hat, he poured some water and scooped handfuls of it to his face, sluicing away some of the dust and grit from long miles on the trail. He slicked back his hair, combing it roughly into place with his fingers. After toweling dry and using his hat to slap off some additional dust from his trousers and shirt, he put his hat back on, then went over and sat on the edge of the bed.

It wasn't as soft as his bed back at the Double M, but it would do. It was a hell of a lot softer than a saddle seat or the hard, cold ground. Firestick's mouth twisted wryly, thinking again about getting soft in his old age. Christ, how many years had he gone without *ever* knowing the feel of a mattress under him? He'd endured—and even enjoyed—those times, but nowadays he damn well appreciated creature comforts whenever he could find them.

But before he got to appreciating the mattress too much, he reminded himself that he had things to do. Heaving a sigh, he got up and quit the room, locking the door behind him. Back at the front desk, he got directions from Rudy to the telegraph office.

Another short hike up the busy street brought Firestick to where he wanted to be. The telegraph operator turned out to be a surprisingly young lad, lanky and red-haired, with more freckles scattered across his nose and cheeks than stars in a clear summer sky. And he probably hated every one of them.

When Firestick asked if any wires had come through in the past day or two for Elwood McQueen, the freckle-faced kid looked almost as startled as if a gun had been shoved in his face and he'd been asked to fork over all the cash in the joint. He recovered quickly, though, snapping shut the mouth that had dropped open and adopting a stern, business-like expression.

"Uh, yeah . . . I mean, yes. Yessir. Got one right here we been holding for you, Mr. McQueen."

He fumbled through some papers on his desk, plucked one out, and handed it to Firestick. "Here you go, Mr. McQueen."

Firestick took the paper, frowning for a long moment at the kid's odd behavior. The freckled operator sat very rigid under his glare, maintaining his stern expression but at the same time looking like he was half ready to bolt out the back door.

Firestick's eyes dropped to the paper and he read the words staring back:

ELWOOD
LAWYER TAGGERT IS STANDING BY TO
TAKE CASE ON A MINUTES NOTICE STOP
MOOSEJAW SAYS TO TELL YOU ALL IS
STABLE HERE STOP GOOD LUCK AND
HURRY HOME SOON STOP MISSING YOU
AND THINKING OF YOU WITH ALL
FONDNESS STOP
KATE

Firestick lifted his face. The kid was watching him anxiously. "Do you wish to send a reply, sir?" There was a catch in the words and you could tell that was the last thing he really wanted.

"No. Not at this time," Firestick grated.

He folded the telegram, slipped it into a vest pocket, and turned to leave. In the doorway he turned and looked back. The kid was still watching him with wide, anxious eyes. "Where can I find the Texas Rose Saloon?" Firestick wanted to know.

CHAPTER 25

Instead of following the telegraph operator's directions, which would have taken him across the street and up to the gaudily painted front of the Texas Rose in the next block, Firestick remained on his current side of the street and retreated only a couple of doors down from the telegraph office until he came to the recessed entrance to a music store. He stepped into the entryway and waited, peering back toward the telegraph office.

He didn't have long to wait before the red-haired operator stepped out of the office and rather frantically locked the door to his place of business behind him. Then, after a furtive look around, he turned and moved hurriedly up the boardwalk in the opposite direction from Firestick. This continued strange behavior, on top of the young man's earlier reaction, caused the marshal's forehead to crease in a thoughtful frown.

Returning to the telegraph office, Firestick saw through the paneled glass of its front door a paper sign hanging on a string. It read: BACK IN 15 MINUTES. Turning his head to look up the boardwalk, Firestick saw the red-haired kid, now in the next block, suddenly turn and disappear into the doorway of some business. The marshal stood very still for a minute, running through his mind all that had happened since he first showed up to ask if there were any wires for him.

He could only conclude one thing—the operator's initial startled reaction and subsequent odd behavior seemed to indicate he had been expecting Firestick with a measure of trepidation and now had hurried to report to somebody that he was here. Who that somebody was and how he knew the marshal was on the way seemed easy enough to guess. But what Firestick didn't quite understand was why his arrival would be met with so much apprehension.

He toyed with the idea of following the telegraph operator directly into wherever he'd gone. But then he decided he would proceed with things as he'd planned and wait to see what whoever appeared so interested in him being here had in mind to do next . . . and whatever it was, he'd be alert for it.

For one o'clock in the afternoon, the Texas Rose Saloon was doing quite a brisk business. It was a large, two-story, somewhat gaudy establishment, as Firestick had surmised from back down the street, with a long, ornate bar on one side and a stage for dancing girls—though none were currently performing—on the other. At the near end of the stage sat a grand piano surrounded by other band instruments, none in use at the moment except for a banjo being plunked by an elderly black man with cottony white sideburns sitting on a ladderback chair. The area between the stage and the bar was filled with several round-topped gaming tables. Only a few of these were seeing any action just now, with the majority of the afternoon's patrons being bellied up to the bar.

Firestick took all of this in by gazing over the top of the batwing doors at the entrance. It wasn't the kind of place where he preferred to do his drinking, but he had a different purpose here. This was where Beartooth had gotten into a row with one of the bouncers, a man named Hardy, and that was who Firestick was aiming to have a talk with.

Before pushing through the batwings and entering, however, he paused a minute longer to turn and also have a look at the row of businesses on the other side of the street. From his angle when standing on that side down in front of the telegraph office, he hadn't been able to tell for sure which doorway the furtive red-haired kid had ducked into. But his best judgment was that it had been just about directly across from where he now stood. If that was the case, it appeared the kid had gone to make his report in a competing saloon—namely, the Courthouse Saloon & General Store.

In sharp contrast to the Texas Rose, this was a small, single-story, rather drab-looking affair. In fact, its slightly sagging roof and faded paint made it look like one of the oldest businesses on the street. Giving it some added and more curious distinction was what appeared to be a much newer structure, an addition rising directly behind, tall and sturdy looking and brightly whitewashed.

Why anyone would construct something so imposing as an add-on and not simply rebuild the whole works, Firestick found a bit puzzling . . . which, come to think of it, made it a good fit if that was indeed where the odd-acting telegraph operator had gone.

Putting aside further pondering along those lines, Firestick turned back to the Texas Rose and pushed on through the batwings in order to pursue what he'd come here for. He found a space at the bar where he was able to shoulder in and rest his elbows.

"What can I get you, big fella?" asked the derby-hatted, cigar-chomping bartender who appeared before him.

"A beer. Cold, if you got it," said Firestick.

"You came to the right place, bub. We got the coldest beer in town."

A moment later a tall, foaming mug was shoved in front of him. He pushed some coins across the bar top in return. When he raised the mug he found the beer was indeed crisp and cold and tasted damned good. He was reminded how long it had been since he'd enjoyed a beer, especially after two days on the trail drinking nothing but canteen water and his own bitter coffee.

The bartender had disappeared to serve others down the line before Firestick got the chance to ask him anything. He took another drink of his beer and then looked to the men on either side of him as possible candidates for striking up a conversation.

To his right was a bleary-eyed old-timer who appeared so drunk he was barely able to keep his sagging, weaving head from dropping down onto the half-empty shot glass that sat before him. To the left was a wrangler in a fancy cowhide vest arguing with another man on the other side of him, apparently a rider for the same spread, about which one of them had the best chance of catching the roaming eye of their ranch foreman's unfaithful wife. Neither appealed to Firestick as someone he wanted to trade words with.

So he drained his beer and waited for the barkeep to come around offering a refill. When he did, Firestick pushed some more coins across the bar but kept his hand over them, preventing the stick man from scooping them up and moving on again until Firestick had the chance to say, "A friend of mine asked me to look up a fella who works here—an old pal of his—and pass along a howdy. So I'm wonderin' if you could tell me where I might find a gent named Hardy?"

The barkeep frowned. "Hardy? I'm surprised to hear there's anybody who'd claim that miserable bastard as an old pal. But then, I guess it'd have to be an old one—because he sure don't have no current ones."

Firestick shrugged. "I don't know about that. I'm just a fella passin' word in between."

"You might want to speak to your friend about not doing you any more favors in the future," said the barkeep. "But if you're bent on going ahead with it, there's Hardy right over there." He extended a stubby arm and pointed to a spot off to one side of the front door, opposite from the piano and band area, where a man on an elevated chair—a bouncer's station—sat looking out over the room.

"Tread careful-like, stranger," advised the barkeep. "He's in an even ornerier mood than usual on account of he ain't had no fights to break up or skulls to crack for two or three days now."

"I'll keep that in mind." Firestick took his hand off the coins and the bartender swept them away.

Firestick lifted the fresh beer to his lips and turned as he did so, studying the man who'd been pointed out to him. Hardy was a bruiser, no mistaking it. Thick through the shoulders and gut, with bulging biceps and muscle-corded forearms well displayed by a panel-fronted white shirt with the sleeves cut off at the shoulder seams. His head was cleanly shaven but he had a full beard, thick and black. Across his forehead and around too-close-together eyes that peered out from under brows as bushy and thick as his beard were scars and puckered patches of skin that spoke of many altercations, possibly some from time in a bare-knuckle boxing ring.

Jesus Christ, Beartooth, Firestick thought to himself as he took another sip of beer, *did you have to pick the biggest, baddest-looking* hombre *north of the Rio Grande to get crossways of?*

Placing his still half-full beer mug on the bar next to the old drunk's shot glass, Firestick patted the souse on a bony shoulder and said, "Go ahead and finish that for me, pardner. Just be careful not to drown in it." Then he shoved off and headed toward Hardy.

CHAPTER 26

Drawing up in front of the bouncer on his elevated chair, Firestick said, "Wonder if I could have a word with you?"

Not bothering to glance down, his gaze continuing to slowly sweep the room for signs of trouble, Hardy responded, "Don't know you. Don't want to. We got nothing to have words about."

Firestick shifted his stance a little. "Not meanin' to be contrary, but what I need to talk to you about ain't got nothing to do with whether or not we know one another. What it's got to do with is some information you might have that could help me help a good friend of mine."

Hardy's chin tipped down and he turned his head to glare at Firestick. "What the hell kind of babbling was that? Me help you help a friend . . . Why should I give a damn about helping either one of you?"

"No reason in particular, I guess," allowed Firestick. "But my friend—somebody you *have* met, by the way—is in kind of a tight spot. Facin' what you might call an injustice. A pretty serious one. If you could just answer a question or two, it might help clear up—"

"Shut that yammering hole in your face," Hardy cut him off. "You ain't making a lick of sense, and you're bothering me, distracting me from trying to do my job. Beat it—and make it fast before I take a notion to shoo you away and not be so pleasant about it."

Firestick felt the heat crawl up the sides of his neck and over his ears. He'd been warned by the barkeep to tread carefully with this character. Plus, as a stranger in town and especially considering what he was hoping to accomplish here, he knew it wouldn't be smart to get involved in a fracas barely an hour after arriving.

But neither of those reasons was enough to offset how hard it went against his grain to be talked to in such a manner. "You better haul back on those reins some, son," he replied through clenched teeth, "before that mouth of yours runs away with itself."

Hardy's menacing glare took on a tinge of disbelief. "What did you just say?"

"I think you heard me plain enough."

"Are you *threatening* me?" Hardy's hands gripped the arms of the chair he was sitting on, squeezing so tight the wood creaked and his knuckles turned as white as the bones underneath the skin.

"More like offerin' a piece of advice," Firestick said in a flat tone.

"If you're in the business of giving advice, then you'd better quick-like dish out some to yourself." Hardy sneered. "Like advising your dumb ass to turn around and walk out of here while you're still able."

Firestick sighed. "Okay. Since you're not in the mood for some well-meanin' advice, how about a helpful lesson?"

Hardy's clearly building anger was momentarily stayed by a look of bewilderment.

To that bewildered expression, Firestick said, "A lot of people, for example, have trouble knowin' the difference between a predicament and a problem. This discussion we're havin' here is sort of a good example. Way it stands now, see, you and me have a predicament. I want to ask you a couple of questions, you don't want to give me the time of day. How are we gonna resolve this? *That's* a predicament . . . But if you was to climb down off that chair and commence tryin' to shoo me off in that unpleasant way you say you're wantin' to do . . . then, I guarantee, it will turn into a problem."

Hardy's lips peeled back, roaring a curse, and down off the chair he came. "You want a problem, you old mossback—you got one!"

Used to dealing with men who were mostly drunk and usually of a lesser size, Hardy simply bulled forward, reaching with both hands, meaning to grab Firestick and sling him around toward the door. But Firestick wasn't drunk, and though twenty years older and giving away as many pounds, neither was he a lightweight who hadn't been in his own share of dustups. Anticipating Hardy's bull-rush, he was already braced, his body coiled and ready.

So when the big bouncer's thick arms stretched toward him, Firestick thrust his own arms up between them and swept outward, knocking the clawed, ready-to-grab hands off to either side. At the same time, the old mountain man lunged forward to meet Hardy's rushing momentum. At the last instant, as their bodies were ready to crash together, he snapped his head forward and slammed his forehead against the lower half of Hardy's face, crushing teeth and mashing the big man's nose.

Though they still collided, chest to chest, Hardy's momentum had been partially halted by the head butt. His own head rocked back sharply and the collision sent him staggering a step and a half to one side. Other than that, however, Firestick was surprised to see the impact appeared not to have stunned him as much as it would have most men. The bouncer was every bit as rugged as he looked.

Nevertheless, the blow to his nose was sure to release vision-blurring tears that he could neither stop nor blink away for a minute or so, and the heavy flow of blood starting to clog his flattened nostrils would soon start taking a toll on his ability to breathe.

Recognizing these things, Firestick knew he needed to take full advantage of them before Hardy was able to regain his full vision and surge back with all his strength and experience before his wind started to go. With that in mind, Firestick—fight-seasoned in his own right and also packing a powerful build that the years hadn't diminished all that much—moved quickly to follow up on his initial telling blow.

His target was the sizable gut that Hardy displayed as a counter to his harder-muscled upper torso. Too many hours sitting on his bouncer perch sipping shots and beer chasers to pass the time between outbreaks of trouble had bloated and softened his middle.

Before Hardy had fully regained his balance from the side stagger, Firestick pressed forward and landed a hard right hook square to the middle of his belly. Hardy bent forward instinctively, hugging his gut as if to try and hold in the air that came gushing out. This left his ribs exposed, and that's where Firestick aimed his next punch, reverse-twisting his torso and drilling a left hook this time to those unprotected ribs.

Hardy emitted a loud grunt of pain and rage as more air was driven out of him. He staggered again, several more steps this time, until he bumped hard against an unoccupied gaming table and sent it skidding three feet, spilling chairs to either side.

By this point, all the conversational buzz throughout the rest of the saloon had stopped and all eyes were on the fight that had broken out. No one said a word. Several mouths were hanging open in astonishment at the sight of Hardy getting the worst of an exchange for once.

But the fight was far from over. Getting a bit over-anxious to try and end it, Firestick closed too fast on Hardy and leaned into a sweeping backhand the bouncer threw as he shoved away from the table he'd fallen against. The blow crashed against the side of Firestick's face, spinning him half around and sending him into a stagger of his own. Sensing Hardy would attempt a rapid follow-through, Firestick went with the momentum of the spin and staggered instead of trying to halt and rebalance himself right away. This amounted to a circling maneuver that took Firestick wide away from his opponent. And Hardy, exactly as Firestick had anticipated, in his still vision-blurred state made a awkwardly futile lunge to where the former mountain man no longer was.

His rage refueled over the frustration of having been

outsmarted, Hardy wheeled about and locked a hateful glare on Firestick. He was blinking rapidly, trying to clear his vision, and a thick, bright red smear of blood from his smashed nose had poured down over his lips and chin. His breathing was starting to come in hard puffs.

"Not too late to stop and have that talk now," Firestick suggested, his own breath also a bit quickened as he felt pressure on his rib that was still healing from the alley brawl a few days before. "Be a sight easier than goin' ahead with this."

"Oh, we're gonna talk, alright," Hardy snarled. "Only I'm gonna say what I got to say by breaking you in two!"

To punctuate his threat, the bouncer suddenly snatched up one of the scattered chairs from the gaming table, wielding it in one hand as easily as if it were a scrap of paper, and hurled it viciously at Firestick. The latter got his arms up and one shoulder partly turned, but the impact of the heavy wooden chair crashing against him still packed a punch. The blunt, rounded end of one of the legs hit like a club just above his left ear. He felt hot blood immediately gush down the side of his neck as he was knocked backward.

As Firestick was driven back, pieces of the shattered chair clattering around him, Hardy charged straight after the missile he'd thrown. He lowered his head and shoulders and hurled himself forward, aiming to ram into his opponent like a human spear. Rattled somewhat after being clubbed by the chair leg, Firestick saw what was coming and braced himself as best he could, but this time he had no time to counter Hardy's bull rush.

When the big bouncer rammed into him, Firestick was

driven back even more, until his back slammed hard against the tall legs and cross braces of the elevated bouncer's chair. Though he clenched his stomach muscles as tight as he could, the former mountain man nevertheless felt a great gush of his own breath driven out of him. At the same time, though, the force of Hardy hurtling into him somehow had the strange effect of jarring Firestick back into clear focus.

As the sneering bouncer drew back, thinking he had Firestick in a stunned condition and therefore was preparing to finish him with repeated shoulder slams or perhaps an onslaught of punches, the crafty old mountain man knew exactly what he had to do. When Hardy drew back, Firestick thrust upward with both hands and gripped the legs of the tall chair he was pressed against. And then, as Hardy started to lunge forward again, intending to drill in with another punishing, rib-cracking shoulder blast, Firestick yanked ahead and down with all his might, tipping the bouncer station suddenly forward so that it crashed heavily down on Hardy even as he was propelling his body forward. The crunching impact was so loud it caused the onlookers who heard it to cringe in response.

Hardy dropped to his hands and knees and now he was the one with shattered, broken pieces of wood clattering around him. The durable, stubborn scrapper seemed to teeter in that position, between falling the rest of the way down and trying to get up again. Firestick, crouching bloody and breathing hard, reached out and wrapped his hand around a length of broken chair leg, ready to use it as a club if that's what it was going to take to convince

Hardy to stay down. But he'd scarcely picked it up when the big bouncer finally gave in and flopped heavily onto his chest and stomach.

After a moment, Firestick heard somebody say, "You can drop the club now, cowboy. Fight's over. You won."

CHAPTER 27

Looking around, Firestick saw that the speaker was a man who had just entered through the batwing doors. He was of average height and build, fortyish, with long auburn hair that fell to his shoulders and a drooping mustache of the same color curling around the corners of his mouth. He was clad in a black swallowtail coat and pinstriped pants tucked into high, flat-heeled boots. On his head, cocked at a precise angle, sat a wide-brimmed Boss of the Plains hat, and around his waist was tied a bright red sash. Tucked in behind the sash, on prominent display, was an ivory-handled Remington revolver.

The rest of the men present in the saloon seemed to eye this newcomer with a certain amount of wariness, shifting around somewhat restlessly but remaining quiet. Firestick straightened up from his crouch, letting go of the broken chair leg, and studied the man in the red sash with his own measure of wariness.

"How'd this start? Who threw the first punch?" the man asked as he moved forward, toward the middle of the room. Only then did Firestick notice the glint of a lawman's badge peeking out from behind the lapel of his coat.

The derby-hatted barkeep was quick to respond, "Wasn't exactly a first punch thrown, Reb. This stranger here"—he gestured toward Firestick—"came in looking to talk to Hardy. Something about a mutual friend. They spoke for only about a minute and then Hardy came off his chair like a raging bull, made a grab for the stranger, and . . . well, the stranger didn't, uh, take kindly to that."

The lawman's eyes made a leisurely sweep, touching on the shoved-away table, the scattered and broken chairs, and the bloodied form of Hardy laying facedown on the floor.

"I'd say 'not take kindly' might be a bit of an understatement," he drawled with a touch of Southern accent. Bringing his gaze to rest on Firestick, he continued, "Care to enlighten the rest of us on just what it was about your discussion with Mr. Hardy that made him come chargin' after you that way?"

"Under most circumstances, I'd say what me and Hardy talked about was between the two of us," Firestick replied measuredly. "But if you'd care to introduce yourself proper-like and tell me you're askin' on account of that badge you're wearin', then I expect I'd owe you an answer."

The lawman smiled thinly. "That's a fair enough response. My apologies for not actin' more professional, especially when dealin' with a fellow law officer, Marshal McQueen." He peeled back his coat lapel, more fully exposing the badge behind it, then added, "My name is Reb Davies. I represent the law in Pecos and serve as bailiff to Judge Walter Buchanon. Actin' in either or both of those roles, then, let me ask again that you explain the cause of the trouble that occurred here."

Firestick nodded. "Alright. As far as any discussion between Hardy and me leadin' up to this, there really wasn't none. I was *wantin'* one—I came lookin' to ask Hardy about a friend of mine who'd passed through here a while back. But he wasn't willin' to talk. Not at all. Right off, before I got a single question out, he got almighty rude and mean. Threatened to break me in two and throw me outta here . . . So I let him know I don't hold much for threats and informed him that if he tried to follow through on the noise he was makin' it might turn into a problem."

Davies took it from there. "And that, of course, brought Hardy off his chair and the, er, 'problem' commenced."

"That's pretty much the way it went, yeah," said Firestick.

"That fits with what I saw and heard," the barkeep spoke up again. "The stranger came in acting easy and polite. Told me, too, how he was looking to talk to Hardy about an old friend. But you know how damned ornery and miserable Hardy can be. Most fellas just steer clear when he growls and snorts to be left alone. Reckon this time he ran into somebody who wasn't put off so easy."

The rest of the crowd was stirring more animatedly now, starting to chatter and talk among themselves. From the snatches of conversation he could make out, it sounded clear to Firestick that none of them were feeling too sorry about what had befallen Hardy. In fact, many of the saloon's customers seemed quite pleased with the outcome. He remembered Beartooth relating how there had been a similar reaction back when he'd had his run-in with the hot-tempered bouncer.

"I'm willin' to pay for my part of the damage that was done," he said now to both the barkeep and Davies. "Reckon I *could* have walked away when Hardy tried to brush me off. But if that's the way he treats folks in general, sounds to me like he's owed some push-back at least once in a while."

"Hard to argue that," Davies allowed. "On the other hand, don't you go and forget he keeps any other trouble at a pretty low level in here. That's why the owner sees it as a reasonable trade-off to have him around."

Firestick shrugged. "His place, his call to make."

The barkeep came around the end of the bar with a wet cloth that he held out to Firestick, saying, "Here. You got a pretty deep cut on the side of your head; hold this against it to stop the bleeding."

Firestick thanked him and took the cloth. Dabbing it to the side of his head, he motioned with his free hand toward Hardy and said, "What about him?"

"What about him?" the stick man grunted. "He's left plenty of other men layin' in their own blood."

"Come on, Pastrelli," said Davies. "He's busted up pretty bad . . . you need to send somebody for Doc Peabody."

"I know, Reb. Take it easy," the barkeep told him. "Against my better judgment, I already sent one of the boys to fetch the sawbones."

If "the boys" Pastrelli referred to meant the rest of the customers in the saloon, they were by now well past their quiet gawking stage and were milling and drinking and jabbering with a lot of energy, much of it rehashing—and even partially reenacting, in a couple instances—the events of the fight. A couple of the braver souls had even ventured close enough, drinks in hand, to have a better look at the fallen Hardy, like men approaching to study a dangerous animal that had been brought low.

"Probably be best, for the sake of keepin' things settled down," Davies said, his gaze coming to rest on Firestick again, "if you wasn't present when the doc brings Hardy back around. Plus, my purpose for comin' here in the first place was to extend to you a request from Judge Buchanon for you to pay him a visit. Pastrelli can send Doc Peabody over there to tend to your cut after he's done here. Any objection to acceptin' the judge's invitation?"

Firestick held the blood-smeared cloth away from his head for a moment and examined it before answering, "Reckon I've done enough objectin' to things, leastways for the time bein' . . . Lead on to Judge Buchanon."

CHAPTER 28

Coming as little surprise to Firestick, Davies led him no farther than the saloon across the street from the Texas Rose—the small, somewhat shabby-looking establishment where he estimated the curious-acting telegraph operator had gone earlier. The Courthouse Saloon & General Store . . . if this was where they were going to find Judge Buchanon, Firestick mused, then that gave a whole new and ironic twist to the name.

Ushered through a standard door, as opposed to the batwing style many saloons throughout the West favored, Firestick found himself in a cramped but neatly arranged room. To the right was the general store half, complete with a long, unvarnished counter stacked with candy jars and other snacks and trinkets meant to appeal to youngsters. Barrels containing crackers, flour, pickles, and so forth were lined up in front of the counter, and behind it were shelves and shelves of canned goods, medicines, bolts of cloth, some ready-to-wear clothing, even an assortment of boots.

To the left, separated by a rather flimsy-looking partition reaching only three-quarters of the way to the ceiling, was the saloon half of the business. A narrow aisle ran alongside this partition, ending at a door on the back wall that Firestick guessed must open to the newer, larger addition he had noted from the street. Upon entering, however, Davies promptly turned and led the way into the saloon portion.

This proved to be an area roughly the same size as the store, containing three round-topped tables spread before a short, equally unvarnished bar with beer kegs and shelves of liquor behind it. At the far end of the bar, off to one side, erected before a flat section of the rear wall adorned with the flag of Texas crossed with that of the United States, stood a tall, rather ornate and highly polished wooden stand that Firestick realized after a moment represented a judge's bench.

There were only two customers present, a pair of old-timers seated at one of the tables, hunched over sudsy mugs of beer and the game of checkers they were engrossed in. Behind the bar, another elderly gent stood leaning on his elbows. He had a growth of bristly white whiskers and was dressed in a crisp white shirt with gartered sleeves, a maroon bow tie, and a silk-paneled vest, gold in color. Atop his head sat a tall beaver hat with a band of matching gold silk. Below the hat, a set of quick, alert eyes tracked the approach of Firestick and Davies. Meeting the gaze from those eyes as Davies led the way to a spot at the bar directly in front of the man, Firestick knew before any introductions were made that he was now in the presence of the infamous Judge Walter Buchanon.

"Judge," Davies announced as they neared the bar, "this is Elwood McQueen from Buffalo Peak."

Buchanon straightened up but made no attempt to extend a hand. "McQueen," he said, "I'm Judge Walter Buchanon."

Firestick nodded. "Gathered as much. Pleased to meet you, sir . . . and I hope that cuts both ways."

"We'll see about that," Buchanon responded gruffly. He eyed Firestick up and down, taking particular note of the bloodied side of his head. Snapping a glance at Davies, he said, "He give you trouble getting him over here?"

Davies shook his head. "No, sir. The only trouble he's given anybody is Hardy, back at the Texas Rose. Trouble that Hardy asked for, accordin' to Pastrelli and others over there who saw it."

The judge's eyebrows lifted. "He tangled with Hardy and he's still walking?"

"Hardy's the one who's havin' trouble standin' up," Davies answered.

"I'm not only able to walk," Firestick spoke up, "but I'm also able to talk for myself—in case you want to speak *to* me instead of around me."

Davies showed another of his thin smiles. "He's kind of a stickler for actin' proper and professional, sir."

"Acting *professional*?" Buchanon echoed, aiming a scowl at Firestick. "You call it professional to ride into a town with intent to conduct a criminal investigation yet not bother to give any notification of same to the town's legal authorities? Would you like someone to show up in your town under those circumstances, Marshal?"

"Reckon I wouldn't," Firestick allowed. "But it don't seem like you're lackin' much in the way of knowin' who

I am and why I'm here. I expect I can thank a couple of Texas Rangers back in Buffalo Peak for wirin' that information ahead and the telegraph operator here in your town for spreadin' word plenty quick that I'd showed up."

"Be that as it may," Buchanon said, "it doesn't absolve you from coming forward on your own."

"I only just got in town an hour or so ago," Firestick pointed out. "Had every intention of lookin' you up to talk to you about those murder charges against my friend, Judge, but didn't see it as something needin' done in a big rush before I got squared away and had the chance to check on a couple things."

"Engaging in a saloon brawl is your idea of getting 'squared away'?"

"Not mine, no. But that fella Hardy sorta insisted otherwise," Firestick explained, lowering the cloth he'd been holding to his head long enough to fold it to a spot that wasn't already blood smeared and then reapplying it.

"Doc Peabody will be comin' by to look to that head of his," Davies said, "after he gets done treatin' Hardy over across the street."

"Good. I don't favor having blood dripped all over my place." Buchanon grunted. He regarded Firestick again. "Are you a drinking man, Marshal?"

"Been known to toss down my share," Firestick answered. "And right about now, if you're askin', I'm thinkin' a shot of red-eye would go down mighty good."

Buchanon gestured to the table behind where Firestick and Davies were standing. "Take a seat, then. I'll bring a bottle 'round."

Half a minute later, true to his word, the judge had shuffled around the end of the bar carrying three glasses and a bottle of bourbon, which he placed on the table where Firestick and Davies had seated themselves. He hitched up a chair for himself and sank down onto it. Davies reached for the bottle and began pouring.

"You guessed correctly, of course, about Rangers Arbry and Rodgers wiring ahead about you being on your way here," the judge said to Firestick. He paused to lift his glass and take a pull before continuing. "It may surprise you to know, however, that in addition to feeling obligated to provide that information, they also felt obligated to provide an assessment of you that was most complimentary. They painted you as an honest man who believes earnestly in the innocence of his friend—this man Skinner, now faced with a murder charge issued by me."

Firestick took a drink of his own bourbon, said nothing.

Buchanon continued, "I place a great deal of stock in the opinion of any man who wears a ranger star and particularly in an assessment from Arbry or Rodgers, both of whom I have worked with in the past and hold in high regard. Were it not for the favorable opinion they expressed about you, frankly, I doubt my welcome of you and your purpose in coming here would be quite so friendly."

"I'm not here lookin' to cause grief or make trouble, Judge," Firestick said. "I'm just after the truth, same as you. Only I believe the truth to be that my friend is innocent of killin' that poor girl, and I'm hopin' to find a way to prove it."

"My understanding, from the wire Arbry and Rodgers sent," said Buchanon, "is that your friend is presently unaccounted for, on the run."

"That's not quite accurate, Judge," Firestick was quick

to correct. "Beartooth is out of touch for the time bein', that's true—but it's because he's off on a business trip for our ranch, not because he's on the run. He knows nothing about the wanted papers on him, you see, so nobody can rightly say he's runnin' from 'em."

"In that case, once he does become aware that he's a wanted man, can he be expected to turn himself in?"

Firestick hesitated a moment, wanting to choose his words carefully. "Don't reckon I can say for sure what he'll do if and when it comes to that. Be a stretch, I think, to expect he'd come forward real sudden—not until he can find out more about what's behind those dodgers on him."

"And how would he do that? By contacting you?"

"Could be."

"As an officer of the law, wouldn't you see it as your duty to arrest him in that case?"

"I'm tryin' to avoid it comin' to that," Firestick answered. "My whole reason for bein' here is aimed at findin' something to turn around that testimony against him."

Buchanon frowned. "So you haven't even spoken to Skinner about these allegations against him, yet you're so wholly convinced of his innocence that you're willing to go to such lengths?"

Firestick clenched his teeth. "I don't need to hear Beartooth say it to know he's not the murderer of a young woman."

"Your loyalty to your friend is admirable, Marshal. But by coming to Pecos thinking here is where you'll find proof of his innocence," said the judge, his eyebrows pinching together again, "you are basically implying that myself and Mr. Davies and others involved with us in the investigation of the murder have done a sloppy job and somehow overlooked something."

Firestick shook his head. "Nobody ever heard me say those words. I got no basis to. From what I understand, you issued those murder charges on account of a witness who came forward and identified Beartooth—Malachi Skinner, as you know him—to be the killer. Given that, and reckonin' you got no other strong suspect, I can understand how you'd proceed the way you did. But the way I'm comin' at it is that your witness is badly mistaken . . . either that, or they're flat-out lyin' for some reason, to make trouble for Beartooth."

"Again implying that I and my men could be easily fooled by such a false witness."

"A good liar can fool most anybody. At least for a while," Firestick said.

"Have you seen the wanted posters on your man Skinner? The description—the image?"

Firestick could see where he was going. He nodded. "They're all a mighty good match," he admitted.

"In addition to that," Buchanon said, "the witness was very well versed on other details about Skinner— everything except that he was a deputy marshal in your town. Apart from that, he knew where to find him, knew he had a ranch in the area, and so forth. The witness told a convincing tale about how he and Skinner had spent time together, years past, trapping up in the mountains. He told how they'd run into each other here in Pecos at the time of the murder. In checking hotel records, we found that Skinner did indeed spend two nights here in town . . . One of those nights being the same one as when Miss Katy Carruthers was murdered."

"I'm not denyin' that, the timin' of Beartooth bein' up this way when the murder took place," said Firestick. "As one of his partners in the horse ranch, I recall mighty plain how he came up here back then on a horse-buyin' trip. But he sure wasn't the only one in town that night. It don't take much to see you got a whole lot of folks comin' and goin' here in Pecos almost every day—and I expect that was especially true durin' those days when the Della Devane show was in town."

"That's what made it so difficult," Buchanon said bitterly, "to narrow down who among such a crowd was the fiend who saw fit to take the life of a vulnerable, un-suspecting showgirl . . . Until the sworn statement of a witness finally driven by guilt to come forward gave us the break we so desperately needed."

"This witness got a name?" Firestick wanted to know.

"Of course he does," the judge said somewhat smugly. "It will be revealed accordingly, at the time of the trial . . . or when your lawyer Taggert files the proper papers for evidence due the defense."

A corner of Firestick's mouth quirked upward wryly. "You don't miss much, do you?"

"No, I don't believe I do," Buchanon declared. "You'd do well to keep that in mind. No matter what you may have heard about the sometimes wild and woolly ways I dispense justice around these parts from right here inside my saloon"—he jerked a thumb over his shoulder toward the judge's stand—"I nevertheless do so fairly and even-handedly. That means I don't make a habit of issuing murder charges without good cause and a strong belief they are justified."

Firestick pinned the judge with a very direct look.

"With all due respect, sir, that almost sounds like you've already made up your mind. Ain't that supposed to wait until *after* the trial?"

"And it shall," Buchanon huffed. "But that doesn't prevent me from having certain inclinations ahead of time. Even judges, after all, are only human."

Further discussion was interrupted by the arrival of a spare, bespectacled, ramrod-straight individual of fifty or so carrying a medical bag. He was introduced as Dr. Peabody and wasted no time hitching up a chair beside Firestick and going to work on the gash above his ear.

"I see," he murmured, "that Mr. Hardy didn't entirely lose his touch for inflicting damage on others—though, I must say, this appears rather anemic in comparison to what you dished out to him."

"Speakin' of Hardy," Firestick said, addressing Buchanon in order to focus on something other than the doctor cleaning and probing at his wound, "are you willin' to at least tell me whether or not he had anything to do with this witness who came forward to make the claims against Beartooth?"

"Hardy?" The judge frowned. "What makes you think he had any involvement in that?"

"Guess you'd call it a hunch. After he got back from his trip up this way last fall," Firestick explained, "I remember Beartooth tellin' about a saloon ruckus he got into while he was here. Hardy's name got mentioned—him and some other fella Beartooth was in a card game with. An argument over the cards was how the ruckus started."

"You have a name for the other man, the cardplayer?"

"Don't recall hearin' one. That's a piece of information I was hopin' to get out of Hardy."

The judge's frown was still in place. "This card game and the ensuing ruckus—how does that figure into your hunch about the murder charges against your friend?"

"From Beartooth's tellin', neither Hardy nor that other fella fared too good in the ruckus," Firestick told him. "I was thinkin' that might have left some hard feelin's that festered into enough of a grudge to cause one of those *hombres* to work up a notion of trying to get payback by comin' forward with that phony murder claim."

"That would be a pretty serious damn grudge," Buchanon exclaimed.

"Seen as bad or worse over less," Firestick said steadfastly. "But, like I said, it was only a hunch. A place to start, something to pick at in hopes of diggin' up something to point a different way than Beartooth."

"Anybody getting the better of Hardy is a rarity," Buchanon mused. He turned to Davies. "You recall anything like that—Hardy getting the worst of an altercation from back then?"

"Come to think on it, yeah, I do," responded Davies. "In all the hoopla surroundin' the big show bein' in town and then the murder takin' place, it didn't get a lot of attention. I don't recall catchin' the name of Skinner at the time, but talk had it that it was an old mountain man responsible for leavin' Hardy flattened."

"For what it's worth, I can add my confirmation of the event also," spoke up the doctor. "It was another occasion where I had the pleasure of patching up Hardy instead of merely another of his victims." Addressing Firestick directly, he added, "You fellows from down Buffalo Peak way seem to come with a pretty thick layer of bark. Which you'll be thankful for here in a minute because I need to throw some stitches in this cut of yours . . . You ready?"

"Do what you have to," Firestick said through gritted teeth. "I'm tired of havin' blood dribble down the side of my neck."

"Something else I remember from that fracas," said Davies, "was that the cardplayer who was part of it was a fella named Weickert. You should remember that name, Judge—he was the four-flushin' little weasel who got shot by Bob Teeler right here in your place last winter and died with two aces up his sleeve."

"Ah, yes. Justifiable homicide, plain as day," declared Buchanon.

"That's rich," said Firestick, biting off the words as Peabody's needle pulled tight on the first stitch. "The pipsqueak who accused Beartooth of cheatin' and caused that whole ruckus last fall turned out to be a card cheat himself?"

Davies nodded. "That's the way it went."

"I'll be damned," Firestick grated.

"I don't know about that," the judge said, "but what I trust you will be is reasonable enough to see that your hunch hasn't panned out. Hardy had no relationship with the witness who came forward against your friend. And the other man who might have borne a grudge stemming from the fracas with Skinner was long dead before the witness spoke up."

"I'll add something else," said Davies. "I've had my share of run-ins with Hardy over the way he goes overboard dealin' with troublemakers in the Texas Rose. You get a pretty good idea of what a fella like that is capable of, after a time. As a lawman yourself, you probably know what I mean, McQueen. My hunch is that Hardy just ain't shrewd enough to try and get even with somebody by causin' him trouble from some outside angle. He's too much like a blunt instrument. He has a grudge against somebody, he'll hunt that somebody down and try to pay him back direct . . . Leastways, like I said, that's my opinion."

"I'll keep it in mind," Firestick replied tersely.

"Let me give you something else to keep in mind," said Judge Buchanon, leaning back in his chair and regarding Firestick. "I'm pretty good at reading men, too. And it's not hard to see you're unsatisfied by what's been revealed here. Whether or not you accept that neither Hardy nor Weickert had anything to do with the testimony against your friend, you're not ready to give up. You think there must be some kind of answer to helping Skinner here in Pecos.

"As I previously said, I admire your loyalty to your friend, and as I also said, I hold in high regard the assessment of Rangers Arbry and Rodgers. Based on that, I won't stand in the way of you trying to find your answer. Within reason. Inasmuch as you are well out of your jurisdiction and therefore have no legal standing to conduct an investigation, I will require you to show some discretion and be neither inflammatory nor disparaging to our existing authority, and it should go without saying, I further expect that if you turn up anything of significance, you will promptly share it with Mr. Davies and myself."

"That sounds reasonable enough, Judge. I'm obliged," said Firestick.

His expression flat and emotionless, the judge added, "One other thing that should go without saying. As soon as Skinner is apprehended, my intent remains to bring him swiftly to trial on the charges that have been issued against him."

CHAPTER 29

Firestick headed out of the Courthouse Saloon feeling at loose ends. He was weary, sore, and discouraged. With his hunch about Hardy and the shady cardplayer now known as Weickert seemingly dead-ended, he had no alternate course in mind to try and pursue. He'd been banking too much, he realized, on one of those two being a key to shifting the focus—or at least introducing some doubt—when it came to Beartooth as the murderer.

The testimony of an anonymous former mountain man, that's what he was up against. More to the point, it was what Beartooth would be up against if he was to get nabbed and brought before Buchanon. And while Firestick had found the cantankerous old judge likable to a certain extent, it was still uncomfortably clear that he had his mind as good as made up and wanted a conviction for the killing of that showgirl as bad or worse than he wanted the absolute truth.

Some insight into what was driving this inclination came to Firestick after he left the saloon portion of the judge's building but lingered for a few minutes before exiting entirely. Despite the plight of Beartooth ever-churning in his mind, he was still intrigued and curious about the newer addition that towered at the rear and contrasted so sharply with the drabness of the store and saloon in front. This curiosity caused him to wander down the aisle that ran alongside the partition separating the two halves until he reached a door at the far end that opened to the add-on. The door was closed and bolted from the other side, but through the eye-level glass panes he could look through into the spacious addition.

What he saw was essentially an auditorium, a scaled-down show palace complete with rows and rows of chairs—enough to seat at least three hundred people by Firestick's quick estimate—with a wide, deep performance stage at the far end. A large, ornate chandelier hung high over the center of the stage, and above the seats ran two rows of smaller chandeliers, three along each side. A colorful banner spread across the front rim of the stage proclaimed: DELLA DEVANE'S ORLEANS QUEEN ENTERTAINMENT EXTRAVAGANZA.

Firestick stood taking all of this in when a familiar voice spoke just behind his left shoulder. "Quite a layout, ain't it?"

"Yeah, it sure is," Firestick agreed, turning to glance at Reb Davies, who had moved up quietly behind him.

"The judge built it special just for her . . . Miss Devane, that is," said Davies. "She put on three shows here and the place was packed to bustin' at the seams every night. Folks came from miles around. The judge had a smile near as wide as the whole room and was so pleased and swelled up with pride I thought he might bust out his own seams."

"That the only thing this whole structure has been used for?" Firestick asked.

"Uh-huh. The only thing it ever will be, too. Leastways until Miss Devane and her extravaganza return," said Davies.

Firestick gave him a look. "Is that likely, seein's how one of her showgals got killed here?"

"The judge is countin' on it . . . once he's able to bring the killer to justice," Davies replied.

Firestick held his eyes, didn't say anything right away.

"I know what you're thinkin'," Davies went on, his own gaze and tone steady. "Everybody knows how the judge feels about Della Devane. I heard somebody once say he's 'obsessed' by her. I had to ask around to find out what the word means—do you know?"

"Reckon I got a pretty good idea."

"Uh-huh. Well, I guess it fits right enough." Davies's mouth pressed momentarily into a tight, straight line. Then: "So what I figure you're thinkin'—and, in your place, I expect I might be, too—is that the judge wants so bad to catch and punish a killer, in order to satisfy Miss Devane so's she'll come back again, that he might be overly quick to judge anybody who looks good for the part."

"Pretty plain he wants real bad to see those wanted dodgers served on my friend," Firestick said. "And you heard him say he's already inclined toward thinkin' he's got the right man."

"I also heard him say he won't make up his mind all the way until the trial's done." Davies' expression grew sterner. "I've been with the judge for a long time, McQueen. I know better than most how he longed to get Della Devane to come here, how he wrote her letter after letter, how he sent off for newspaper accounts and playbills from the shows she and her troupe did in other parts of the country . . . That word. Obsessed. Yeah, that's how he is when it comes to her.

"But I'll tell you something else he's obsessed with. That's *justice.* Oh, I know all the yarns that have spread about him over the years . . . how he never goes by lawbooks and conducts court in his saloon. How he once fined a man found dead in the street for litterin'. How he packs a .45 under his robe when he's on the bench and how I myself ain't nothing but a hired gunslinger on his payroll . . . I ain't gonna begin to go into which parts of those got some truth and which ones are flat lies. A lot of 'em, both ways, go back to the old days, the wilder times when it took a certain amount of noise and flamboyance to grab things by the nape of the neck and start tamin' 'em down . . . But through it all—past, present, and future—I'll defy anybody to show me where the judge ever railroaded an innocent man. His idea of what form justice should take might skew away from the notion of other folks' sometimes, but it never got dished out to anybody who didn't deserve it."

By the time Davies was finished, his eyes were burning with the intensity of red-hot coals, and gazing into them, Firestick was thoroughly convinced of one thing: Whether he was right or wrong, the man fiercely believed everything he had just said.

"There's an old sayin' about bein' a first time for everything," Firestick replied in a measured tone. "If what you say is true, then let's hope that old sayin' never finds its way to the judge—not now, not ever."

CHAPTER 30

After returning to his hotel room long enough to grab a bundle of clean duds, Firestick walked back up the street until he spotted a barbershop that advertised also having hot baths available. Once he'd occupied the chair for a shave and trim, he was led to a tent area in the back where he then occupied a galvanized tub of steaming, sudsy water, scrubbing and soaking in it until the water turned tepid.

From there, decked out in the clean attire he'd traded his blood-spattered shirt and other trail-worn clothes for, he found a café that served up an excellent steak with all the trimmings.

As Firestick leisurely enjoyed the meal, he ran through his mind the session with Judge Buchanon and Reb Davies. Grudgingly, he had to admit he'd heard enough to convince him that neither Hardy nor Weickert held any potential for having anything to do with the charges against Beartooth.

So that left the actual witness, the one only sparingly described by the judge. Another former mountain man, an alleged old friend of Beartooth's from that bygone time up in the high reaches. Yet Beartooth had mentioned nothing about running into anybody from the old days during his Pecos trip last fall. Surely such a meeting wouldn't have slipped his mind.

It was a given that the witness was a liar—that much was established by his identification of Beartooth as a murderer in the first place. Therefore, though it seemed unnecessarily elaborate, did that mean he was also lying about having ever been a mountain man? Or—to still fit with Firestick's original hunch, but from a different angle—could that much be true but instead of being a friend from back then was he perhaps somebody harboring an old grudge he was now seeking to settle? Disputes over traplines or hunting territories had certainly cropped up now and then in the high country, and Beartooth had been involved in his share. In some instances, men had died as the result of such disputes; other times, the intruders had merely been run off, empty-handed and bitter.

Firestick was hesitant to remain stuck on a grudge or revenge—especially one tracing back that far—as being behind all of this. But he couldn't think of anything else in the way of a possible motive. None that made sense. There had to be a purpose—a gain—involved in trying to make so much trouble for somebody. The only ones who would benefit materially from Beartooth being sent to prison or facing a hangman's noose, as far as Firestick could see, was him and Moosejaw by turning the Double M split from thirds to halves. But that reasoning was too ridiculous to waste even a fraction of a second's thought on.

The only other possibility, and a slim one it was, could be that the witness made a horrible but honest mistake.

Meaning he must have seen or heard something that caused him to erroneously conclude Beartooth truly *was* the killer. Yet if he stayed convinced of that, mistakenly or not, his testimony would be just as damning. The only hope, in that case—and it would be slimmer still—was that the sight of Beartooth should he be brought in for trial might jolt the witness into realizing his mistake . . .

But no, Firestick wasn't willing to bank on that. He had no intention of letting things reach that point. He didn't know, didn't want to think, what extreme he might go to in order to avoid the risk of letting Beartooth be tried here in Pecos, not the way things stood. He just knew that he—and he had no doubt Beartooth and Moosejaw would feel the same—could never allow it to come to that.

If he only knew the name of that damn witness! If he could have just a handful of minutes alone with him . . .

Unlikely as the latter seemed, finding out the alleged former mountain man's name was another matter. Judge Buchanon had said that much would have to be revealed to Taggert, acting as Beartooth's lawyer, if he filed proper papers as a representative for the defense. Whatever else he did from this point, Firestick decided, what he would take care of first thing in the morning would be getting a wire off telling Kate to set Taggert in motion and sic him on getting that name as soon as possible.

During the time Firestick spent eating and pondering, other diners came and went around him, marking the dinner hour. The place never grew overly crowded, however, so the murmur of conversation and clink of silverware remained at a low level. In the course of this, Firestick gradually became aware of frequent furtive glances aimed his way. Accompanying these came a few faintly amplified words, enough for him to gather that this interest in him stemmed from his getting the best of Hardy in that saloon brawl. He found this bitterly amusing. Here he was, in town on a life-or-death matter, and it was a minor scrape with the town bully that was earning him attention and a certain amount of notoriety.

By the time he left the café, the long shadows of late afternoon were thickening into evening darkness. The weariness and aches Firestick had felt earlier, temporarily dulled by the barbering and long soak, were returning. And the restless grinding in his mind had never let up. This, he knew, would prevent sleep from settling in any time soon, despite feeling weary.

But the quiet confines and soft bed of his hotel room nevertheless beckoned as a place where he could stretch out and continue to think. Also there, and also beckoning, was the bottle he'd brought along in his war bag to help cope with cold nights on the trail. A lonely hotel room in a strange town could have a way of seeming mighty chilly as well . . .

The first knock was very tentative, almost too light to rattle the hotel room door. The second one was only slightly harder, but by then Firestick was up off the bed and gripping the .44 he'd skinned from his gunbelt hanging on the bedpost. He glided in stocking feet across the floor's thin carpet and took a stance off-center of the door.

"Who's there?" he called.

A muffled voice responded. "It's Strousel . . . Uh, Stuart Strousel. From the livery barn."

Firestick pulled out his pocket watch and checked the time. It was past ten. He'd fallen asleep stretched out on the bed, fully clothed except for his boots.

He went to the door, threw back the lock, and then stepped to one side again. "Come on in," he said.

The door opened slowly, with the same tentativeness as the knock. Strousel poked his head forward, sort of peeking ahead, before the rest of him entered.

"Close the door," Firestick told him.

Strousel reached behind himself, pushing the door shut with one hand. In the other hand he was clutching his hat, which he held up in front of his chest like a shield. "Sorry to come around botherin' you so late, Mr. McQueen," he said.

"What brings you? Is there something wrong?" Firestick wanted to know.

Strousel's forehead puckered. "I sure hope not. But I, uh . . . I'm kinda worried about one of your horses. The sorrel . . . She was fine up till a couple hours ago, but now she's laid herself down and don't seem to want to get up. Not for nothing . . . I even tried coaxin' her with some fresh grain, but she won't budge. She don't seem to be in pain or frettin' any, just don't want to move. You seemed to have some savvy about horses and was clearly fond of those two when you brought 'em in. I thought you'd want to know, maybe come see for yourself."

By that point Firestick was already stomping into his boots. It took only a moment to strap on his gunbelt and grab his hat. He motioned to the door and said, "Let's go have a look."

The night air was chilly and the town was quiet at this hour except for some music and the infrequent whoop drifting out of the saloons farther up the street. A row of street lamps combined with the bluish silver wash of illumination from a clear sky overhead lighted their way as they made for the livery barn. Strousel was silent and somewhat nervous-acting, which Firestick read as a man showing genuine concern for an animal in his care.

When they reached the barn, one of its double doors was standing open. Entering, Firestick saw a lantern burning dimly back near the far end of the center aisle.

"She's back there, back by that lantern," Strousel said at his shoulder.

Firestick strode forward, his own anxiety increasing a bit. The sorrel was a fine animal. He would hate for this trip to have exposed her to some illness. As he proceeded down the length of the barn, he failed to notice Strousel fading back, not keeping pace with him.

When he reached the stall, Firestick saw, in the yellow glow of the hanging lantern, the sorrel standing there. She turned her head to look back at him, calmly munching a mouthful of hay.

"Well, how about that. Looks like she just took a notion to get up when she was good and ready," he said, his mouth spreading in a relieved grin as he reached out to pat her flank. "Appears to me like there's no problem after all."

"Maybe the horse ain't got a problem. But the same can't be said for you, you meddlin' bastard!"

CHAPTER 31

The voice came from the deep shadows just outside the circle of light thrown by the lantern. It didn't belong to the liveryman Strousel. Though Firestick knew he'd heard it before, recently, it took a moment for him to place it.

Then he did—it belonged to Hardy, the bouncer from the Texas Rose Saloon.

Firestick turned around slowly, his right hand drifting down to hover above the .44 on his hip.

"Don't get no foolish notions about tryin' for that hogleg. You're the one standin' in full light and there's already a gun drawed and aimed at you."

To emphasize the claim, there came the metallic sound of a pistol's hammer being thumbed back to full cock.

Firestick's lips peeled back, baring his teeth in a sneer. "So that's the game. You couldn't whip me in a straight-up fight, so now you're aimin' to settle things with a yellow-bellied ambush."

Strousel's voice, trembling slightly, floated through the murkiness from the front of the barn. "I'm sorry, McQueen.

They forced me to fetch you here with a false yarn . . . They threatened to beat me. B-beat me real bad . . . I gotta live in this town, McQueen."

"Shut your mealy mouth, Strousel," growled Hardy. "Best thing for you is to set those horseshit-caked feet of yours in motion and clear on out of here. And make damn sure you forget you know anything about any of this."

Strousel made a half-whimper sound like he wanted to say more. But nothing else came out and then there was the sound of him making a hurried departure.

"You're just like all bullies, Hardy," grated Firestick. "Tough as hell, but only when it comes to shovin' around weaklings and knee-walkin' drunks."

Hardy responded, "I've busted more skulls in this town than you can count, meddler. And a helluva lot of 'em were mighty tough fightin' men who found out the hard way they'd bit off more than they could chew! You'd've found out the same, you old mossback, if you hadn't got lucky by smashin' that chair down on me."

"You brought a chair into it first," Firestick reminded him. "All I wanted was to ask you a few simple questions."

"To hell with you and your questions!" As he hurled these words, Hardy edged forward so that he became dimly visible on the edge of the light. There were purplish circles under each of his eyes, tufts of cotton poked out both nostrils of his thickly packed nose, and his lower lip was swollen to almost double its normal size. "All the time all you wanted was to drag me into the murder of that poor little showgirl. And now you're still goin' ahead and spreadin' dirty lies about me somehow bein' a part of it. I won't stand for that! I'm gonna make you take back every word, and then I'm gonna help by crammin' 'em down your lyin' throat!"

"Wait a minute," protested Firestick. "You got things twisted around. I never accused you of havin' anything to do with that killin'. I just had a notion you might've had a grudge against my friend and were maybe tryin' to get back at him by spreadin' the idea *he* had had something to do with it."

"I ain't buyin' it! I know what I heard, what's spreadin' all over town about me. That ain't gonna hold, by God." Hardy edged forward another half step, raising his balled fists. "I never hurt no woman ever in my life, but I'm damn sure gonna hurt you for tryin' to make folks think so!"

"Nobody who counts thinks that," Firestick told him. "Not the judge, not Davies—they're the ones who convinced me you got no involvement."

Hardy rolled his shoulders. "Ain't good enough. I'm gonna make you pay for makin' *anybody* think it, even for a second."

Firestick gave it one final try. "This is crazy. You're in no shape for this—or is your gunman gonna put a bullet in me to balance out your injuries?"

"He's only there to make sure *you* don't bring gunplay into it—that's the only balancin' I need." To make the claim a convincing one, Hardy turned his head slightly and growled over his left shoulder, "Make sure you're damn clear on that, Rufe!" Then, his bloodshot eyes swinging back to bore once more into Firestick, he said, "Now. All you got to do is shuck that gunbelt, meddler, and we can get on with this. There ain't no chairs for you to get lucky with this time—just the dirt floor you're gonna be eatin' by the time we're done!"

Firestick realized there was no way out of fighting Hardy again. As he accepted this, he also came to a couple other realizations. Number one, he found himself believing that Hardy's backup, the man in the shadows he had referred to as Rufe, was truly there only to prevent gunplay. Secondly, Firestick discovered that, in a cockeyed kind of way, he was feeling a measure of respect for Hardy. No matter his past deeds or the reputation that had sprung out of them, the man was showing enough pride to strain against having his name tarnished further by a deed he clearly found loathsome.

However, none of that meant Firestick wasn't going to defend himself against what was being forced upon him and fight as hard as he could to end it in his favor. Damaged though he still was from their earlier encounter, Hardy was too dangerous and too much of a seasoned fighting man to cut any slack.

Unbuckling his gunbelt and dropping it off to one side, Firestick shrugged into a fighting stance of his own. With fists raised, he said, "If you insist, Hardy. We'll see who ends up tastin' that dirt."

The two men began circling one another warily, staying just within the pool of light cast by the lantern. The sorrel shifted somewhat nervously in the closest stall, and other horses in other nearby stalls could be heard chuffing and scraping their feet, sensing the tension in the air.

Hardy didn't come in a bull rush this time. His previous ruckus with Firestick clearly had instilled some caution and respect in him as well.

So it was Firestick who made the first move. When he had his balance set the way he wanted, he suddenly feinted with a high left hook. Then, changing up, he dropped his right shoulder and drove his right fist straight for Hardy's middle, once again targeting that bulging weakness.

But Hardy was quick to react. He hopped straight backward in a rather awkward but effective move, causing Firestick's reach to come up short so that the punch only grazed what it had been intended for. Still, it caught enough to make Hardy expel some air with a short grunt.

Before Firestick could close in and try to follow up, Hardy continued moving backward until he momentarily dissolved into the shadows. Firestick stopped advancing, not daring to get close enough for Hardy to tag him with a blind punch thrown out of the darkness. Firestick did some backing up of his own, retreating into the heart of the lantern glow. Hardy eased back into the light and they returned to circling each other.

Then, suddenly, unexpectedly, Hardy resorted to the tried-and-true tactic that had worked for him so many times in the past. Leaning forward while at the same time lowering his head and shoulders, he came at Firestick in a rush!

Because the big bruiser had initially delayed such a maneuver, it caught Firestick by surprise. What was more, it came when he was positioned exactly where Hardy wanted him—with the upright post of the sorrel's stall partition directly at his back. So when the bouncer's full weight hurtled into him, he was slammed back and pinned against the post.

Firestick hadn't had time to duck away from the rush, but as Hardy's head drilled into his chest and drove him back, the former mountain man got his arms up and then pounded down with doubled fists onto the back of his attacker's thick neck. The impact took its toll on both men. Firestick had much of his air driven out of him and continued to be pinned against the post while Hardy, the rabbit punch sending a shock wave down through his spine, was half-stunned and staggered even as he kept ramming ahead.

They remained locked together like that, pummeling one another, both struggling desperately to gain the advantage. Firestick fought to suck some air back into his lungs while simultaneously trying to struggle free from Hardy's crushing weight and the sharp-edged post chewing into his back. Hardy, in the meantime, kept his feet churning, instinctively continuing to grind against Firestick as his head was clearing and the tingling sensation was starting to leave his hands and arms.

Reaching awkwardly down and around Hardy's massive shoulders, Firestick kept slamming first one fist and then the other into the man's ribs. He wasn't able to get a lot of steam into the punches that way, but he figured if he landed enough of them it was bound to start adding up and enable him to get the bouncer shoved off to one side or the other. While Firestick was doing that, Hardy kept slamming upward with the top of his head, trying to either clip Firestick on the point of the chin or crush his windpipe.

Finally, one of Firestick's punches with his right fist managed to knock Hardy a half step to one side and slightly off balance. In that moment, Firestick was able to twist his upper body and swing his left arm over the top of Hardy's head. With that leverage, the wily old mountain man quickly twisted back the opposite way and at last shoved Hardy away and off to one side.

The two men staggered apart from one another, each bent partially forward at the waist, puffing hard, grim-faced. Fresh blood streamed out of Hardy's nose and a long, dripping string of the cotton stuffing trailed from one nostril.

With the feeling returned to his hands and arms and seeing his opponent was still struggling to regain his breath, Hardy charged forward again, this time swinging his mallet-like right fist in a whooshing roundhouse meant to knock Firestick's head off. But the latter, even sucking air, was faster. He ducked to the right, and as Hardy lunged past, lashed out with a short, choppy jab once more to the big man's rib cage. Hardy stumbled sideways, howling with a mixture of pain and frustration.

Now Firestick charged. As Hardy was righting himself and turning back, the mountain man was suddenly right there throwing a piston-like jab straight to his already tortured nose. The blow popped loudly in the silent livery barn, and Hardy's head rocked back like it was on a hinge.

Bracing himself, planting his feet wide, Firestick whipped first a right and then a left hook into Hardy's bulging belly. When the big man folded forward, Firestick's fist, the right this time, met his face again in a sweeping uppercut brought all the way up from knee level.

The blow caused Hardy to snap upward to his full height and then topple straight back, crashing to the ground flat on his shoulders.

Firestick edged forward warily, balled fists hanging at his sides. A trickle of blood ran from one corner of his mouth, the result of Hardy's head slamming up under his chin. His breathing was still ragged, coming in rapid gasps, but he was managing to gradually pull more and more air back into his craving lungs.

On the ground, Hardy was down but not out. His bleary eyes stared up at the high ceiling of the barn and he was working his mouth like a fish out of water. He kept trying to lift his arms, grunting unintelligible words, attempting to push himself to a sitting position.

"For Christ's sake, stay down," rasped Firestick, taking another step forward, hovering over him. "It's over. You made your point. Nobody thinks you had anything to do with that showgirl's death or tryin' to frame my friend. I was wrong."

Hardy glared up at him and squirmed on the ground, still trying to rise up. "Make you pay . . . for the lies," he grunted. "Everybody's got to know . . . I didn't . . . didn't do none of that."

"Everybody does know," Firestick told him. "I'm admittin' it. You got what you wanted."

Hardy didn't try to talk anymore, but he reached up with a wavering arm and lifted one shoulder, still trying to rise up.

Firestick turned and looked back into the shadows. "Damn it, Rufe . . . whoever and wherever you are," he said. "Get out here and talk to him if he's your friend. Tell him it's over, he made his point. I don't want to, but if he gets up and comes at me again, I'll knock him down again."

After a moment, a man eased out of the shadows. He was a frail-looking individual of forty or so, unshaven and dressed in shabby clothes. Under a slouch hat his eyes darted around furtively. In the waistband of his dusty, patched trousers was thrust a Navy Colt with a chipped handle.

Firestick motioned him toward where Hardy lay. "Talk some sense into him. I don't want to keep goin' on with this."

Rufe circled wide around Firestick, watching him suspiciously out of the corner of his eye, like he feared some kind of trick. When he reached the fallen Hardy, he dropped to one knee beside him. Hardy clutched his pant leg and pulled himself up on one elbow. He grunted heavily with the effort, blood bubbling from both nostrils.

"Take it easy," Rufe said. "For God's sake, lay back and stay down. It's over. You heard him, nobody's accusin' you of nothing no more. You got what you was after."

"Make that . . . that sumbitch eat his words," Hardy gasped stubbornly.

"He already ate 'em. Didn't you hear? Leave it be, man," Rufe pleaded. "You'll only get busted up worse . . . and for nothing."

For the first time, Hardy seemed to waver somewhat, appearing to relax from trying to keep sitting up. He passed the back of one hand across his mouth, wiping away blood, and fought to suppress a gag from more blood draining back into his throat. His shoulders sagged a little.

Firestick watched him, feeling guardedly relieved. He wanted this to be done with.

At that moment, the sound of voices and hurried footfalls came from the front of the livery barn. Turning to look, Firestick saw the forms of two men, backlit by the open door, striding purposefully toward where he stood.

When they got close enough, he saw it was Reb Davies being urged along by Strousel, the liveryman.

Coming to a halt, taking in the scene with a sweep of narrowed eyes, Davies said, "What the hell's goin' on here? Didn't you two get enough of each other the first time?"

Rufe stood up and eased back to the edge of the light, looking like he was ready to bolt. "Don't even think it, you!" Davies warned him harshly.

"Take it easy, Marshal," Firestick said in a soothing tone. "Everything is okay here. Me and Hardy were, uh, finishin' up our discussion from before. He finally agreed to answer some of my questions, and er, wanted to make sure I was clear on him havin' no part in my friend's trouble."

Davies scowled. "You think I'm stupid enough to swallow that line of crap?"

"It's the truth," Firestick insisted. "Leastways, that's the bottom line we arrived at. Okay, yeah, we growled and shoved each other around some more before we got it settled. But everything's under control now—ain't that right, Hardy?"

The bouncer cut his eyes back and forth between Firestick and Davies. Then, licking his lips, he said in a raspy voice, "Yeah. Yeah, that's right . . . We got things settled now."

Davies continued to scowl. Then, grudgingly, he said, "Okay. Long as you two fools didn't do no harm except to each other, I'm willin' to cut you some slack one more time. But this better be the end of it."

He pinned Hardy directly with a hard look. "I've warned you too damn many times about settlin' things with your fists, mister. You walked a thin line when you always kept it inside the Texas Rose before, but takin' it outside of there is pushin' over that line and damn near to the limit. Any more trouble like this, you'd better believe I'll be runnin' your ass out of town."

Now that same look found Firestick. "And you. No matter your good intentions, I mark you as a trouble magnet. The judge might have given you the go-ahead to keep after your so-called investigation, but don't ever think that can't change in a quick hurry. If the testimony of that old mountain rat Ripley is what's causin' so much grief for your pal, then he's the one you ought to—"

Davies stopped abruptly, his eyes widening and his mouth clapping shut as he realized what he had let slip.

Suddenly, Firestick was the one scowling. "What did you just say? Ripley!? What the hell does he have to do with any of this?"

CHAPTER 32

"It's all on me, Judge. I got mad and let the name slip." Reb Davies stood with sagging shoulders and a dejected look on his face. "Once I'd done that—and especially after McQueen recognized who it was—there didn't seem no way to backtrack out of it. So I figured we might as well come here and clear the air the rest of the way."

"You might say I sort of insisted," Firestick added.

Judge Buchanon glowered at him. "And you think you're in a position to be making demands?"

"Pick whatever word suits you," Firestick grated. "What it comes down to is that I'm in the position of wantin' some answers and feelin' mighty stubborn about gettin' 'em."

The three men were standing in the parlor of Buchanon's home, a small one-story house on a side street only a short distance from the Courthouse Saloon. The judge, rousted from bed, was wrapped in a rumpled, faded bathrobe, belted loosely around the middle. Minus his beaver hat, he had sparse white hair that poked out at odd angles above and around his ears.

"How is it, considering the vastness of the Rockies and other mountainous regions," he said, continuing to glare at Firestick, "that those of you who traipsed those lonely reaches somehow all seem to have ended up knowing each other?"

"It can happen, over a period of time," Firestick answered. "You meet a lot of fellow trappers at Rendezvous. Others, if you don't meet 'em face-on but they run their lines in the high country long enough, you still tend to hear about 'em."

"And the name 'Ripley' is so distinctive you're certain you know this fellow Davies happened to mention?"

"If it's Cuthbert 'Rip' Ripley—yeah, he's pretty distinctive," Firestick said.

Buchanon twisted his mouth ruefully and released a sigh. "I don't recall hearing the 'Rip' part, but I can't say it sounds inappropriate . . . and assuming it *is* the same man, does it also fit that he knows your friend Skinner?"

"He does right enough."

"But Skinner made no mention of meeting Ripley when he was up this way last fall?"

"None," Firestick admitted, frowning.

"How long since *you* have seen Ripley?" the judge asked.

Firestick's mind raced. Once again he found himself in a position of having to respond but needing to be very careful about what he did or didn't say.

"Matter of fact, he passed by our way not so very long ago."

"Since the murder that occurred up here you mean?"

"For a fact."

"Yet he nor Skinner, either one, ever mentioned running into each other here in Pecos?"

"No, they didn't."

"That seems rather odd, don't you think?" Buchanon didn't wait for an answer before adding, "You wouldn't happen to know where Ripley is now, would you?"

"He's your witness. Don't *you* know?" said Firestick, seizing the chance to turn the inquiry around.

In what Firestick guessed was a rare instance, the judge looked momentarily flustered. Then, quickly regaining his composure, he replied, "Regrettably, no. After coming forward with his testimony and providing his sworn and signed statement, Mr. Ripley apparently felt his obligation was sufficiently met and has since left town."

Firestick clenched his teeth and said in a challenging tone, "Yet no longer havin' a witness didn't stop you from issuin' those wanted dodgers and siccin' the Texas Rangers on Beartooth?"

"Did you not just hear me say I have a sworn and signed statement?" the judge snapped back. "What was I supposed to do—lock Ripley up, detain him indefinitely while the manhunt for Skinner was being conducted?"

"Might be wishin' you had, if it ever comes time for a trial. Leastways, a proper-conducted one," said Firestick. "Don't recall ever seein' or hearin' of a signed piece of paper takin' the witness stand."

Buchanon's face flushed with color. "You let me worry about that, mister. What you'd better worry about is watching that impertinent tongue of yours. I've gone out of my way to be reasonable with you, but if I choose, I could just as easily change my mind and have Reb here bring fully deserved charges of disorderly conduct and disturbing the peace against you. How well do you think you could conduct your investigation from a jail cell or making dust as you are being run out of town?"

"Far as I can see," said Firestick, fighting to keep his voice level and his own anger in check for the sake of not letting things get out of hand any worse, "my time here has run its course anyway. How about I make it easy on both of us by not wastin' no more? Just as quick as I can gather my gear and get saddled up, I'll be happy to make dust leavin' this town of yours."

Chapter 33

KATE
ON MY WAY HOME STOP THERE LATE
TOMORROW STOP TELL NO ONE BUT
MOOSEJAW STOP WARN CLAYBURN IF
HE BLABS I WILL MAKE HIM EAT HIS
TELEGRAPH KEY STOP
E

Kate Mallory stood in the Buffalo Peak marshal's office, watching Moosejaw read the telegram she had handed him a minute earlier. When the big deputy finished, he lifted his eyes and regarded her with an expectant look.

He said, "This is pretty good news, don't you think? That Firestick is headed back so quick, I mean. He would've barely had time to get there and now he's already returnin'."

"That wire was sent from a place called Toyah," Kate pointed out. "Isn't that a little settlement this side of Pecos?"

Moosejaw frowned down at the telegram and murmured,

"Yeah. Yeah it is." He looked up again. "You think that means something?"

"I don't know for sure," said Kate. "Like you, I want to think it's good news. But at the same time, if that's the case, I can't help wondering a little about the emphasis on being so secretive—wanting only you and me to know he's on his way back."

"You think that means Beartooth, too? That Firestick don't want him knowin', either?"

"If we take it literally—which I think we need to—that's what it says. It's addressed to me and states pretty plainly, 'no one but Moosejaw.'"

Moosejaw's frown deepened. "Yeah. Yeah, it does, don't it? Did you make sure Clayburn, the telegraph operator, understood that, too?"

Kate gave a little nod. "Well, for starters, he's the one who originally received it. But yes, I made a point to advise him he'd best follow what it said."

Moosejaw's brow puckered as he glanced at the clock on the wall. It was a little before nine in the morning. Bright sunlight poured in through the jail building windows.

"So I guess that's the advice we need to follow, too. Dang, when I first read that Firestick would be back tomorrow, I thought that seemed pretty quick and it made me glad. Now, wonderin' for sure what's goin' on and havin' to wait that long to find out—it don't seem very quick at all."

Kate flashed a brief smile. "I know what you mean. But at least things around here have stayed mostly tame while he's been gone. Right? Those wanted dodgers on Beartooth didn't stir up near the bluster or arguments that

I, for one, rather feared. And Beartooth, thank God, is staying put the way he's supposed to. Also, from what I've seen, those two Texas Rangers have even been keeping a relatively low profile, haven't they?"

"If, by that, you mean they been stayin' out of my hair—yeah, that's true enough," said Moosejaw. "The thing about that, though, is that they been stayin' out of most everybody's hair. That sorta bothers me. I can't quite figure out what they're up to. They ride out of town for hours at a time. I got a hunch they've gone back to spyin' on our ranch, the Double M. But if that's what they're doin', they're bein' mighty slick about not gettin' themselves spotted. Miguel ain't no slouch when it comes to such things and he ain't been able to catch sight of nothing . . . But I still can't shake the hunch they're out there somewhere, lookin' on."

"Have you tried following them?" Kate asked.

"What with havin' to stick close and keep an eye on the town, I really ain't had much of a chance. I even been stayin' in town nights, sleepin' here at the jail," Moosejaw explained. "I did ride out to the ranch evenin' before last, though, to check on Beartooth and have a word with Miguel. While I was there, I rode a loop around the perimeter of the house and buildings." He shook his head. "Wasn't able to spot no sign, though."

"Well," said Kate. "Even if the rangers *are* doing some spying, so long as Beartooth stays inside out of sight, they're not going to have any luck."

Moosejaw made a sour face. "That's the rest of it. The rest of what's got me worried. You see, Beartooth is gettin' antsier by the minute from bein' cooped up the way he is. One of these times, I'm afraid he's gonna bust out of what he sees as nothing but a cage. And I can understand feelin' that way, if I was in his same position. Even if he steps out for only a handful of minutes, though, to look up at the sun and sky and breathe in some fresh air . . . if he picks the wrong handful of minutes, when the rangers are lookin' on like I suspect . . . then things could take a mighty serious bad turn." His eyes dropped to the telegram still in his hand. "I just hope things hold together until tomorrow when Firestick gets here . . . and that he's bringin' some good news with him."

After leaving Pecos, Firestick had ridden through most of the night. The illumination from a clear, star-filled sky gave him plenty of light to follow the trail south over open, rolling terrain. Sleep had been out of the question anyway, what with all the questions and speculations whirling so wildly inside his head, so he'd figured he might as well eat up some miles while he was wrestling with his thoughts.

Ripley! Cuthbert "Rip" Ripley turning out to be the witness who'd come forward to testify against Beartooth on a charge of murder! What in flaming hell was that all about? Firestick couldn't begin to wrap his head around it. Especially not with Rip then showing up in Buffalo Peak, *after* he'd made such outrageous claims, and acting like butter wouldn't melt in his mouth. Full of nothing but old-time good cheer and friendliness. Right up to acting so surprised and concerned when the two Texas Rangers arrived with their wanted papers for Beartooth.

That lowdown scoundrel, a onetime trusted friend, was clearly up to something. But what could it be? Firestick didn't have an answer, couldn't even begin to make a halfway sensible guess. But what he did know—what every instinct in him was urging—was that he needed to get back to Buffalo Peak as soon as possible. For two reasons: to try and figure out whatever it was Rip was involved in and then to hopefully be in time to get in his way.

An hour before daybreak, with the lights marking the settlement of Toyah winking faintly in the distance ahead, Firestick had finally stopped to give himself and his horses a break. He'd stripped the animals, watered and hobbled them where they had graze, then stretched out in his bedroll, weary enough now for some sleep, albeit only a short amount.

In addition to knowing it wasn't smart to try and push himself and the horses too hard, he needed to give Toyah time to wake up and be open for business when he got there, in particular the telegraph office, where he meant to send a wire ahead to Kate—something he would have avoided doing in Pecos even if the hour hadn't been too late to try. Regardless, he suspected it was likely either the judge or Reb Davies would take the soonest opportunity to notify the rangers in Buffalo Peak he was on his way back, but Firestick still didn't want the word that he was returning so soon to spread too much.

He'd slept only until the sun barely cleared the horizon. Then he rose, saddled up again, and rode the rest of the way into town. There, he'd sent off his wire to Kate and took time for a good full breakfast in Toyah's only café. Within minutes of cleaning his plate, he was on the trail once more. His intent was to push on steadily through the day, with limited breaks, until stopping for a proper night camp. Sticking to this schedule would get him to

Buffalo Peak the following day, as he'd told Kate in his telegram . . .

"Judgin' by the peek out the window I snuck a little bit ago, looks like it's shapin' up to be another nice day out there." Beartooth made this observation at the breakfast table in the Double M dining room. He'd meant it as just a remark to make conversation, but his tone didn't quite mask the bitterness and melancholy simmering in him from his days of being penned up in the house.

Ignoring that part, however, Miguel, also present for the meal along with his nephew Jesus, replied, "*Sí, patrón.* The days are quickly showing the change from spring to summer. The nights, too, are losing most of their chill."

Beartooth sighed. "Reckon I'll have to take your word on that. I ain't been out in the evenin' air since the night we cornered that griz. The air was still plenty chilly then, I'll tell you."

Victoria, who had just settled into her own seat at the table after dishing heaps of scrambled eggs and bacon onto everyone's plates, said, "It won't be long, once the heat of full summer is upon us, when a chilly evening will seem like a blessing."

"Yeah," Beartooth said around a mouthful of eggs, "maybe by then I'll get a chance to actually step outside and discover that for myself."

Victoria gave him a look. "Or," she said tartly, "maybe you'll still be so busy feeling sorry for yourself you won't be able to enjoy it anyway."

Beartooth stopped chewing. "That's a pretty unchari- table thing to say, don't you think? You, of all people, ought to understand how hard it is for me to stay bottled up all the time like a damn prisoner in my own house."

"Of course I understand. I see you struggling with it every day, every minute." Victoria's tartness abruptly gave way to a sympathetic softness. "Being out of doors, out in the wind and under the sky and sun, is as much a part of you as breathing. And I can appreciate how hard it must be, being kept from that and having to remain 'bottled up,' as you say. What's been thrust upon you is unfortunate and unfair. But others—Firestick, Moosejaw, all of us here—are going through it with you. None of us understands why this has happened, but we're all on your side, trying to help each in our own way—either to merely help you cope or, in the case of Firestick, going to considerable lengths to get to the bottom of that ridiculous charge and trying to find a way to get it disposed of."

Miguel and Jesus looked decidedly uncomfortable, being present for this exchange. Each concentrated very hard on eating their bacon and eggs and studiously avoided making eye contact with anyone.

Beartooth frowned throughout most of what Victoria had to say. By the time she was done, however, the corners of his mouth had lifted into a straighter, though still tightly pressed line. Then he said, "You're right. I know I ain't goin' through this alone . . . and believe me, I'm grateful to each and every one of you." His gaze touched Victoria and also the two *vaqueros* with heads still lowered over their plates. "A man with friends like y'all has no call to feel sorry for himself. That ain't ever been my way, no matter what, but I guess it's how I was soundin'. For that, I apologize. It's just that the hardest part is feelin' so damn helpless, not bein' able to go out there and fight this thing for myself. Along with bein' all closed in, it's eatin' me up."

"You owe no one an apology, *patrón*," Miguel said quietly, lifting his head. "What you are going through would be difficult for any man."

"And you *are* making your own fight," Victoria insisted. "The battle of staying inside, knowing it's for the best in spite of it going against the grain of all your past experience and instincts . . . Like you just said, it may be the hardest fight you've ever faced."

Beartooth heaved a heavy sigh. "Knowin' those blasted rangers are lurkin' out there, waitin' and watchin', ready to pounce if I make the smallest wrong move . . . gives me moments when I want to just strap on my guns and charge out that door. Put the challenge to 'em—force 'em to either take me if they can, or I make a run for it and ride free and clear."

"Only you wouldn't be free," Victoria pointed out quietly. "You'd risk having to run—and hide—for the rest of your days. And if you happened to shoot one of those rangers in the process of making such a break, that would cause it to be virtually impossible for Firestick or anyone else to ever find a way to clear your name."

"I know," Beartooth muttered grudgingly. He stabbed through a piece of bacon so hard that the prongs of his fork threatened to chip the plate underneath. "I just hope to God that Firestick is able to turn up something in Pecos. If he comes home empty, I don't know how long I'll be able to hold myself back."

CHAPTER 34

When the two men rode up to the hitchrail in front of the jail, Moosejaw was sitting outside with his chair tipped back against the front of the building. He'd been propped that way for a while, watching the comings and goings up and down Trail Street, waiting for one of the waitresses from the Mallory House to show up with lunch for Ripley. The air was still and starting to turn hazy in the rising heat from the sun blazing high overhead in a cloudless sky. After Ripley had eaten, the big deputy had plans to join Daisy and take his own lunch with her. He knew she'd have a big pitcher of cold buttermilk ready, and he was looking forward to that as well as spending time with his ladylove.

The two men who rode up had the look of wranglers, though Moosejaw recognized neither one of them from any of the surrounding spreads. The older of the two was a narrow-eyed, sun-and wind-burned specimen, closing in on fifty, with prematurely bone-white hair and an average build that nevertheless gave the impression of being rangy and plenty tough. His companion was six or eight years younger, a couple inches taller, and slightly stockier, dark-haired and dark-complexioned with a gambler's quick, calculating eyes. Both men were dusty and sweat streaked, indicating that they had been on a long, hard trail for a spell.

"Howdy," said the older man, reining in and leaning forward to rest one forearm on his saddle horn. "I take it you're the law hereabouts?"

"Part of it," Moosejaw replied with a nod. "I'm one of the deputies. Marshal's out of town for a few days. Can I help you gents with something?"

The older of the pair spoke again. "More like we're just stopping by on a courtesy call, Deputy. Our hope is, for the time we plan on being in your town, we won't have any need to bother you after this."

"Sounds reasonable enough," Moosejaw said. "But I ain't exactly sure I'm followin' what you mean."

"My name's Wilson. Trav Wilson. I'm ramroddin' a horse herd up out of Mexico, headed for sale as remounts to the cavalry at Fort Leaton. This here"—Wilson waved a hand to indicate the dark-haired man—"is Matt Corbain, one of my wranglers."

Moosejaw gave a little nod, waited for more.

"We've ridden ahead," Wilson went on. "The rest of our boys will be bringing the herd to a halt later on, not too far south of town. We plan on holding them there for the night and another day and night, resting them and letting them take on a good feed before pushing the rest of the way. I know this is open range all through here, but I already paid a visit to the rancher down where we aim to lay over and cleared it with him. We're not looking for trouble."

"That's a good, sensible way to be lookin'," Moosejaw agreed.

Wilson thumbed the front brim of his hat back a ways on his head. "The thing is," he said, "while we're laid over, I plan on splitting my crew into . . . well, shifts, you might say, and letting them have a turn at coming into town for a while. They've been out on the trail for a pretty long stretch; I figure they deserve a taste of something besides dust and chuckwagon grub for a change."

Now Moosejaw saw where this was going. He tipped his chair level and stood up.

"I got a good, seasoned crew. About half Mex, half white like Matt and me," Wilson went on. "They've all got a few years on 'em, none too green nor too wild in their ways. All the same, they *are* wranglers, and like I said, they've been out on the trail for a spell. So they've naturally got some thirst and some other needs built up. I plan on being in town each night, too. Not so much for seeing to my own needs, but more for seeing to it my men don't get out of line."

Moosejaw smiled. "I appreciate that. Of course, I'll be around, too, to help make sure of it."

"That's why Mr. Wilson said this was a courtesy call," spoke up Corbain for the first time. "No need to take a hard line about it."

Moosejaw's smile faded and so did his relaxed expression. He said to Corbain, "Mister, if I get me a notion to take a hard line, that's pretty much what I'll go ahead and do. And if it comes to that, you won't have any trouble recognizing the difference between that and makin' a simple statement."

"Hey, both of you take it easy," Wilson was quick to say. "That was the whole purpose for this visit—to make sure we avoid any unpleasantness."

"And I appreciate it," Moosejaw responded. "You stoppin' here, takin' time to speak with ranchers to the south where you'll be passin' through and layin' over—those are sensible steps to keepin' everybody calm. Believe me, I'm all for that. And all I meant when I said what I did is that I'll be around if you need help keepin' your men out of trouble. I don't want that any more than you do. And I sure understand how fellas comin' in off the trail are gonna feel the need to howl some, so it ain't like I'll be poised to pounce on the first squeak out of one of 'em."

"Glad to hear that," Wilson said.

"Look, boss," Corbain said, turning to him. "How about I peel off and go find someplace to wash some of the trail dust out of my own throat? You don't need me here to finish talking this out. You can trust me to behave until you catch up."

"Yeah, I reckon I can," Wilson agreed. "Go ahead. Me, I'm more interested in a shave and hot bath before I worry about washing down my insides—but you darn well better save me something cold for when I'm ready."

Corbain nodded, swung his horse away, and trotted off up the street.

Wilson looked after him for a moment and then returned his attention to Moosejaw. "He's not a bad sort.

Good hand. Maybe just a little too quick to get his hackles up."

"Can't fault a man for bein' loyal to his own," Moosejaw allowed. "Speakin' of your bunch—how many you got?"

"A baker's dozen, counting me."

"For how big a herd?"

"Eighty when we started out."

Moosejaw's eyebrows lifted. "That's pretty good sized. Surprised, though, it takes that many men to wrangle 'em."

"It wouldn't, ordinarily," Wilson answered. "But we had to pass through bandit country south of the border. I brought the extra men for their guns as much as for their wrangling skills. Turned out we didn't have any trouble. But being safe rather than sorry is usually the better way. It's important for my boss—the ranch owner—to get these horses to the army without a hitch. Make a good impression for setting up future deliveries."

"Yeah, I wondered about that," said Moosejaw. "Kinda surprised to hear the army's buyin' stock from south of the border."

Wilson shrugged. "All I know is that my boss, a fella named Bart Howell, is American, too. He served with distinction during the war. For the winning side. Seems that left him with some close ties to the brass at Fort Leaton. In the meantime, following the war, he went to Mexico and married well. His father-in-law set him up with a nice spread of land—the Santa Rosalie, named after Howell's wife—for raising horses, tough little desert mustangs that will serve the cavalry well. They're getting a price that's fair to them but a lot better than Howell can get in Mexico. So it works out to be a good deal both ways."

"Sounds like," Moosejaw agreed. "I'll be sure to keep it in mind. Might just be givin' your Mr. Howell some competition one of these days."

"How's that?"

"Me and my partners—the marshal and the other deputy here in town—also run a small horse spread on the side," Moosejaw explained. "We ain't got all that big a herd built up yet, we been concentratin' on careful breedin' to improve our quality, sellin' off mostly small lots until we can claim top of the line all the way through. Then we aim to get bigger."

"Sounds like a good plan," Wilson said. "Speaking of which, I think I'm ready to set my own plan—the one about a shave and hot bath—into motion. You recommend any particular place?"

"Moorehouse's barbershop, just up the street. You can't miss it and you'll find no place better."

"Sounds good. I'll be seeing you around, Deputy." Wilson started to swing his horse away but then held up. "Say, one more thing . . . Our cook tells me he's running a mite low on certain supplies. He'll be wanting to bring his chuckwagon in, probably tomorrow after breakfast. Got a good general store where he can do his stocking up?"

"Greeble's, just a ways farther up from the barbershop, on the opposite side of the street. He should have everything your cookie needs."

Wilson touched a finger to the brim of his hat. "Obliged, Deputy. Be seeing you."

Moosejaw stood watching the ramrod head up the street. Before too long, though, his eyes narrowed and his gaze turned toward the Mallory House Hotel. Where was that waitress with Ripley's lunch? The talk about restocking the chuckwagon reminded the big deputy he was getting hungry. As soon as he was able to shove some grub in front of ol' Rip, he'd be making a beeline for Daisy's and the feed she would have waiting for him. When it came time to eat, Moosejaw didn't have a lot of patience.

CHAPTER 35

A freshly shaved and scrubbed Trav Wilson caught up with his man Corbain in the Lone Star Palace Saloon. Corbain was leaning against the bar with no one close around him, half a glass of beer and a full shot of whiskey on the bar top in front of him.

There was a pretty good crowd of other customers on hand, most of them seated at tables where they were socializing and doing their drinking along with enjoying sandwiches they'd built from the spread of meat, cheese, and bread the saloon made available through the noon hour.

When Wilson came up beside him, Corbain said, "They've got good cold beer here and plenty of it. So it wasn't no trouble to save you some."

"Uh-huh," said Wilson. "See you been sampling some of the red-eye, too."

"This is only my second one," Corbain replied. "Didn't figure you'd want me hitting it too heavy."

"You figured right. You've still got work to do before the day is done."

"I know."

When a bartender appeared, Wilson said to him, "I'll have a shot and a beer. Give my friend here another short beer, too."

"Thanks, boss," Corbain said.

"It's alright," Wilson told him. "When you've finished it, I want you to head on back to the herd. I'll catch up in a bit. You know the spot I picked out to bed down for the night. You happen to get there ahead of me, you inform the rest."

"I'll be informing them of more than that," Corbain said. "You see, I been looking things over and talking to some folks. I got this whole town scoped out. They got sporting girls here, but it's the only place. There's another saloon, but they only serve drinks. And there's a Mexican *cantina* down at the far end of town for our *vaquero* buddies, but they don't have girls, either."

Wilson grinned. "Sounds like you got all the important things covered."

"You bet I do."

"And since you're in the first group of men scheduled to come back later tonight, you can lead the way."

"Which is what I intend to do."

The additional drinks came. After he'd paid, Wilson wasted no time throwing down his own shot and then following it with a long pull of beer.

"Ah, yeah," he exclaimed. "That is good and cold."

Corbain downed his shot also and chased it with the rest of the beer he'd previously had in front of him. As he reached for the fresh one, the one his boss had bought, Wilson said to him, "Now I've already made it clear which men are in which group when it comes to riding into town. Some tonight, some tomorrow night. Everybody will get their chance and I'm pretty sure the town ain't gonna run dry. What I want you to make extra clear to everybody is that if there's any squabbling about who gets to go when, or if some fool gets here and turns too damn loco and wild—I'll call the whole shebang off. It'll be spoiled for everybody. You got that?"

"Damn straight, boss. Some idiot starts turnin' too rowdy, I'll be the first one to chunk him over the head with a Colt barrel and tame him down a mite."

"I'm glad to hear that. I'm counting on you to help me keep things under control so we won't have to have that big deputy step in. He takes a notion to club some of our boys, he's liable to put 'em out of commission for a week."

Corbain grunted. "Yeah, he's a big 'un, ain't he? What the hell was I thinking, spouting off to him like I did? Half a second after the words came out of my mouth, I knew it was a dumb idea. I'm glad all he did was bark back at me and not take it any farther."

"Well, you got away with one," Wilson said, grinning. "And that's what you'd best be doing again. Getting away, I mean. Finish your beer and head on back to the herd. I'll follow along shortly."

"Okay. See you there."

Corbain finished his beer, then squared his hat on his head and took his leave. Once he was gone, Wilson motioned for a refill. After it came, he took a short pull and then settled into nursing it slowly. As he did so, he appeared to pay little or no attention to anything that was going on around him. His face took on the expression of a man lost in deep thought.

Before Wilson's beer was drained even halfway, another man sauntered over from one of the tables and leaned against the bar beside him. This individual was maybe forty, maybe forty-five and craggily handsome with a long, thin nose and deep, sun-baked crinkles around his eyes and mouth. He was dressed in standard trail garb that bore little sign of hard use. Not new, just carefully brushed and pressed and neatly fitted. Flat-crowned Stetson cocked just so on a headful of wavy black hair, short-waisted jacket of brown suede, tan slacks with a crease, polished boots. An ivory-handled Colt .45 rode low on his right hip, encased in black leather as shiny as his boots.

The newcomer carried a bottle and a shot glass with him. He set the glass on the bar top, poured, then put the bottle down. After he'd thrown back the shot, he said in a low, matter-of-fact voice, "'Bout time you got here."

Without turning his head, Wilson lifted one corner of his mouth and replied, "Funny thing about pushing eighty half-broke nags across a big stretch of open, rugged country—they don't seem to care one little bit about keeping a tight schedule. Now, the *old* Clete Halsey, the fella I used to know who got involved with wrangling horses or cattle from time to time, would've remembered such a thing. But I guess maybe this new version has forgot. Could have something to do with all the time it must take to bend over in order to keep those boots polished so bright. Probably caused too much blood to rush to your head and washed away part of your memory."

Halsey's own mouth formed a wry grin. "The memory of punching cows *or* horses all day, eating their dust and smelling the stink of what comes out of the south end of the damn critters . . . Yeah, I'd trade that for the smell of boot polish anytime."

Now Wilson turned his head, face once more taking on a sober expression. "So how long have you been waiting?"

"Only a couple of days. I sent Pauley out yesterday to look for the dust of a moving herd, see how far off you were. So I knew you were closing in."

Wilson nodded thoughtfully. "Pauley's a good man. Who else did you bring?"

"Muldoon, Mud River Neelan, and a young kid named Beevey. He's young, but I've seen him work. Damned fast with the Remington he carries, but not cocky about it like a lot of young punks. Trust me, he'll do."

"So six, counting me and you," Wilson said. "That should do it. Where's the rest of 'em now?"

"They're holed up in the foothills of those mountains off to the north. I've been sticking closer to town, keeping an eye on things. I figured it was best not to have too many new faces hanging around. Town ain't that big, didn't want to be too . . . what's the word? . . . conspicuous."

Wilson drank some of his beer. "What about the old man?"

Halsey picked up his bottle, poured himself another shot, and then filled Wilson's glass, too.

"Hope you're going a little easy on that."

"Don't worry about me," said Halsey. "But you're gonna want a stiff one when you hear this. The old man's in jail."

"What!?" Wilson blurted the word louder than he meant and then immediately looked around to see if he'd drawn any undue attention. But no one else was anywhere close to where he and Halsey stood, and nobody seemed to be paying them any heed. Lowering his voice to an aggravated hiss, Wilson then said, "How did the old bastard manage that?"

Halsey calmly took a sip of his whiskey. "Believe it or not, he wanted it that way. But before you blow your stack, hear this out. The main thing is that the old rascal did what he said he was going to do. He cleared out two of the three lawmen from here in town. Just like he promised. The only one left is a big, slow-moving ox who looks equally slow between the ears."

"I met him a little while ago," Wilson said, teeth still clenched. "I ain't so sure I agree about the slow between the ears part. But never mind that. How did the old man get rid of the other two?"

"All I know is that both of 'em are out of town and the word all over is that they'll be gone for a spell. Before he went into the hoosegow, the old man got word to me," Halsey explained, "saying not to worry, that he had things going according to plan and he'd have the third law dog taken care of, too, then be there to join us when we took the wagon."

"I'd like to know how he's going to do that," Wilson muttered as he frowned down at the bar.

"The thing we do know is that, just like he said he would, he cleared out two-thirds of the town law already." Halsey tossed down the rest of his drink. "But here's the fly in the buttermilk on that. The reason one of 'em is away is that he's on the run for a murder charge. Whether or not the old man had anything to do with that, I ain't sure. But the fact remains, he's gone. The problem, though, is that now there's two Texas Rangers in town looking for him."

Wilson scowled fiercely. "Sounds to me like this is going to hell in a handbasket! The last thing we want is to end up with the Texas Rangers on our ass."

"I got no argument with that. But with them right here so close at hand, I ain't sure there's any way around it. Way I see it, we got two choices," Halsey said. "Either we call the whole thing off . . . or we make an adjustment to our plans."

"Adjust how?"

"We hold off. You go ahead and do your layover tonight and tomorrow, then push on with the herd. We wait until you're well away from here, away from where the rangers are lurking, and then we hit the herd farther down the trail."

Wilson's mouth pulled tight. "Doing it that way would mean taking down most or all of the wranglers in order to get it done. They'll put up a fight, a fight to the death. Thinking it's for the herd. That's why I brought so many along, in case we ran into *bandidos* before we got out of Mexico. Our six would be outnumbered two to one."

"We'd have the element of surprise," Halsey argued. "We'd be able to cut most of them down before they knew what hit 'em."

Wilson suddenly threw back the shot Halsey had poured him. When he brought the glass back down, he said firmly, "No! I've ridden with these men for close to two years now. Before this other business ever came up. They're good boys . . . they look up to me. They're simple, hardworking horse wranglers; I don't want to see them sacrificed for the sake of some lousy gold they know nothing about! That's why I was so careful to set it up this way—isolate the chuckwagon, grab the gold, vamoose before anybody knows what happened. By the time they do, we'll be long gone and those boys will be left hungover and having to look after the herd. I ain't ready to think about doing it no other way."

Halsey matched his scowl. "You're being awful damned sentimental about a bunch of ranch hands with a hundred thousand dollars' worth of gold on the line, ain't you? You're the one who set this in motion. You're the one who contacted *me*, remember? And I brought in the others—men I also owe something to. How willing you think they'll be to just ride away from this kind of take if I was to try explaining to 'em we're calling it off on account of you not wanting to see a bunch of un-washed wranglers get hurt?"

"Don't try to bluff me, Halsey, and damn sure don't try to threaten me," Wilson said, baring his teeth. "Like you just put it, I'm the one who set this in motion, and I can derail the whole works even easier. All I have to do is get the ear of those rangers. And if you think you're man enough to stop me, you'd better remember that fancy holster you got polished to match those shiny boots don't mean you can skin a hogleg any quicker than you ever could. I always was faster than you and I always will be."

For an intense moment it looked like Halsey might be ready to test that challenge. His eyes narrowed, his body went rigid.

Then, abruptly, the heat left those narrowed eyes, and the set of his jaw relaxed. "What the hell are we doing,

Trav? This thing is too big for us to let it fall apart now. And me and you butting heads sure ain't no way to help get it done."

Wilson expelled a measured breath and shifted his weight, resting more of it on the elbow he had planted atop the bar. "Yeah, you're right. This thing *is* big. Why do you think I was tempted by it to begin with? A deal like this could damn near set a man up for the rest of his life. But even for all that, I just ain't got it in me to hand over my whole crew of wranglers to be slaughtered like a pack of mongrel dogs. In days past, when we was younger and wilder, hell, I probably wouldn't have even thought twice about it. But I ain't like that no more."

"What then?" Halsey wanted to know.

Wilson sighed again. "I think we lathered ourselves into worrying too much about those blasted rangers. If we go ahead and hit that chuckwagon like we've been planning all along—in between the herd and town— there's as good a chance as ever it will be hours before anybody even realizes it. And when they do, there still won't be none who know about the gold that was in the false bottom. Not until word gets back to Howell clear down in Mexico . . . And he's gonna be tongue-tied over what he can safely say on account of he was the one illegally smuggling out the gold to begin with."

"So a lousy chuckwagon getting robbed and ransacked," Halsey joined in, his voice growing more excited, "ain't gonna be a big enough deal for the rangers to get worked up about, not hardly at all. Especially since the horse herd will be left intact."

"There's bound to be some puzzlement and concern

about me suddenly coming up missing," said Wilson. "But not enough to sidetrack the rangers, not if they're already on the trail of a killer. And my crew will have no choice but to concentrate on getting the herd on through. Once again, when word reaches Howell down in Mexico, he'll add it up right away. But he'll still be stymied as far as what he can say or try to do about it."

Halsey smiled eagerly. "So everything's back on again. We're less than twenty-four hours away from getting our hands on all that sweet, sweet gold."

Wilson didn't appear quite so ready to consider everything settled. "As long as that screwy old man don't do something to trip us up. I still don't feel comfortable with him being in a jail cell, no matter how much he thinks he's got it under control."

"He's held up his end of everything so far," Halsey pointed out.

"Yeah. So far. What if he can't worm his way back out of his cell in time to join us at the wagon? That would leave him behind, maybe needing to blab on us in order to make some kind of deal for himself. If he spills on a hundred thousand dollars' worth of smuggled gold having been in that chuckwagon, that would sure as hell give those rangers something to get involved in."

"Maybe so," allowed Halsey. "But that kind of take can't possibly come without some kind of risk. Let's not start doing it again."

"Doing what?"

"Worrying ourselves to death about those damn rangers." Halsey grabbed the bottle and poured two more shots for Wilson and himself. Then, lifting his glass, he said in a determined tone, "Let's drink to it. Enough fretting and fussing. Let's by damn settle on doing what we came here to do."

Wilson gave it half a beat before picking up his own glass. "Alright. Have your men in place tomorrow morning. We'll make it happen."

CHAPTER 36

"It wasn't quite so bad the first day or so," Roy Arbry was saying. "But that doggone sun is getting *hot*. Laying here like this, right out in the open, I'm starting to feel like a slice of bacon on a griddle."

"You've been on stakeouts before when it was hot, haven't you?" replied his partner, Gene Rodgers. "Being in uncomfortable situations sort of comes with being a ranger."

"I know, Grampaw," Arbry said sarcastically. "I'm not exactly a greenhorn when it comes to packing this star. I don't even mind being in situations where the discomfort comes from bullets making it hot. But being hot from the blasted sun *and* being bored to tears at the same time . . . that's what's really gratin' on my nerves."

The two men were sprawled on the slope of an ancient buffalo wallow. They were facing southeast, looking down on the main house and outbuildings of the Double M ranch. They peered cautiously over the rim of the wallow, hats removed, heads poked just above eye level. On the dry, dusty fringe of grass at the lip of the depression lay a pair of binoculars, hooded to prevent sun glare.

From time to time, one of the rangers would raise the field glasses and use them to scrutinize the scene below even more closely.

"What's grating on my nerves," Rodgers said, "is *knowing* Skinner is down there. I can feel it in my bones. It's just a matter of time before he pokes his head out and we can be positive."

"If you're that sure—and I'm not saying I disagree, mind you—why don't we ride on down there and conduct a thorough search like we were going to do before?" asked Arbry.

"They've got to have about as strong a suspicion we're watching them as we do that our man is down there," Rodgers answered. "That means they're prepared for us. First sign of us riding up, they'll have an even deeper hidey-hole for Skinner to duck into. We'd have little chance of turning him up in a simple search."

"What's the difference if we spot him poke his head out and *then* go riding down? They'll still see us coming and hide him out."

"The difference is we can say with conviction that we spotted him. They'll be able to tell we're putting it to them straight, that they're not fooling us, not even for a second." Rodgers paused and frowned, looking concerned. "Then it'll come down to how hard Skinner is willing to resist."

"You think he'll put up a fight?"

"Could be. It's been hinted at more than once that's he's still the wildest of those three former mountain men. Even the marshal as much as said so."

"If Skinner is holed up down there, then the marshal

has to know about it," Arbry pointed out. "He had me fooled into believing he was on the level."

"I still think he is—in his own way. He's a decent man."

Arbry's forehead puckered. "That doesn't jibe. A decent man, especially one who wears a badge, shouldn't let himself be part of hiding out a wanted fugitive."

"He would if the wanted man was a friend whose innocence he believed strongly enough in. More than the law, he'd worry about making sure his friend didn't get a raw deal."

The creases above Arbry's brows only deepened. "You sound awfully willing to cut him some slack. You almost sound like you're as worried as he is about Skinner getting a raw deal."

"Maybe I am," Rodgers said quietly.

Arbry gave him a look. "Come on now, partner. You know damn well that part ain't ours to worry about. I've heard you say it dozens of times—our job is to haul 'em in and let the court pass judgment. And you saw the telegram we got this morning from Judge Buchanon. McQueen's on his way back and nothing is changed. The judge wants us to close in on Skinner 'posthaste.'"

"Yeah, I know what the judge's telegram said. And I know what I've said all those times in the past. I still stand by all of that. But it don't mean I can't have a personal feeling sometimes—a hunch, if you want to call it that— about how I think the outcome of a given case should go." Rodgers cut his eyes away from Arbry and scowled down at the ranch house below. "And this time I got one of those feelings, a mighty powerful one. I can't help thinking that if a man like McQueen is so sold on Skinner being innocent that he's willing to risk his badge and reputation . . . well, then there must be something to it."

"You put an awful lot of stock in McQueen, don't you?"

Rodgers swung his eyes back. "Yeah, I do . . . Don't you?"

Now it was Arbry who shifted his gaze and stared down at the ranch house. "Yeah, I guess I do, too," he admitted. "I wasn't so much at first. But he's got such a steady, solid doggone way about him. He didn't have to show up in that draw the other night when Eckert and the others had us pinned down. If all he was interested in was helping Skinner get shed of us, he had a prime chance to do it right there and let somebody else carry the load."

Neither man spoke again for a full minute. Until Rodgers said, "The hell of it is, no matter any of that, we still got to do the job assigned to us."

In a weary-sounding tone, Arbry responded, "Yeah . . . that's the hell of it alright."

Miles to the north, Firestick and his horses were also being hammered by the prematurely hot day. He was switching mounts regularly, yet setting such an aggressive pace that both animals were worked into a lather. The urgency Firestick felt when he first rode out of Pecos had only increased, driving him harder with each mile.

He had to get back to Buffalo Peak, and get there fast. That was all there was to it. There were clear, obvious reasons why, but there also were nebulous ones that seemed to be tugging at him as much or more.

What would make Ripley bring such unspeakable

claims against a solid, longtime friend like Beartooth? What was he up to?

Those were the big questions, the mystery so deep and troubling it twisted Firestick's guts. He not only couldn't think of any motive that made sense, he couldn't think of one no matter how far or outrageous he tried to stretch his imagination. And lacking anything remotely sensible only left the ominous category of insanity.

With everything and everyone he held dear located back at Buffalo Peak, Firestick felt a stab of dread like he'd seldom known when he thought about what was at risk if Ripley's apparent madness and intent to do harm suddenly spread wider than just Beartooth. He had to get there, had to stop the old devil from doing . . . whatever it was he was bent on doing.

But running his horses past the point of exhaustion wasn't going to help him achieve that goal. Far from it. If even one of his horses went down, the urgency driving Firestick wouldn't matter a damn. He'd be slowed to an agonizing pace. At one point, feeling fully relentless inside himself, he'd actually toyed with abandoning his original idea of stopping for a lengthy night rest and instead making a shorter one and pushing on sooner for the sake of getting back all the faster. But he saw now that he couldn't do that to his horses. Especially not with the toll this heat was taking on them.

From this realization, however, sprang an idea for a different plan. In his early days of traveling the wild places, after his first stint in the Rockies and long before joining up with Beartooth and Moosejaw, Firestick had experienced the calling to head farther west, beyond the Rockies and all the way to the Pacific Ocean. In the course of doing that, he'd fallen in with some explorers and long hunters who had experience crossing the desert regions. Without them, in fact, a young Elwood McQueen might not have survived. But he did survive, and what he learned about traveling over a harsh desert was the trick of laying up during the hottest part of the day and traveling in the coolness of the night.

While these West Texas plains did not rate as a harsh desert, today's sudden spike in temperature nevertheless qualified as similar conditions. And so, with a clear sky showing all signs of lasting into the night and a route he felt comfortable following, Firestick made the decision to utilize that old lesson. He'd lay up for the balance of this boiling afternoon, resting himself as well as the horses in a shady spot such as the stand of cottonwood trees he already had his eye on in the near distance, and then push on through the cool, clear night. That way, barring any unforeseen complications, he felt he could better his earlier estimation of making it back in the afternoon. In fact, he reckoned he stood a good chance of getting there sooner . . .

CHAPTER 37

"A herd of mustangs driven up out of Mexico, you say? And the army's buyin' 'em?" Ripley scrunched his face into a distasteful expression. "That sort of rankles me, don't it you? Why ain't the army buyin' good American stock, instead of doin' their shoppin' south of the border?"

Moosejaw appeared unfazed. "I guess they must figure that's where they can get their best bargain. They got a right to shop around in order to stretch their dollar like anybody else, don't they?"

"But it's the government dollar they're stretchin'," argued Ripley. "Tax money—paid in by Americans. That's why I say it oughta get paid back *to* Americans. You and the other fellas are in the horse business, for cryin' out loud, wouldn't you like to have a crack at the cavalry buyin' off you?"

"Sure, when we get our herd built up big enough to where we're ready to sell off eighty at a time," said Moosejaw. "But we ain't ready for that yet. And even when we are, we're still gonna have to be . . . what's the word? Competitive. Yeah, competitive to other folks' prices."

"You got to be aggressive, grind your competition into the ground. *That's* what you got to be! That's how you succeed in business," Ripley insisted. He gave a dismayed shake of his head. "I hope to blazes Firestick and Beartooth got a better grasp on this here business than you seem to. If they don't, you fellas are the ones gonna get ground down to nothin'."

Moosejaw just smiled. "I guess we'll have to see. We're doin' okay so far."

The two men were seated in Ripley's cell, having supper together, the meals being provided again by the Mallory House. Rip was perched on the edge of his cot, Moosejaw on a straight-backed wooden chair he'd dragged in from the office area. The cell door was standing ajar, and through the high, barred window in the cell's back wall, the last rays of fading daylight reached through as evening began to settle outside.

"One thing about it, if you're worried about money gettin' spent on this side of the border," Moosejaw said as he chewed a bite of food, "is that some of those wranglers are bound to be layin' down a few coins here in Buffalo Peak tonight. Tonight and tomorrow night both, as a matter of fact. That's how Wilson, the fella ramroddin' the outfit, is splittin' up his crew so's they all get a shot at lettin' off some steam before movin' on the rest of the way."

Ripley stabbed at his own food and grunted. "Sounds like the kind of ramrod I wouldn't mind ridin' for—*if* I ever took the fool notion to hire on for nursemaidin' cows or horses or such, that is."

"As far as ridin' on a trail drive, I gotta go along with you on that. Buildin' up our own herd out at the ranch is one thing, but spendin' days and weeks in the saddle like this bunch is doin' . . ." Moosejaw shook his head. "Nope, that wouldn't be for me."

"That's why they're all rowdied up and ready to cut loose their wolves by the time they hit town."

"I suppose."

"Meanin' it sounds like you might have your hands full a little later on tonight."

Moosejaw shrugged. "Won't be the first time a cattle drive crew hit town. But Wilson's only sendin' in about a half dozen at a time. And he figures to be around to keep 'em tamed down himself. No matter, I figure I can handle it okay."

Ripley set his emptied plate aside. "I just hope they don't cut loose to the point where you have to arrest some of 'em and end up throwin' a few in here next to me. Nothing worse than being stone sober around a gaggle of slobberin' drunks!"

"I'll do my best to spare you," Moosejaw told him dryly.

"You can do better than that," Ripley said, his eyes suddenly brightening.

"How's that?"

"I know Firestick's got some bottles of confiscated whiskey out yonder in his desk. How about you slip me one of them?" Ripley licked his lips. "You know, strictly as a measure to fortify myself in case things get out o' hand."

Moosejaw stood up, balancing his own empty plate as he reached to gather Ripley's as well. He grinned.

"Nice try, you old fox. But no dice. I can't loosen things up quite that far."

"Aw, come on! Who'll know?"

"I will." Moosejaw backed out the door, clutching the plates and dragging his chair after him. Then he kicked the cell door shut and locked it.

"All that talk about those wranglers ridin' into town to gorge themselves on drinkin' and frolickin'—that's pure torture to a man who's been bone dry for goin' on three days now," Ripley wailed as Moosejaw, still grinning, retreated through the door leading from the cell block out into the front office. "Moosejaw, you're as stubborn and evil as that dad-blasted Firestick!"

The sun hung low above the horizon now. The air had cooled some, though it was still plenty warm. But a gentle, welcome breeze had also wandered in out of the northwest, making things reasonably comfortable.

Firestick had slept, and slept well, for the better part of four hours. He was feeling refreshed and eager to get on the move again. What was more, the horses also looked rested and ready. He'd stripped them, watered them, and left them to graze in their own patch of shade while he dozed.

Over a small campfire, Firestick cooked coffee and fried some bacon that he ate along with a few grease-softened hardtack biscuits. He was finishing his final cup of coffee, getting ready to kick out the fire and go saddle the horses, when he saw the riders headed his way from the west.

There were two horses, one of them burdened in some

unusual way that puzzled Firestick for a few minutes until they drew close enough for him to make out that the animal was carrying double. As they slowly came closer still, he saw that they were a sorry-looking lot, men and animals alike, ragged and filthy and mighty hard used.

Continuing to eye their approach, Firestick stood motionless except for the slow sweep of his hand thumbing the keeper thong off the hammer of the Colt holstered on his hip.

The one riding alone was a man of indistinguishable age due to the streaks of dust, sweat, and whiskers covering his face. Somewhere in his thirties was Firestick's best guess. He was a shade over average height, lean and wiry, with faded blue eyes that were the only facial features not caked with dirt. It was like they were peering out from behind a mask.

As far as the two on the other horse, one was a close copy of the loner, maybe a few years older, with eyes tinted even a more washed-out blue. The other, sitting in front in the saddle with the other riding behind, was a much bulkier specimen with a ragged black beard and greasy tendrils of equally black hair spilling around his fleshy face and down the back of his thick neck.

"Evenin', stranger," said the lone rider. "The sight of that campfire and the smell of coffee makes your simple camp look like the richest oasis on the desert to the weary eyes of us poor wretches who have suffered nothing but a string of bad luck."

Firestick noted that, despite their overall shabbiness, each of the men was sporting a handgun and holster that looked well cared for. The big one also had a set of bandoleers crisscrossing his heavy chest, their rows of ammunition clearly meant for the Winchester 73 snugged in the saddle scabbard thrusting up just ahead of his right knee. What he was faced with here, Firestick decided with full confidence, were three men on the run—escapees from a jail or prison somewhere to the west. Desperate. Dangerous.

"This here ain't hardly a desert," he replied easily to the one who'd spoken. "But you're plumb right about my camp bein' a simple one. Not so simple, though, that I can't spare some coffee or fresh water, maybe a few biscuits. I warn you, though, those biscuits are hard enough to dull your teeth."

The big one grunted. "Hot coffee on a hot day never made no sense to me. And as far as damn hardtack—"

"Never mind, Jasper," the apparent leader cut him off. Keeping his gaze locked on Firestick, he went on, "We're being offered the best hospitality available from Mister . . . ?"

"McQueen," Firestick finished for him.

"Mr. McQueen, let me present to you my cousin Jasper Twitchell. He's the oversized *hombre* who just addressed you. Behind him is Ludlow Ames, my brother. And I am Teaford Ames . . . Reckon those names are familiar to you, right?"

Firestick gave a slow wag of his head. "Can't say they are."

"He must be new to these parts, Brother T," said Ludlow.

"That's right," agreed Firestick. "I'm just passin' through, and as a matter of fact, that's what I need to keep on doin'. So you're welcome to the fire, and I'll even leave you some coffee if you're short. There's a spring over there in those trees where you can fill your pot and water your horses. I won't be joinin' you, though, as I have to be on my way."

"Now hold on a minute, McQueen." Teaford's voice suddenly took on a less friendly tone as he swung down from his saddle. "Before you go anywhere, there's some business needs tendin' to here."

"That's right. Are you hard of hearin' or something? Your damn coffee ain't no part of it," said Twitchell, dismounting heavily after Ludlow had shifted behind him and slipped off the horse's rump.

Firestick planted his feet a little wider and squared himself to face the men. "Whatever you gents got in mind, make it quick," he grated. "I got business to attend to as well—but it ain't here, and it's something important for me to get to."

"Well, that'll work out just fine then." Teaford's mouth smiled but his eyes didn't. "You can hurry off to all the business you want—you just can't leave for it on either of those horses you got over there."

"We need 'em worser than you." Ludlow chuckled.

"What we don't need is your stinkin' coffee," grumbled Twitchell.

"Now don't get the wrong idea," Teaford added. "We ain't meanin' to leave you afoot. Nossir, we ain't low-lifes like that. A way to look at it is that we're offerin' a trade—your two horses for one of ours. Hell, you can even pick which one you want. Can't be much fairer than that, can we?"

"That's a real interestin' offer," Firestick said, low and soft. "But no thanks. I'll be obliged to keep the ones I got."

"The hell you will," growled Twitchell.

"Be sensible, McQueen," said Teaford. "We're three men on two mounts; you're one man on two. That just ain't right. What do you need two horses so bad for anyway?"

Firestick gave it a beat and then replied, "Maybe you're right. For what I got to do, could be I'd be better off with four."

The implication of his words hung in the air, growing heavier and more tension-filled with each heartbeat. Gradually, the expressions on the faces of the Ames brothers and their cousin turned from puzzlement to disbelief to anger.

And then, suddenly, with everyone realizing that any more words would only be wasted, four hands streaked for holstered iron and the scene erupted into one of blazing guns and hot lead sizzling through the air.

Firestick's innate skill with any firearm—from his beloved Hawken to repeating rifles to handguns—had come to also include a mastery of the fast draw. Never was this more on display than there in that remote stand of cottonwoods in the slanted rays of a setting sun.

Twitchell's hand was the first to jump toward the gun on his hip. For that reason, Firestick responded by shooting him first. The big man's hand had barely closed over the grips of his Colt before a slug from Firestick's .44 slammed into his chest, just above the V of his intersecting bandoleers. The impact staggered Twitchell back a half step and caused him to drop to his knees.

Working in descending order based on who he calculated to be the most dangerous, Firestick swung his arm and centered the .44's muzzle on Teaford. The man had cleared leather with a short-barreled Schofield and was in the act of raising it when Firestick triggered his second shot and planted a pill square into the older Ames brother's heart. Teaford spun away, his gun arm jerking upward and his spasming finger snapping two shots skyward as he toppled to the ground.

When Firestick wheeled to face Ludlow, the remaining would-be horse thief had his gun drawn and was extending his arm toward the old mountain man. If he'd fired from the hip instead of trying to take aim, he might have gotten off an effective shot.

As it was, he and Firestick squeezed their triggers simultaneously. Ludlow's bullet came close enough to sting the tip of Firestick's earlobe. But in the same instant, while Ludlow had to settle for that near miss, Firestick's slug punched into his throat, a half inch below the chin, plowing all the way through and exiting in a gout of blood and mangled tissue.

With both Ames brothers down, Firestick returned his attention to Twitchell. The big man was still on his knees, still fumbling stubbornly with near-dead fingers, trying to draw his Colt even as his life's blood was pumping from the hole in his chest. Firestick spent a second bullet on him, planting the shot smack in the middle of his broad forehead, finally knocking him back and down.

Except for his hands busying themselves with replacing spent cartridges in the .44, Firestick stood very still for a long moment. His eyes lingered on the three dead men. The last crack of gunfire faded into nothingness and bluish wisps of powder smoke drifted away in the gentle wind.

Abruptly, Firestick holstered his Colt and then turned to the tasks he'd been about to perform before being interrupted. He kicked out the fire, gathered up his gear, walked over and saddled his horses. Leaving them hobbled for the time being, he then approached the horses his three visitors had arrived on.

The critters had skittered away at the burst of gunfire, but only a short distance. Clucking soothingly, Firestick had no trouble getting them to hold for his touch. The animal that had been carrying double looked past its best years to begin with, and the hard load it had been forced to endure clearly took still more of a toll. It wouldn't be of much use to him, Firestick decided.

So he stripped it of all its gear and then slapped it on the rump, setting it free. He figured it should be fine; there was graze and water close at hand, and in due time, the animal would likely find its way back home—back to where Firestick was convinced his visitors had stolen the two mounts to begin with.

The remaining horse was a tall steeldust with decent lines. Given some rest from carrying a rider, at least for a while, Firestick judged that this one still had some miles left in it—enough to be of use to him as a third switch-off mount so he could ride all the harder and steadier through the night. Leading the animal over to the spring, allowing it to sufficiently slake its thirst, he then treated it to a couple handfuls of grain from one of his saddlebags, instead of allowing the animal time to graze.

Half a minute later, after removing the hobbles on his

original horses and attaching a tether line to the steeldust, Firestick climbed into a saddle and swung all noses southward. His face was expressionless as they passed the fallen bodies, and he didn't bother to toss another glance in their direction.

CHAPTER 38

The one aspect of being cooped up in the house that Beartooth absolutely refused to go along with involved the matter of relieving himself. Accepting that the house and Double M grounds likely were being watched by the rangers much of the time, he understood the risk of exposing himself via trips to the outside privy. Therefore he grudgingly made use of the chamber pot in his room.

But he was damned if he was going to leave the task of periodically emptying the vessel to anyone else, namely Victoria. For this reason, he'd adopted the habit of making a quick trip outside, first thing each morning, to take care of the task himself.

This morning, while Victoria was preparing breakfast out in the kitchen, he once again followed this routine. He could see that, weather-wise, it was the beginning of another beautiful day. Because he knew that too much thinking about being shut away from enjoying any of it would only gall him into a sour mood, he took care of his business quickly and went back inside.

* * *

"I'll be damned," muttered Gene Rodgers, lowering the field glasses he'd been gazing through.

Beside him once again in the high buffalo wallow, Roy Arbry grinned broadly. Even without the binoculars, he'd been able to see well enough what his partner had been focused on.

"You hate it when I'm right, don't you?" Arbry said. "But it only stood to reason. We spent hours watching at night and then at different times during the day—trying it first thing in the morning, before anybody might figure we'd even be up and about, seemed worth a try."

"I got to hand it to you," Rodgers allowed as he pushed back from the lip of the wallow. "It panned out, no two ways about it. We've got the evidence we needed, giving us every right to go down there and demand Skinner be turned over."

"Yeah. We got our certain answer to whether or not he was actually holed up there. Now," Arbry added with a wry twist to his mouth, "all that's left is finding out how hard it might be to actually root him out."

Having already called out to Beartooth, advising him breakfast was ready, Victoria stepped out onto the front porch to ring the triangle bell that would notify Manuel and Jesus of the same. It was as she was reaching to do this that she noticed the pair of riders approaching, coming down a long hill to the northwest. Her heart sank. Even though Victoria had never laid eyes on or even heard a description of the two rangers so often discussed over the past few days, she somehow instinctively knew that's who the approaching riders were. The thing she *didn't* know—yet nevertheless feared—was what would happen now.

"It's a good thing you called when you did," came Beartooth's voice through the open door as he entered the kitchen behind her, "because the smell of that fryin' bacon was drivin' me to the point where—"

Victoria wheeled and stepped back inside, saying in a hushed voice, "They're here!"

Beartooth looked blank.

Hastily closing the door, Victoria explained, "There are two men riding up. I believe they're the Texas Rangers."

Beartooth hurried forward and parted a window curtain ever so slightly in order to look out. Like Victoria, he'd never had a firsthand look at the two rangers in question. Yet, also like her, one look convinced him that's exactly who the two approaching riders were. And then, removing any shred of a doubt, the lapel on the jacket of one of the men sagged open wider and revealed the unmistakable star-within-a-circle badge pinned to his shirt.

"It's them, alright," Beartooth said, stepping back away from the window. "Damn!"

"Go back to your room," Victoria said. "I'll deal with them."

Beartooth thought of his recent trip to the outhouse and realized if the rangers were showing up this early in the day, there was a good chance they had spotted him carrying out the errand.

"That might not be so easy."

"You don't know how convincing I can be. At least let me give it a try," Victoria urged.

Beartooth glanced into the adjoining dining room and the parlor beyond, with the Hawken rifle hanging over the door. "I wish to heck Firestick was here," he muttered under his breath.

"Just go!"

Half a minute later, Victoria stepped back out onto the front porch to greet the arriving horsemen. She stood wiping her hands on her apron and smiling pleasantly as they reined up at the hitchrail in front of the house.

"Good morning, gentlemen," she said. "We seldom get visitors out this way, especially so early in the day."

"Taking care of business, as I expect you know from running a ranch, sometimes requires an early start, ma'am," said one of the newcomers, a man about thirty years old with a smooth, roundish face and mild brown eyes.

"Oh? You're here on business then?" Victoria said.

"That's right," confirmed the second man, somewhat taller and leaner with a narrow face and slightly squinted eyes. "We're here looking to speak with a Mr. Malachi Skinner."

Victoria blinked innocently. "Oh. I'm sorry, I hope you didn't ride too far. But I'm afraid Mr. Skinner is not present. You see, he's away on—"

"Pardon me for interrupting, ma'am," said the round-faced man, "but we happen to know that's not true. This whole thing would go a whole lot easier if you'd just accept that fact and have Skinner come out."

"Really! Are you calling me a liar?" Victoria demanded, putting on a good show of indignation and anger.

"We'd truly like to avoid that, ma'am," said the lean rider. Spreading back the lapel of his jacket and showing his ranger's badge, he went on to say, "My name's Roy Arbry, and this is my partner Gene Rodgers. We're here on official business for the Texas Rangers, and it would be unwise for you to interfere."

"You may as well know," added Rodgers, "that we spotted Skinner outside this house only a few minutes ago. We know he's here. So, like my partner said, please make this easy and just have him come out."

Victoria was momentarily flustered. The cool insistence of these men was hard to stand up to. This wasn't going at all like she'd intended.

Looking past the rangers in the direction of the bunkhouse, she felt a surge of momentary relief when she saw Miguel and Jesus walking her way. Although she'd never gotten around to ringing the breakfast bell, they had apparently seen the men ride up and whether sensing who they might be or merely out of curiosity, they were coming to see what was on the visitors' minds.

Sensing the approach of the *vaqueros*, the rangers twisted in their saddles and watched them walk up. Miguel gave them an indifferent glance as he moved past their horses and went to stand before Victoria on the porch. His nephew followed silently in his footsteps.

"Good morning, Miss Victoria," Miguel greeted. "We saw you come out on the porch and thought you were going to ring the breakfast bell."

"Yes. Yes, I was," Victoria confirmed. "But then these men showed up. They rode out looking to conduct some business with Mr. Skinner."

Miguel's eyes passed back and forth between Victoria and the rangers. "That is too bad," he said calmly. "Mr. Skinner is gone and not expected to return for some time." He fixed his gaze earnestly on the rangers and said, "If it is a matter of horses, however, maybe I can help. I work very closely with Mr. Skinner when it comes to—"

"Knock it off," snapped Arbry, losing some of his patience. "We met the other night, Mr. Santros, when you assisted against those ambushers who attacked my partner and me. You demonstrated yourself to be a man of good character in that matter and earned our gratitude. Please don't sully that impression now by participating in an attempt to obstruct justice."

"There may be some doubt about your so-called justice!" Victoria exclaimed.

"Look," said Rodgers, "we've already told you—we know Skinner is here. If he's listening, like I suspect he is, then he knows we're here and he knows *why* we're here. We have an arrest warrant to serve and the courts will take it from there. That's how it's going to be, whether you like it or not."

"Well, I *don't* like it," Victoria informed him. "And it remains to be seen how you're going to serve your warrant on someone who is not present."

"Alright, then," Arbry said, swinging down from his saddle. "If you insist on sticking with that—and if Skinner insists on remaining in hiding—then we'll move this case along another way. We'll arrest you, ma'am, on charges of interfering with law officers in the line of duty. Maybe the sight of you behind bars will convince Skinner to suddenly return from his 'trip.'"

"You wouldn't dare!" Victoria protested. In spite of her outward bravado, however, her already fair complexion notably paled.

Young Jesus, who harbored an achingly deep crush on

the lady of the manor, stepped forward to block Arbry from advancing on her.

Also dismounting hurriedly, Rodgers said, "Don't make it worse, son. Be smart and don't involve yourself in this."

"That's enough!"

The voice, coming from the open doorway behind Victoria, turned all heads.

Beartooth stood there, mouth set in a tight, grim line, balled fists hanging loosely at his sides. His chest rose and fell as his eyes raked the two rangers.

"Leave 'em alone," he grated. "It's me you want—not them."

CHAPTER 39

Moosejaw opened his eyes, but a stabbing sensation of light and blurred shapes caused him to quickly shut them again. When he tried to speak, the words came out only as a groan. Pain throbbed behind his ear and down the back of his neck. An attempt to lift his head was met with a bolt of increased pain shooting through him, and he immediately flopped back again.

At least he was lying on something soft. Soft and furry. That was somewhat comforting, though not enough to make the pain behind his ear go away. He tried to open one eye this time. Just one. Very slowly. As he did so, his breathing quickened in anticipation of another jolt of increased pain.

"Aw, come on. I didn't clip you that hard," said a voice.

Moosejaw knew the voice. He thought he did, anyway. But when he tried to concentrate, to remember, it made his head hurt worse and he still wasn't quite able to place it.

The voice spoke again. "You're so damn big I had to put some beef behind clubbin' you. But thunderation,

I seen the day you could've took a tap like that and barely staggered. You must be gettin' soft."

Now Moosejaw was sure. He forced his eyes open, forced himself past the pain until he was able to make out the blurred outline of a face that seemed to be floating above him. He groaned again, meaning for it to be a curse.

"I'd splash some water on you to bring you around, but I don't want to get Daisy's bearskin all wet. Don't you go bleedin' on it, neither. I put in a lot of work to get that rascal done, and it turned out pretty darn good if I do say so myself."

Moosejaw finally managed to croak out some words. "Rip . . . What the hell happened . . . W-what did you do to me?"

Ripley sighed. "I had to thump you one, old son. A pretty hefty clout, like I said, on account of you're so blamed big. The other two I was able to get rid of without doin' 'em any harm, leastways not no physical kind. You I had to get a little rough with. No other way to do it."

Moosejaw's vision became clearer. He saw that he was lying on the floor of one of the jail cells—the one Ripley had been occupying for the past few days. He was sprawled on the bearskin rug Ripley had been fashioning for Daisy.

"Don't try to strain and struggle too hard," Ripley told him. "Your wrists are handcuffed behind your back. Lord, don't think that wasn't a chore, tryin' to yank those tree trunk arms of your'n around."

Increasing anger was making Moosejaw forget his pain and sharpening the clarity of his vision. But there were still many other things he wasn't clear about.

"What the hell is this all about, Rip? A lousy jailbreak?

All you had to do is wait for Firestick to get back, like you agreed, and it won't take no time before he—"

"Quit your yappin' and listen," Ripley growled. "Give me a minute and I'll explain. But listen tight, 'cause I ain't got a lot of time to spend goin' over it."

Moosejaw glared at him but held his tongue.

"This is bigger than me just bustin' jail," Ripley began. "Hell, I coulda done that anytime, the way you was bein' so friendly and loose with how you treated me. This is part of something that's gonna see me through the rest of my days. See me through in style and comfort like I thought I'd never know. Sure as hell like I wasn't gonna find otherwise in this here so-called civilization where I stood no chance of fittin' in the regular way."

Ripley's eyes took on a gleam that appeared part anger and part something else as he went on, "It's about gold, old son! Gold I got me a chance to get a slice of. Yeah, it means sidin' in with some fellas who don't make a habit of stickin' to the rules of the law. But so what? Your civilized rules and laws was never meant to work for me anyhow. I finally figured that out.

"That horse herd comin' in out of Mexico? It's got more than horses runnin' with it. In the false bottom of the chuckwagon there's a hundred thousand dollars' worth of gold bars. That big rancher, Howell, found a vein of it on the property he married into. But the Mexican government has a strict policy about takin' a healthy cut of any gold or other minerals mined inside their borders. Plus, the cash-out for any amount a body *can* claim down there is a whole lot less than what's paid up here. So Howell got a healthy clump of the shiny stuff dug out, melted into bars, and then set it up for his ramrod, Wilson, to smuggle it out with the remount herd he was sellin' off to the army. All on the up-and-up, the horse part. But on the sly, somewhere in the Fort Leaton area, Howell also has a buyer waitin' for the gold . . . Only trouble is, Wilson decided to out-sly Howell and made his own plans for that sweet haul. That's where I came in, seein's how I was already runnin' with the pack of fellas Wilson contacted to throw in with him for snatchin' the gold away."

"So why involve Buffalo Peak or any of us here with your sneaky double-dealin'?" Moosejaw wanted to know.

"Because here—strictly with no put-in from me, mind you, is where it was decided to do the snatch," Ripley answered. "It's up across the border, clear of any *bandido* threat, and still a long ways from Fort Leaton. Only thing to consider was a nearby little town, out in the middle of nowhere, with nothing for law but three old mountain men that somebody slapped badges on . . . That's where I *did* do some puttin' in. I know you fellas well enough to know that if a robbery took place practically in your backyard, you'd damn sure try to get in the way. And I know this pack I'm runnin' with well enough to know they wouldn't hesitate to blast each and every one of you down." Ripley paused a beat, frowning. "And even though I've took a turn down the owlhoot trail, I didn't want to be any part of that."

"That's mighty big of you, Rip." Moosejaw sneered.

Ignoring the remark, Ripley continued. "So I convinced the others that I could get the three of you out of the way ahead of time, to make dang sure you didn't try to interfere. I was up in Pecos last year, see, back when that showgirl got killed and when Beartooth also showed up there. I didn't make no contact with him then on account of I was in pretty sorry shape at the time, drinkin' heavy and scrapin' mighty low in the gutter. I didn't want him to see me that way.

"But then, after I crawled out of the gutter and throwed in with the pack I'm runnin' with now and this gold deal came along, I thought back on that time. Thought back on that terrible murder and how it was still unsolved. That's what gave me the idea for testifyin' against Beartooth and gettin' that wanted dodger put out for him. I figured it was bound to do one of two things—either put him on the run or behind bars."

"You did that?" Moosejaw said through clenched teeth. "You're the one behind that?"

"Better than havin' him go down under the gun, ain't it?" Ripley challenged. "It got him out of the way, got him out of danger. And I knew that you and Firestick would be bound to go to work on tryin' to find a way to clear him. I figured a trip to Pecos would be called for, hopin' you'd both ride up there. Well, it only worked for Firestick, but at least it was one more out of the way. That only left you, and now you're took care of, too. As soon as that little waitress left after deliverin' our breakfast, I clunked you over the head and . . . well, now here we are. That's how the story is gonna end."

"The hell it is!" Moosejaw snarled. "We'll track you down. Every mother's son of you."

"Maybe you'll try. For a day or so. But we aim to scatter to the four winds and more—and you, Beartooth, and Firestick can't afford to leave your town and your ranch behind to stick with trailin' us for too long. Besides, the gold ain't no skin off your noses. Leave it to the rangers."

"You can bet they won't give up!"

Ripley shrugged. "They're welcome to try. This pack I'm runnin' with has a knack for stayin' out of their reach."

"Think what you're doin', Rip," Moosejaw pleaded. "This is no good! You'll stain yourself an outlaw for the rest of your days. That ain't you!"

Ripley shook his head sadly. "What ain't me, old friend, is this critter who's been bumpin' around ever since I came down out of the mountains, tryin' to fit into civilization. It ain't ever come close to workin', and it ain't ever gonna, not the way I was tryin' before. My only other choices are to end up dyin' in a gutter or go back up and freeze in the mountains. This way, I might still be takin' the gutter by your way of lookin' at it . . . but it will, by God, be a gutter lined with gold!"

Moosejaw couldn't find words for a response.

"I left a short note out on the marshal's desk," Ripley said, "tellin' how my testimony against Beartooth was false. You be sure and show that to the rangers; it should be enough to get him cleared."

Moosejaw just glared at him.

Sighing, Ripley produced a towel he'd taken from the washstand out in a corner of the office. "I gotta go now, old son. Got me a date in a dry wash south of town where that chuckwagon will be comin' through in a spell. Before I go, I'm gonna gag you so's you can't holler loud enough to draw attention too soon. I'm hopin' you'll be smart enough to hold still for it. If not, I'll have to clunk you on the head again. But, one way or t'other, it's what I aim to do . . ."

CHAPTER 40

The sun had been up just a little over an hour when Firestick angled in past the east end of the Vieja Mountains and came in sight of Buffalo Mound, the butte thrusting up out of the prairie below the mountains and the source for the name Buffalo Peak being applied to the town a ways farther west. Buffalo Mound . . . Buffalo Peak . . . home. Almost there.

Firestick felt pleased and relieved, along with a fresh surge of energy. He'd ridden hard and steady all through the night. With the moon and stars lighting his way and three horses to regularly switch off riding, he had made better time than he'd dared hope.

Now, as he continued pushing hard, closing in on the town, his destination was near. And so was the confrontation that had to take place once he got there.

The feeling of trepidation that suddenly passed through him as part of that thought was somewhat surprising. Firestick had faced hostile Indians, marauders out to steal his furs, gunmen and various types of outlaws, and scores of rowdy drunks without knowing fear. But the prospect of facing an old and once-trusted friend now responsible for betrayal on a scale as high as Ripley had reached touched an emotion so deep and raw in Firestick that he suddenly did have a fear—a fear of what he might do once the double-crossing cur was within his grasp.

CHAPTER 41

"Howdy, boys," Ripley greeted as he nosed his horse into a stand of cedar trees, leaning forward in his saddle to duck under one of the low-hanging branches.

Clete Halsey, mottled in shadows thrown by the thick branches, stepped forward. "I'll be damned," he said. "You old rascal, you did worm your way out of that jail cell."

"Worm my way out hell," Ripley replied, swinging down to the ground. "I walked out standin' straight up. What's more, I got all three of those lawmen back yonder cleared out of the way, just like I said I would. Two of 'em are clean out of town, and one of 'em is havin' hisself a turn in that cell I just left."

"You're a slippery devil, I got to give you that," Halsey allowed with a grin.

"I don't see the big deal," muttered Mud River Neelan from where he sat leaning against a tree trunk. He was a bulky *hombre* with stringy, straw-colored hair and a V-shaped knife scar tugging down the outside corner of his left eye. "Those mossy old law dogs from that pissant of a town weren't never no threat to us. In the first place, we're more than a mile out of, whatyacall, their jepperdiction. In the second place, whether they was around or not, we'll be long gone before they ever know we was here doin' anything anyway."

"Maybe so. But having three *less* law dogs to worry about," said Halsey, "is a plus in my book."

"Especially after what you told us about a couple of Texas Rangers also hanging around," spoke up Billy Beevey, a whip-thin young man with sleepy eyes and a slouched posture that belied the speed in his gun hand. "That's plenty enough to worry about right there."

"Shit, that ain't so much of a worry," claimed lantern-jawed, derby-hatted Buford Muldoon. "We've had Texas Rangers snortin' on our tail before and none of 'em ever got close enough to take a bite."

"Sometimes one bite—a big enough one—is all it takes," remarked Liam Pauley, a tall, lean specimen sporting twin Colts in a double-holster rig decked out with silver studs. "And a hundred thousand dollars in gold just might be what it takes for them to stretch their necks a little farther and spread their jaws a little wider."

"The thing to remember about that, though," pointed out Halsey, "is that first they have to *know* about the gold. When our ransacking of this stupid chuckwagon is first reported, the only ones who'll know there was gold involved will be rancher Howell and Wilson. Howell is going to be forced to play it mighty tight-lipped because he arranged to illegally smuggle the shiny stuff to begin with. And Wilson"—Halsey chuckled—"well, I guess we know he ain't going to be doing too much blabbing about it, right?"

"Where is Wilson?" Ripley asked.

"Don't worry. He'll be along when he needs to be."

"Wilson can show up or not, far as I'm concerned. If he decides to stay with his horses, that's a bigger cut for the rest of us," said Muldoon. "The thing I'm anxious to see is that blamed chuckwagon. It ought to have been here by now, oughtn't it?"

"How can we be sure it's going to come this way?" asked Beevey.

"Because Wilson scouted ahead and told them. Remember?" A hint of annoyance crept into Halsey's tone. "He told them about this dry wash and how the shallowest, least rocky place to cross is here by these cedar trees."

"Hey. Another thing," said Muldoon. "If we don't want this business about the gold spread too far too fast, what about the fella drivin' the chuckwagon? The cook, I suppose he is. We don't want to leave him having seen us break open that false bottom, do we?"

"No problem. We bash him over the head as soon as we get his wagon stopped. Wilson don't want no killing unless it absolutely can't be avoided," explained Halsey. "We leave the cook knocked cold and he stays in the dark—literally—about us slipping away with the gold he never knew he was carrying in the first place."

"I just want to get to it," Beevey said.

"The cook is an older fella, so we don't want to bash him too hard," Halsey told everybody. "He's got a helper, a young Yacqui boy, who might be riding along with him."

"An Injun, you say?" Mud River's mouth spread in a nasty smile. "Say now, there's some gravy I didn't expect. I ain't killed me an Injun in nigh onto three years. And I don't think I ever did me a Yacqui before at all."

"You heard what I said about unnecessary killing," Halsey reminded him.

"Yeah, yeah, I heard you," Mud River grumbled. Then, under his breath, he added, "Never saw an Injun yet, though, where it didn't feel necessary he needed killin'."

"Well, it so happens you're about to get another chance," Ripley stated. "The wagon's practically on top of us."

Everybody looked around.

"Where?"

"What do you mean?"

Ripley pointed. "There. Across the wash, on the other side of that rise just yonder. I can hear it clankin' along. Can't you fellas?" The former mountain man emitted a bitter chuckle. "Hell's bells, if you boys ever ventured up into the high reaches with shit-clogged hearin' like you seem to have, you wouldn't last between new moons before your scalps was lifted or you ended up supper for some critter."

"What's that old buzzard cacklin' about?"

"Never mind," Halsey hissed in a hoarse whisper. "Just get in your positions. Get ready for that wagon."

Bristly-browed Hamp Nabor spat a gob of tobacco juice off to one side of the wagon box and squeezed the bushy growths above his eyes into a fierce scowl as he drew back on the reins of his team. The matched pair of black pullers came to a halt on the near edge of the wide, rocky-bottomed dry wash that looked like it hadn't had any water pass through it in decades.

"Holy flamin' toadfrogs!" exclaimed old Hamp. "If this

here is the best crossin' spot, I'd sure in blazes hate to see the worst."

"But it is good and dry, Mister Hamp," said the brown-skinned, black-haired lad sitting on the seat beside him. "Is that not a good thing?"

"It's good as far as it goes," snorted Hamp. "Means we won't get washed away or drownedified. But look at all those sharp, jagged rocks scattered full across the width. Hit one of them a little bit wrong and we could bust a wheel or maybe even an axle, then be left sittin' here until another flood *did* come along."

The boy, who was only fourteen and was called Jorto, displayed a puzzled frown. "But if we took too long getting back to the herd, would Señor Wilson not come looking for us?"

"Yeah, I reckon he would." Hamp sighed. "And if I'm sittin' here just frettin' about crossin' and he shows up, he'll be sore about that. But if I try to cross and *do* end up bustin' a wheel or axle, then he'll be sore about that. Some days a body just can't win for losin'."

"What will we win if we make it across without breaking anything?"

"It was just an expression, Jorto. Don't worry about it." Hamp sighed again. "Hang on tight. Here we go. This is the way Trav steered us, so we gotta put some trust in it. We'll just take it slow and easy and we oughta be okay."

Hamp gave his reins a slap, and the blacks tugged the wagon into motion again. Down the last few yards of the incline they slowly rolled, then over the crumbled low bank and out into the rocky-bottomed wash. Sand and pebbles crunched under the iron-rimmed wheels and some of the larger, irregular-shaped rocks clattered loudly when they got bumped out of the way. The wagon rocked side to side, creaking and thumping as the wheels rolled up and over rocks embedded solidly in the ground yet with sizable portions still sticking up.

When they were halfway across, six men on horses emerged from the stand of cedar trees and spread out before them along the opposite bank.

"Whoa there, old-timer," called Halsey, curving half of his mouth in what was meant to be a friendly-looking smile.

Not liking the look of this, Hamp pulled back on the reins and halted his team again. "You're blockin' the way," he growled. "This is rough enough goin' without you *hombres* makin' it any more so."

"That's just the thing," said Halsey. "We saw you were having a rough time, so we thought maybe we could help. The way you're clunking and bouncing over those rocks, you're apt to shake that wagon apart."

"This ol' wagon has held together for a lot of miles so far. I reckon she's good for a few more." Hamp squinted under his ledge of gnarly brows. "Besides, what do you reckon you can do to smooth this crossin' anyway? Shovel all those rocks out of my way?"

"That's real funny," said Halsey. "I like a fella with a sense of humor."

"That's real pleasin' to my ears. Now that we've had ourselves a good laugh," suggested Hamp, "how about you and your boys move aside so we can be about our business?"

Halsey nodded. "See, now there's another funny thing.

Because your business and our business sort of runs together."

Beside Hamp, Jorto whispered, "I do not like these men, Mister Hamp. I do not think they are good men."

"Just be quiet, son. Let me handle this," Hamp told him.

"If you'd have taken it more serious when I said we were willing to help you, I could have explained this right from the get-go," Halsey continued. "The way it's going to work is—we're going to lighten your load for you. Then, after we do that, you'll be able to roll on across this rough ol' wash a lot easier. You'll go on your way, we'll go on ours, and that'll be it."

"That's a real generous offer," Hamp said in a measured tone. "But the way the mornin's buildin' up to be another hot day, I truly hate to see you fellas go to all that work. So I'll just say I'm much obliged, but no thanks. And we'll leave it at that."

As Hamp was talking, Jorto slipped one arm slowly, carefully behind him to reach for the short-barreled, bolt-action .22-caliber rifle, his prized possession, lying just behind the wagon seat. Mister Hamp had given it to him and taught him to use it for hunting jackrabbits and sage hens to provide added meat for the stew pot. Jorto never thought he would ever aim it at a man, but if these six before them now tried to force trouble or threatened harm to Mister Hamp, he knew he would not hesitate to do so.

"Okay. Enough of this talk," boomed Muldoon. "The old goat was right about one thing—it's getting hot. Too hot to drag this out any more than we have to. Tell him what's what, Halsey, and let's get on with what we came here for."

"I agree," spoke up Mud River. "I'm sick of pussy-footin' around. We want what's in that wagon, and we're gonna by-God have it!"

Halsey let his men have their say and then looked appealingly at Hamp. "You see how it is, old-timer. I tried to be pleasant about it, but my men are short on patience. So, if you're smart, climb down off that wagon, stand out of the way while we help ourselves to certain items, and neither you nor the boy has to get hurt."

"You bastards better not harm that boy!"

Quick as an eyeblink, Beevey's gun flashed out of its holster and leveled at Jorto. "That's strictly up to you, old man," he said softly.

CHAPTER 42

"Urrrmph!" . . . "Unnenhrr!"

Moosejaw was trying to shout words, but due to the handkerchief stuffed in his mouth and held there by the towel knotted tight around the lower part of his face, all that came out were muffled, unintelligible grunts and growls. He'd begun these attempts as soon as Ripley was gone. After a while, realizing the futility of it until there was some sign that somebody might be close enough to hear, he'd let up.

Instead, he managed to shove himself to his feet and tried slamming his shoulder against the closed and locked cell door—which was even more futile. Some further attempted shouts under the small, barred window high on the back wall of the cell also failed to get any results.

For a time, he wasn't sure how long, the big deputy sat dejectedly on the hard, narrow cot. A torrent of thoughts, alternating between rage and disbelief, ran through his mind. How could Ripley have turned into such a low-down skunk? How could he turn on old friends this way? More than his own mistreatment, what infuriated Moosejaw the most was the way Rip had set up Beartooth, branding him a murderer and aiming him down a path that could very well lead to the gallows! Supposedly there was a note meant to erase all of that—but was the note really out there on the marshal's desk and would it truly be enough to curb everything already set in motion?

As if bidden by his thoughts of Beartooth's plight, Moosejaw suddenly imagined he could hear his close pal's voice . . . and then other voices, too . . . and the clumping of feet and movement out in the front office of the jail. But no, it wasn't just his imagination—somebody was out there, talking and moving around!

Moosejaw rammed his shoulder against the cell door again, causing it to clatter loudly, and also renewed his grunting and guttural efforts to call out, trying to draw attention to himself.

The connecting door between the cell block and front office swung open. One of the Texas Rangers—the narrow-faced one, Moosejaw couldn't remember what name he went by—poked his head in. His eyes went wide at the sight of Moosejaw, handcuffed and gagged inside one of the cells.

Behind the narrow-faced ranger, somebody said, "What's that noise? What's going on?" On the heels of those words, the round-faced ranger crowded into view. "Holy Jesus!" he exclaimed when he saw Moosejaw.

The two men pushed into the cell block and then, in the doorway to the front office, a third man appeared. It was Beartooth!

A flurry of excited chatter and activity followed as keys to Moosejaw's cell and handcuffs were found and put to use freeing the big deputy. Beartooth provided some advice on where to find the keys but otherwise stayed out of the way, standing still and looking on anxiously, his own arms chained behind his back.

As soon as his gag was removed, Moosejaw spat and released a blue streak of curses. One of the rangers gave him a dipper of water. Then came the questions: "What happened here? Who did this to you?"

Moosejaw's eyes found Beartooth before he answered, "Ripley! It was Rip, Beartooth—he's turned bad on us, and gone down the owlhoot trail!"

"You mean that old mountain man friend of yours who helped with the attempted ambush on us the other night?" asked Rodgers.

"The same. Only he ain't no friend of ours—not no more," Moosejaw said bitterly.

"What set him off? What made him do—" Before Arbry could finish, Moosejaw cut him short.

"No time for a lot of long-winded explainin'," the big deputy said. "We got a gold robbery to stop. If you fellas will follow my lead and put some quick trust in what I've got to tell you, we can clear up a heap of bad business."

Arbry and Rodgers exchanged glances. "We're willing to go along up to a point," Arbry said. "But you've got to give us something more than what you just said."

Alternately rubbing his wrists and swinging his arms to work circulation back in them, Moosejaw said, "There's a horse herd camped south of town. Up out of Mexico, on their way to be sold as remounts to the cavalry at Fort Leaton. Unknown to the men pushin' the herd, all except the ramrod, a fella named Wilson, a false bottom in the chuckwagon is carryin' a stash of gold bars. The gold was mined in secret and melted down by the ranch owner down in Mexico and is bein' smuggled out so's not to have to pay what the Mexican government would otherwise lay claim to. Wilson is workin' in cahoots with a gang of robbers—includin' Ripley—primed to steal the gold when the chuckwagon is on its way into town this mornin' for fresh supplies."

Beartooth shook his head in dismay. "And Rip has let himself get mixed up in something like that?"

"Right smack in the middle. And it's even worse," Moosejaw said bitterly. "The murder charge against you? That's Rip's doin'. He worked it out with the rest of the gang to be the one to get the three of us out of the way for when the robbery took place. The way he told me, he figured testifyin' against you on that murder charge would put you either behind bars or force you to go on the run. Then he counted on Firestick and me settin' out—likely up Pecos way—to try and clear you." The big deputy spread his hands. "When I stayed behind, he changed his plan for dealin' with me to waitin' until the last minute, cloutin' me over the head, and leavin' me locked away like you just found."

"That mangy old sonofabitch," Beartooth bit off through clenched teeth.

"Any idea where this robbery is supposed to take place?" asked Rodgers.

"Rip said something about a dry wash south of town. I think I know where he means. We'll have to follow it and hope we get to the right spot before it's too late."

"Take these cuffs off me! Give me a gun so I can join in," Beartooth said in a strident tone. "You heard what Rip said about the charges against me bein' phony!"

"That's only the word of a declared criminal, a known trickster . . . On top of that, we're getting it third hand," replied Arbry. As soon as he spoke the last, he glanced apologetically over at Moosejaw. "I'm sorry. But put yourself in our boots."

"Come on, man! I give you my word I won't try to run afterward," Beartooth swore to the rangers.

"Wait a minute. There's something out on the desk that might help," said Moosejaw, suddenly breaking toward the office door, crowding through the others. His heart was thudding in his chest—hoping that Rip had been leveling about the note, that it would be where he'd said it was and that it would be convincing.

It was there. Right in the middle of the broad desktop, anchored by a crusty old ink well. A sheet of plain white stationery containing the cramped, careful scrawl of someone who wasn't used to putting pen to paper, yet plainly legible in spite of misspellings.

> To the judge and raingers—What I said about
> Bear Tooth Skiner being the kiler of that
> girl wasnt true. I don't knoe who killed her,
> but it wasnt him. I lyed for my own perpus,
> which you will find out why—Cuthbert Ripley

After the others had all scanned the note, Moosejaw said, "I don't know how many are in that gang Rip is part of. But if we're gonna have any luck stoppin' 'em, we need to get a move on—and Beartooth is too good a gun to leave behind."

Once again, Arbry and Rodgers exchanged looks.

And then Rodgers abruptly began digging in the watch pocket of his pants for the handcuff key.

CHAPTER 43

Surprisingly, Jorto did not feel fear when the young *pistolero* aimed the gun at him. He felt only anger. And determination. His own hand was resting on his hunting rifle and he was confident he could shoot and kill the *pistolero*—or any of the others—if he had to. And if they tried to hurt Mister Hamp or steal from the chuckwagon, he wouldn't hesitate. Señor Wilson and Mister Hamp and all the other wranglers on this drive had put their trust in him, had given him this great chance to earn money for his family and an opportunity for a lasting job. He would not let them down. He would not let these bad *hombres* steal food or any of the other supplies so important to the men he was making this drive with.

The six horsemen gigged their mounts closer. They fanned out as they did so, making it so there would be riders pulling up on each side of the wagon. As they came closer, the remaining five also drew their guns, though not with the speed the young *pistolero* had.

"Damn it, old man, are you hard of hearing?" demanded Muldoon as he reined up alongside the wagon on Hamp's side. "You were told to climb down off there—now get to doing it!"

Jorto stood up and said angrily, "He has bad knees, and it is hard for him to get up and down. I need to help him!"

On Jorto's side, Mud River snarled, "You shut your damn Injun yap and worry about gettin' your own skinny ass down. If the old man has trouble, he can *fall* off for all we care. But the two of you better get the hell out of the way, if you know what's good for you."

"Do as he says, boy. Don't sass him and make it worse," urged Hamp.

But Jorto wasn't listening. It had become clear to him that these bad *hombres* meant to do harm to him and Mister Hamp, no matter if they cooperated or not. So all he could think was to put up a fight, try to chase them away, and with that decision made, he jerked up his .22, whirled partway around, and shot the big, bearded man who was closest to him.

Jorto's action was so unexpected that, even though the hardened men gathered around the wagon all had their guns drawn, they were so caught by surprise that nobody responded for a stunned moment. Mud River Neelan, in that same second of time, took Jorto's bullet in his right cheek. Because he jerked his head away and opened his mouth to shout a protest just as the boy fired, the slug passed through Mud River's opened mouth, burned a crease across the top of his tongue, and punched out through his left cheek. The big man rocked back in his saddle, howling in pain and throwing his arms wide, unbalancing himself to the point of pitching off his horse and falling heavily onto the rocky bottom of the wash.

Then the other guns opened fire. Beevey shot first, planting a round just above Jorto's hip as the lad was bending over to grab a fresh cartridge from the box behind the seat. The impact of Beevey's bullet knocked Jorto off his feet and deposited him roughly back into the bed of the wagon. This fall saved him from further hits as more slugs sizzled through the air where he'd been standing and chewed into the seat he'd suddenly vacated.

With those same bullets whizzing so close by him, Hamp blurted, "Oh, hell no!" as he simultaneously hurled himself backward off the seat and toppled into the rear area next to where Jorto had fallen. More bullets riddled the emptied seat and pounded high and low into the space behind it.

But Jorto's little .22 wasn't the only gun riding in the chuckwagon that day. Old Hamp wasn't much good with a handgun, but for as many years as he'd been dishing out grub to trail herds, he'd carried a double-barreled Greener shotgun under his seat. He'd only ever pulled it out from there once or twice in all that time, but this morning he drew it as smoothly and quickly as if he'd practiced the move for hours every day.

Screaming, "You sonsabitches kilt little Jorto!" he reared up from behind the seat, thrusting the twin muzzles ahead of him, and pulled the first trigger. Loudmouthed, threatening Muldoon was less than two yards away. He took the full blast square to his face. To those looking on, it was like his head dissolved. One second it was there, the next it was gone; everything between his derby hat and his shoulders disappeared in a red mist. The hat toppled to the ground, and the body tipped to one side and slipped slowly from the saddle.

By the time Hamp pulled his second trigger—wildly, without careful aim—the men still left on horses were scattering and spurring back toward the cedar trees. A wounded Mud River—half running, stumbling, and at times scrambling on hands and knees—hurried after them as fast as he could, praying he could make it before the old bastard in the wagon got his Greener loaded again.

Coming from the south, Trav Wilson heard the sound of gunfire up ahead. He swore under his breath. Damn it to hell, he had stressed again and again how badly he wanted to avoid any shooting or killing. His stomach knotted at the thought of Hamp's helper, the young Indian boy Jorto, who had ridden out of camp with the old cook. *Jesus*, he groaned inwardly, *please don't let this mean they gunned down the boy.*

With that anguished thought in mind, he spurred his horse harder toward the long rise that he knew would crest and then slope down to the wash and cedar stand where he and Halsey had laid out the ambush spot. The gunfire ahead had turned sporadic, the crack of handguns punctuated at intervals by the dull roar of a shotgun.

At the top of the rise, he checked down his horse and took a moment to study the scene below. The chuck-wagon was stopped in the middle of the wash, just like he and Halsey had planned. The body of a man lay on the ground to one side—a body without a head, something that certainly hadn't been part of the plan. Nor had the slaughter of the team of horses pulling the wagon, their bullet-riddled carcasses dropped in their traces.

From inside the chuckwagon, somebody was continuing to periodically blast away with a shotgun. In the cedar trees on the far bank, Halsey and the rest of his men were peppering the wagon with repeated barrages.

Abruptly, the shooting from inside the wagon ceased. Several more shots poured in from the trees before they stopped also.

With the knot in his stomach tightening, Wilson gigged his horse on down the slope. As he approached the rear of the wagon, Halsey and the others emerged cautiously from the trees across the way and once again they also moved toward the wagon.

Wilson was the first to reach it. He came up on the side where the headless body lay on the ground. The buzz of gathering flies could already be heard swarming, both on the dead man and on the nearby horses. As if that wasn't enough, when Wilson looked into the wagon box behind the seat and saw both Hamp and the boy, motionless and blood-spattered and pocked by numerous bullet holes, his stomach knotted in a different way, threatening to void itself. "My God," he groaned under his breath.

Halsey and the others came riding up, guns still drawn.

"What the hell happened?" Wilson demanded. "Why the need for this savagery? I specifically said—"

"They opened up on us!" Halsey cut him off. "What did you expect us to do, throw rocks back at 'em?"

"Look what they did to Muldoon, for Chrissakes," pointed out Pauley. "Do you need any more of an answer than that?"

"An' lug ah mah face," said Mud River through his damaged mouth. "Li'l Innin bassard—I hah his sca'p fore we done!"

"The hell you will," Wilson said. "You've splashed this robbery with too much blood already. All you've done is give the rangers and every other law dog in the territory all the more reason to come hunting for us."

"Gold spends all the same, blood on it or not," said Beevey. "What's done is done. But what's still left for us to do is *take* that gold. That's what this is all about, so why are we yapping and not getting to it?"

"The kid's right," said Halsey. "That still stands as what we came for."

Wilson set his teeth on edge and raked his eyes over the faces around him. Exhaling a ragged breath, he said, "This sure ain't the way I wanted it. But you're right, the gold is still what it's all about." He jabbed a thumb over his shoulder, indicating the slope he'd just come down. "Ripley, get on up to that high ground and keep a sharp lookout in all directions while the rest of us start tearing apart the false bottom. All this shooting might have drawn attention from one of the surrounding ranches. Make sure nobody comes riding up on us unexpected."

CHAPTER 44

As soon as he crossed the city limits of town, Firestick sensed something was wrong. He didn't know what, but it made the short hairs on the back of his neck stand up stiff like a cold breeze had touched them.

The street wasn't very busy. But it was early . . . he wouldn't expect it to be. As he rode along, leading his spare mounts, a number of faces turned to look his way. Nothing uncommon there; he was something of an imposing figure. A few heads bobbed in acknowledgment when he met their eyes, a couple hands raised in short waves.

Halfway up the street from the jail, his gaze fell on the first sign of something that seemed to fit with the uneasy feeling he had. The front door of the building was standing wide open. He watched as he continued on, waiting for some sign of activity, someone perhaps making a delayed exit. But there was nothing, only an ominous stillness from beyond the doorway.

And then, to his right, Kate, looking as lovely and fresh as the morning, came out onto the front porch of the Mallory House. Rather than the joy he would have expected to see on her face at the sight of him, her expression was one of mild confusion, a trace of concern.

"You're back," she said somewhat breathlessly. "I'm glad."

"Is something wrong?" Firestick wanted to know.

Kate tucked her bottom lip momentarily between her teeth. "I . . . I'm not sure. But certainly something is odd."

"Odd how? What do you mean?"

"Just a short time ago . . . Moosejaw and those rangers went tearing out of town, toward the south . . . and Beartooth was riding with them."

Atop the rise overlooking the site of the chuckwagon ambush, Ripley was also feeling uneasy. A sourness was building deep in his gut. He didn't like being part of this no more. Not nohow. Robbing, maybe killing . . . he'd thought he was ready for that.

But seeing that young boy go down under a bullet and then, afterward, peering behind the seat where he'd fallen and seeing how his spare little body lay all twisted and punched full of more bullet holes . . . Knowing how he had joined in pouring lead at the wagon and knowing further how the powerful punch of his big Sharps would have chewed through that flimsy seat, he had to own that some of those wounds likely came from him . . . It was an awful thing to face and he couldn't erase the sight from his mind's eye. He felt half-sick, almost like he wanted to weep. Either for the boy, or maybe for his own miserable hide, he didn't know which.

Down below, the others had removed much of the contents from inside the wagon and strewn it about to get at the false bottom. They had the hidden compartment broken open now and were starting to pull out some of the gold bars. There were lots of smiles and whoops of joy over this.

But, looking on, Ripley felt none of that joy. The sight of the gold—the sight of what he'd ached for, thinking it was the answer to everything he would ever want or need for the rest of his days—stirred nothing in him now. He looked at the gold, but all he saw was the twisted, bloody body of the little boy.

He groaned, cursing himself inwardly for being part of such a terrible thing. The only sliver of salvation he was able to cling to was the thought of how he had—although by betrayal—saved his three old friends from very possibly meeting the same fate.

Barely had this thought crossed his mind when Ripley's agony-blurred eyes caught sight of something. Movement to the west and north, riders coming from the general direction of town, following the twisting path of the dry wash. The dust cloud swirling about them made it impossible to make out their features or even guess at their number. But they were coming at a pretty good clip, and by following the course of the old waterway, it was just a matter of minutes before they would be in sight of the chuckwagon.

Ripley started his horse down the slope, shouting ahead, "Company's on the way!" As he rode, he waved his arm to indicate which direction the trouble was coming from.

By the time he got to the wagon, the others were all poised and tense, facing northwest along the wash with guns drawn once more.

"How many?" Wilson wanted to know.

Ripley said, "Can't say for sure, too much dust. 'Bout half a dozen, I'd guess."

"Damn! Must be wranglers from some close-by spread, heard the shooting," said Wilson. "We're too far from the horse herd for any of the boys there to have picked up the sound."

"So how are we gonna play it?" Halsey asked.

Wilson looked around. Then: "Halsey, you stay here with me. We're going to try and make them think—for a minute anyway—that we're the ones who got attacked. We'll try to draw them in close, with their guard down. The rest of you men hightail it back to the trees. Take all the horses with you, and keep 'em quiet. Don't start shooting unless I do. If it comes to that, we'll try to catch them in a crossfire. Cover up that loose gold, and for Christ's sake, somebody throw a tarp or something over what's left of Muldoon!"

Ripley joined the other three men in the trees. He crouched within the cluster of trunks, his hat removed and held over his horse's snout to keep it quiet. In the other hand he gripped his loaded and ready Sharps.

To his right was Mud River, his damaged mouth hanging slack, his brows knitted against the pain he had to be suffering. But he was a tough cuss, you had to give him that much, Ripley thought. Other than what he'd said to Wilson about wanting to scalp the Indian boy, he hadn't uttered a single complaint about his injuries. It was like handling those gold bars had a healing—or at least pain-numbing—effect on him.

Ripley wished he had something to counter the kind of pain he was feeling. Here he was, getting ready to throw more lead at some oncoming riders who were total strangers to him. Men guilty of nothing more than showing up at the wrong time. Maybe Wilson's bluff would fool them, but Ripley doubted it. And maybe they'd even manage to throw some lead in return—but the crossfire wouldn't give them much chance.

Ripley felt so soured on the whole business he seriously considered climbing onto the horse he was quieting and just riding away. Would the others let him go, rather than risk a commotion that might warn the men coming down the wash . . . or would he be stopped by getting shot in the back in order to prevent his flight?

A moment later, the approaching riders rounded a bend in the twisting wash and Ripley got his first good look at them, particularly the hulking form riding at the front. Suddenly, he knew that he wouldn't run—*couldn't* run—and just as suddenly, he knew what he had to do to try and counter the feeling of self-disgust inside him.

Ripley straightened up suddenly, taking his hat away from the horse's snout and using it to swat the animal away. At the same time, he pointed his Sharps skyward and triggered a shattering blast as he shouted, "Moosejaw! Ambush!"

Then, turning immediately to his right, he swung the heavy rifle in a backhanded sweep that crashed the barrel as hard as he could across the side of Mud River's head. The Indian-hating outlaw blurted a sharp grunt of pain and surprise that mixed with the *craack!* of his snapping neck as he collapsed in a loose, lifeless heap.

Wheeling back the opposite way, Ripley braced to make a lunge for Pauley and Beevey. But the young gunny's reflexes and speed never gave him a chance. Without even a heartbeat's hesitation, Beevey's Remington spat flame and thunder, twice, and both slugs hammered into Ripley's chest, driving him back and knocking him into a sprawl that left him lying across the legs of Mud River.

CHAPTER 45

Ripley's warning bought precious seconds for Moose-jaw and the others. What was more, it stopped them from advancing far enough to be positioned for Wilson's cal-culated crossfire. Also adding to their swift reaction was Moosejaw's recognition of Trav Wilson as soon as he came in sight of the ransacked chuckwagon—recognition based not just on the ramrod's deceptive introduction of himself but, more importantly, the complete picture sub-sequently painted by Ripley.

"Hit the dirt!" Moosejaw hollered, springing from the saddle and dragging his Winchester from its scabbard as he did so.

Behind him, Beartooth and the two deputies promptly followed suit. Though without the full recognition and in-formation Moosejaw was privy to, they had enough faith in his instincts—especially combined with the shouted warning and rifle shot they'd all heard—not to hesitate.

Moosejaw hit the ground hard and immediately scram-bled toward the north side of the ancient streambed, dropping in behind a couple of pumpkin-sized boulders jammed against a pile of smaller rocks, as if all had been swept together and then left by a long-past rush of water that had once coursed through the spot. His position gave him decent cover but limited his effectiveness for return fire without dangerously exposing himself.

In the center of the wash, Beartooth pulled his horse down with him as he skinned from the saddle, crouching behind the barricade thus presented by the prone animal. Though it ultimately meant sacrificing the beast, it was his best option for quickly shielding himself.

Arbry and Rodgers both dismounted and went into diving rolls for the southern edge of the wash, where a low, ragged embankment of gravel-packed soil provided decent cover especially from the angle of the cedar trees. Unfortunately for Rodgers, the two men at the chuckwagon—Wilson and Halsey—were quick to open fire, even as they scurried to gain cover for themselves behind the wagon, and a slug from one of them hit Rodgers in the thigh as he was making his dive. The impact dropped him short of his goal, and when his partner reached to drag him to safety, Arbry took a hit to his left shoulder. Together, both men collapsed against the gravelly shoulder and pressed themselves tight against the protection it provided.

The next half minute was like a drawn-out explosion of blazing guns and sizzling bullets that scorched the very air throughout the scene. Despite the warning provided by Ripley, the four newly arrived men were at the disadvantage of being caught relatively out in the open while those firing on them were already in place, in position. True, Wilson and Halsey had to make the adjustment of hurrying around to the back side of the chuckwagon, but that was a comparatively minor maneuver.

Still, the men spread across the width of the wash were hardly defenseless. All were veterans of gun work, and none lacked grit when it came to standing their ground and holding their own.

"How bad are you two hit?" Beartooth called across to the rangers when the gunfire went into a brief lull as chambers were being reloaded.

"My leg's not bad. Chewed some muscle but I got the bleeding mostly stanched," reported Rodgers. "Arbry's shoulder is tore up worse, and he's losing quite a bit of blood."

"Don't worry about me," Arbry insisted. "I got lots more where that came from, and my shooting arm is still good. I say we can spill the blood of those ambushing skunks long before I run dry."

"That's a bunch of phony bluster, you meddling bastards!" Halsey hollered from behind the wagon. "We got cover and shade and we got you pinned down like sittin' ducks. You ain't got a chance. If we don't pick you off one by one, you'll either bake or bleed out before nightfall."

"Here's a little something to warm you up, in case you get chilly in all that shade!" Moosejaw reared up and levered three rapid-fire blasts that hammered the side of the chuckwagon before he dropped back down.

An immediate volley of return fire from both the wagon and the trees peppered the boulders he was behind, kicking up plumes of dust and throwing shards of broken rock.

When the volley subsided, Beartooth called over to his big pal, "You might want to save some of that ammunition until you've got a clearer target."

"Yeah, yeah," Moosejaw growled. "I was just givin' 'em something to think about."

In a lowered voice, Beartooth said, "Something else you might want to do, speakin' of things to think about, is to ponder a bit on how we'll handle it if one of the varmints over in the trees decides to skin outta there and try to work wide around on that brushy ridge to the south and come at us from high or behind."

But Moosejaw wasn't much in the mood for pondering. "That's easy. Any sorry sonofabitch pokes his head up, we'll shoot 'em."

Beartooth ducked his own head low as a couple of fresh rounds pounded into the carcass of the now-dead horse he lay behind. "Yeah," he muttered, "don't I wish it'd be that easy."

Moments later, a strange sound drifted down from somewhere along the brushy ridge that Beartooth had just expressed concern about. It was the trilling of a bird. To those less discerning, it might only seem strange that a bird would still be anywhere close, given all the shooting that was taking place. To the ears of both Beartooth and Moosejaw, however, it was a signal that meant something quite different . . .

"If you think it's such a good idea," challenged young Billy Beevey, "why don't you be the one to slick around and try to blindside 'em?"

"Look at the two of us," said Liam Pauley, spreading his hands. "You're fifteen years younger, at least twenty-five pounds lighter, you're sprier and quicker moving . . .

you got a way better chance of successfully 'slicking around,' as you put it, than I do. And everybody knows how fast and dead accurate you are if you get 'em anywhere in your sights. You could have two or three of them cut down before they ever knew what hit 'em."

"Yeah, and you know where you can stick your flattery," Beevey sneered. "You're the one wearing two tie-down Colts and always hinting you're as fast or faster than me. Well, here's your chance to show it. Me, I like throwing lead from right here with all these nice thick tree trunks around me, so here is where it suits me to stay . . . Besides, you heard what Halsey told them a few minutes ago. We'll have 'em baked out or bled out in a few hours. Why add extra risk to ourselves if we don't have to?"

Now it was Pauley's turn to sneer. "Yeah, and I also heard Halsey say, along with this old mountain goat here"—he jerked his chin disdainfully toward Ripley's sprawled body—"how all the close-by law had been taken care of. Remember? Well, what is it I see shining on the shirts of two or three of those *hombres* out there if it ain't law badges? The longer we diddle around, how do we know there ain't the chance of more of 'em showing up?"

"Like me, you mean?"

The question was posed by a deep, steady voice speaking from a slight upslope of high grass on the fringe of dappled shadows thrown by the cedar branches—about six yards above and off to one side of where the two outlaws crouched jawing at one another.

Pauley and Beevey were momentarily frozen by surprise and indecision, afraid to look around . . . but also afraid *not* to.

CHAPTER 46

Firestick had been riding the dry wash for more than a mile, following the signs in its rocky bed of freshly chewed ground and scattered stones made by the recent passage of horses' hooves. Taking time only to check the jail in order to determine that Ripley's cell was empty, he'd ridden south out of town since Kate had said that Moosejaw, Beartooth, and the rangers had headed that way. He'd picked up their trail easily and was able to stick with it even while holding his own horse to a hard gallop.

As he rode, a whole new swarm of questions and concerns had filled his head. Why wasn't Rip still locked up? How did it come to be that Beartooth was riding with Moosejaw and the rangers? Were the two things connected? Were the four lawmen on Rip's trail, chasing him? Had they somehow discovered he was behind the phony charges against Beartooth, or had he done something more, perhaps even worse?

The sound of gunfire from not too far up ahead had suddenly swept away all those questions without answers and forced Firestick to focus on the immediacy of what he was riding into. Quickly, he swung his horse out of the wash and up onto the southern bank, out of the rocks upon which the click of a horseshoe could give unwanted warning.

He chose the southern side because a low, brushy ridge dotted with occasional clumps of trees ran along there, providing cover for him to continue forward unseen. To the north it was mostly a series of open, rolling, treeless hills.

A hundred yards ahead, the wash made a twist to the left and dipped out of sight behind the brushy ridge. Shortly beyond that turn, Firestick judged, was where the shooting was taking place.

After first grabbing his Yellowboy from its saddle sheath, he abandoned his horse and proceeded on foot, running bent over low at the waist, through the brush and high weeds along the ridge. In short order, he arrived in full sight of the shoot-out that was playing out. He dropped onto his belly in a high clump of weeds and gave it a quick but thorough appraisal.

He had no idea who the men behind the ransacked chuckwagon or in the cedar grove were, but all that really mattered was that they were shooting at his friends and had them in a tight spot. He could see, thankfully, that both Moosejaw and Beartooth seemed okay so far. And though he saw splashes of blood and signs of injury on the two rangers, they were still well enough to be making a fight of it.

His course was obvious. Joining the fight from this vantage point would do little to help his friends except make it five guns to four. Yet the advantage would remain with the other side because they were still better positioned. Though with some patience, caution, and a smidge of luck, Firestick reckoned he had a good chance to turn that around.

But first he wanted to give at least Beartooth and Moosejaw a warning of his presence to make sure they wouldn't attempt anything reckless before he got himself situated.

During their time together in the mountains, the three of them had developed a clever and useful method of communicating with one another in situations where— usually due to the close proximity of hostile Indians—it was ill advised to speak or otherwise make any sound that would reveal their presence. They came to refer to this means of communicating as "killdeer talk" because it was mimicry based on the wide range of calls used by the commonly found killdeer bird, so named because of the range of sounds it made stemming from the basic "*k-deer*" trill.

On this occasion, before moving ahead with the plan he had in mind, Firestick gave a simple notification to his comrades. "*K-deer*" . . . "*k-deer*" he trilled, telling Moosejaw and Beartooth: "*I'm close by.*"

Then, pausing only to make sure he saw recognition and understanding on each of their faces, he moved on . . .

Once he'd succeeded in using the cover of brush and weeds to make his way unseen along the southern ridge as the shoot-out continued in sporadic bursts down below, Firestick emerged above and slightly behind the two men in the cedar trees just as they were bickering about one of them possibly using the route he had just navigated in an attempt to outflank those they were shooting at.

He smiled a wolf's smile when he heard the one with twin tie-down Colts say, ". . . how do we know there ain't the chance of more of 'em showing up?"

The words he said in response came out almost of their own volition. "Like me, you mean?"

He watched the reaction of the two men with a clarity that almost made it seem like everything was playing out in slow motion. He saw them freeze . . . saw their flicker of indecision . . . knew with certainty what they were going to do next. But despite the fact they were ambushing skunks who'd been trying like hell to kill his friends, it wasn't in him to simply mow them down in cold blood. He tried to give them a chance, saying, "One twitch other than to drop your guns, I'll kill you where you stand."

But of course, they didn't listen.

Two of them, two hardcases who each thought they were top guns and already had their hoglegs drawn, challenged by a voice without a face who might be all thumbs when it came to pulling a trigger . . . they had to try.

When they made their spins, they actually came closer than many others would have. Each of them even managed to get off a shot—only not before a .44 slug from Firestick's Colt was already planted in their hearts and they were knocked backward by the impact, their gun hands jerked awry and the rounds they triggered veering off harmlessly. As each buckled at the knees and started to sink down, Firestick spent two additional make-sure bullets and hurried their falls.

Then, holstering the Colt and swinging up the Yellowboy he'd been holding in his off hand, he moved forward into the thick of the cedar trunks and called out to Wilson and Halsey behind the chuckwagon, "This is Marshal Elwood McQueen from the town of Buffalo Peak! In case you gutless peckerwoods didn't recognize it, that little burst of gunfire you just heard was the last of your men over here bitin' the dust. So that leaves you outnumbered and outflanked and outmatched every way from Sunday. Makes no never mind to me—in fact I might even lean in favor of it—if you two want to keep this up and go the way your friends did. But I'll give you one chance to throw down your guns and step out with your hands high. Make up your minds quick. Which'll it be?"

CHAPTER 47

Wilson and Halsey gave up with a whimper.

Once they were disarmed and secured by being handcuffed to opposite wagon wheels, focus quickly shifted to tending the wounds of the two rangers. Both were brought over to the shade of the cedars and laid out as comfortably as possible. While this was being done, rapid exchanges of conversation brought everybody roughly up to date.

As Rodgers had indicated earlier, his injury was less serious than Arbry's. The bullet had passed through, so, apart from the discomfort it left him in, the application of a fresh bandage to keep the bleeding stanched was all that was immediately required for him.

Arbry's shoulder was in considerably worse shape, with damage to bone and joint having been done and the slug still lodged somewhere in there. Once they got most of the bleeding stopped, though, he insisted he'd be able to stay on a horse long enough to make it to town to receive care from the doctor there.

They were in the process of preparing to do that when

a low moan and slight stirring from Ripley—who'd been taken for dead up to that point—suddenly drew everyone's attention to him. As the four lawmen who were on their feet loomed close around him, the old mountain man's eyes fluttered open and he looked around in pain-dulled confusion. Until his gaze settled on Firestick and recognition brought apparent clarity.

"Firestick . . . Y-you made it back?"

"I'm here."

Ripley swallowed. "Hell's bells, fellas . . . I sure sunk awful low . . . C-can't tell you how sorry I am . . . Reckon I didn't fit no better with bein' an outlaw, though, than I . . . than I did fittin' into civ-civilization."

"You were never meant to be civilized, Rip," Beartooth said, his voice thicker than usual. "But we're gonna get you patched up and then you can take another crack at—"

"N-no," Ripley cut him off. "Don't waste time talkin' about what ain't . . . ain't gonna be." His eyes found the faces of Arbry and Rodgers. "Important you read the note I left in the jail . . . Now the words of a dyin' man . . . Make sure the judge believes."

"We'll tell him. We'll make sure he sees the note," Rodgers said.

Ripley's breathing grew heavier, more ragged, then very shallow again. "So s-sorry . . . everybody," he wheezed. Abruptly his eyes opened, very wide and clear, and he locked them once more on Firestick. "That bounty on me . . . Make sure you by-God collect it, you hear? . . . M-make that damn Cotton Bailey pay his lousy dollar!"

His mouth curved in a final rakehell smile. And then

his face relaxed and this time when his eyes went shut they never opened again.

Over the next two days, activity in and around Buffalo Peak was at a fever pitch. First, the rangers were hurried into town for the medical care they required. The gold from the chuckwagon was confiscated and held in the West Texas Cattlemen's Association Bank until a legal ruling for its release could be handed down. Wilson and Halsey were locked up in jail awaiting the arrival of replacement rangers to haul them away.

After attending a burial service in the town cemetery for their chuckwagon crew, Hamp and Jorto, the wranglers left to care for the horse herd elected a new ramrod—Matt Corbain—to oversee getting the mustangs on to market at Fort Leaton. What their ranch boss, Howell, would be facing as a result of his part in the gold-smuggling attempt was expected to be a drawn-out matter for the courts to decide.

The bodies of the men who'd ridden with Wilson and Halsey were also buried in the town cemetery—in unmarked graves in a weedy corner with no ceremony.

That left Ripley.

For him, Firestick, Beartooth, and Moosejaw decided something different was warranted. Despite his betrayal of them and the grief he had caused, in their eyes he had largely redeemed himself at the end. And he'd been a good friend for far longer than he'd been something less.

So, on the third day, the three of them took his body— bathed and curried, dressed in fine buckskins selected from their own personal gear, and wrapped in the bearskin he had tanned for Daisy—she insisted it stay with him—and rode high into the Vieja Mountains. There, they pruned the sturdy horizontal branches of a tall pine tree across which they erected a platform that they laid him out on. With a high, clear view of the mountains and sky.

At the base of the tree, they stood with their hats in their hands and Firestick said some words.

"Well, Rip. This ain't the Rockies, where your spirit soared at its finest. But it's the best we can do. We reckon it still counts for the high reaches. All things considered, ain't no tellin' if you'll make it any higher or not. That's for somebody bigger than us to balance out. All we can do is send you on your way and wish for the best. Guess that means hopin' you make it someplace where the trappin' and huntin' shines like the old days. If you get there, mark a path for us . . . We'll keep an eye out for you on the other side."

They didn't talk much on the ride back to town.

When they got there, they received word that Ranger Arbry, who was recuperating in one of the rooms of a boardinghouse that Dr. Greaves had arranged for him, wished to see them as soon as possible. When they arrived, they found Rodgers also present at bedside.

Arbry held out a piece of paper, a telegram, saying, "This came while you were away."

Firestick shook open the paper and read it, with Beartooth and Moosejaw looking over his shoulders. It was from Judge Walter Buchanon and was a terse report that the murderer of the showgirl Katy Carruthers had been apprehended and had given a full confession. The killer turned out to be another member of Della Devane's own entertainment troupe.

"I'll be damned," Moosejaw muttered.

"A rather ironic ending, don't you think?" said Arbry.

Beartooth nodded somberly. "Well, at least it *is* an ending. I'm just glad it's finally over."

"No, it ain't over quite yet," said Firestick. When the others looked his way, his mouth curved in a rakehell smile that was very familiar to all of them. And then he added, "I still got a one-dollar bounty to collect."

Keep reading for more Johnstone action!

NATIONAL BESTSELLING AUTHORS
WILLIAM W. JOHNSTONE
and J.A. JOHNSTONE

HELL FOR BREAKFAST
A Slash and Pecos Western

In a twist of fate, Slash and Pecos are riding hard for the law, dispensing justice as they see fit, and determined to watch their final sunset as heroes . . . not outlaws.

His wicked ways mostly behind him, reformed bank robber Jimmy "Slash" Braddock is getting hitched to his sweetheart. But before the honeymoon, Chief U.S. Marshal Luther T. "Bleed-'Em-So" Bledsoe needs Slash and his former partner-in-crime, Melvin "Pecos Kid" Baker, to don a couple of deputy marshal badges and saddle up for a trip to Nebraska. Seems the town of Harveyville has fallen prey to a trio of murderous badmen blasting away up and down Main Street, and the local law needs some assistance from men who know how to handle a gun.

But Slash and Pecos killed the wrong man. Worse, the town marshal tells them that the outlaws rode on and he doesn't need their help after all. But now Slash and Pecos are wanted men. Tom Gyllenwater's son is dead. He won't rest until Slash and Pecos are permanently relocated to Boot Hill. And as the duo are targeted by every gun-crazy desperado in the territory, Slash and Pecos discover they'll find no help from anyone in Harveyville, a town of ruthless and corrupt folks willing to kill to protect their secrets . . .

Look for HELL FOR BREAKFAST, on sale now!

CHAPTER 1

Danny O'Neil wasn't sure what made him turn back around to face the depot platform. An unshakable premonition of sudden violence?

He'd never felt any such thing before. The sudden stiffening of his shoulders made him turn around and, holding the mail for the post office in the canvas sack over his right shoulder, he cast his gaze back at the train that had thundered in from Ogallala only a few minutes ago.

As he did, a tall man with a saddle on one shoulder and saddlebags draped over his other shoulder, and with a glistening Henry rifle in his right hand, stepped down off the rear platform of one of the combination's two passenger coaches. He was obscured by steam and coal smoke wafting back from the locomotive panting on the tracks ahead of the tender car. Still, squinting, Danny could see another man, and then one more man, similarly burdened with saddle, saddlebags, and rifle, step down from the passenger coach behind the first man.

The three men stood talking among themselves, in the snakes of steam mixed with the fetid coal smoke, until one of them, a tall strawberry-blond man with a red-blond mustache, set his saddle down at his feet, then scratched a match to life on the heel of his silver-tipped boot. The blond man, wearing a red shirt and leather pants, lifted the flame to the slender cheroot dangling from one corner of his wide mouth.

As he did, his gaze half met Danny's, flicked away, then returned to Danny, and held.

He stood holding the flaming match a few inches from the cheroot, staring back at the twelve-year-old boy through the haze of steam and smoke billowing around him. The man had a strange face. There was something not quite human about it. It was like a snake's face. Or maybe the face of a snake if that snake was half human. Or the face of a man if he was half snake.

Danny knew those thoughts were preposterous. Still, they flitted through his mind while his guts curled in on themselves and a cold dread oozed up his back from the base of his spine.

Still holding the match, the blond man stared back at Danny. A breeze blew the match out. Still, he stood holding the smoking match until a slit-eyed smile slowly took shape on his face.

It wasn't really a smile. At least, there was nothing warm or amused about the expression. The man dropped the dead match he'd been holding, then slowly extended his index finger and raised his thumb like a gun hammer, extending the "gun" straight out from his shoulder and canting his head slightly toward his arm, narrowing those devilish eyes as though aiming down the barrel of the gun at Danny.

Danny felt a cold spot on his forehead, where the man was drawing an imaginary bead on him.

The man mouthed the word "bang," and jerked the gun's barrel up.

He lowered the gun, smiling.

Danny's heart thumped in his chest. Then it raced. His feet turned cold in his boots as he wheeled and hurried off the train platform and on to the town of Harveyville's main street, which was Patterson Avenue. He swung right to head north along the broad avenue's east side. He'd been told by the postmaster, Mr. Wilkes, to "not lollygag or moon about" with the mail but to hustle it back to the post office pronto, so Wilkes could get it sorted and into the right cubbyholes before lunch.

Mr. Wilkes always had a big beer with an egg in it for lunch, right at high noon, and he became surly when something or someone made him late for it. Maybe he was surly about the lunch, or maybe he was surly about being late for the girl he always took upstairs at the Wildcat Saloon after he'd finished his beer. Danny wasn't supposed to know such things about Mr. Wilkes or anyone else, of course. But Danny was a curious and observant boy. A boy who had extra time on his hands, and a boy who made use of it. There was a lot a fella could see through gauzy window curtains or through cracks in the brick walls of the Wildcat Saloon.

Wilkes might be late for his lunch and his girl today; however, it wouldn't be Danny's fault. His grandfather, Kentucky O'Neil, knowing Danny spent a lot of time at the train station even when he wasn't fetching the mail for Mr. Wilkes, had told Danny to let him know if he ever saw any "suspicious characters" get off the train here in Harveyville. There was something about the infrequent trains and the rails that always seemed to be stretching in from some exotic place far from Harveyville, only to stretch off again to another exotic place in the opposite direction—that Danny found endlessly romantic and fascinating.

Someday, he might climb aboard one of those trains and find out just where those rails led. He'd never been anywhere but here.

For the time being, he had to see Gramps, for Danny couldn't imagine any more suspicious characters than the ones he'd just seen step off the train here in dusty and boring old Harveyville. They had to be trouble. They sure *looked* like trouble!

As Danny strode along the boardwalk, he kept his intense, all-business gaze locked straight ahead, pinned to the little mud-brick marshal's office crouched between a leather goods store and a small café roughly one block ahead.

"Mornin', Danny," a voice on his right called out to the boy.

Not halting his stride one iota, Danny only said, "Mornin'," as he continued walking.

"Hey, Danny," Melvin Dunham said as he swept the step fronting his barbershop. "You want to make a quick dime? I need to get Pearl's lunch over to her—"

"Not now, Mr. Dunham," Danny said, making a beeline past the man, whom he did not even glance at, keeping his eyes grave and proud with purpose beneath the brim of his brown felt hat.

"Hello there, handsome," said another voice, this one a female voice, as Danny strode passed Madam Delacroix's pink-and-purple hurdy-gurdy house. "Say, you're gettin' taller every day. Look at those shoulders. Carryin' that mailbag is givin' you muscles!"

Danny smelled sweet perfume mixed with peppery Mexican tobacco smoke.

"Mornin', Miss Wynona," Danny said, glimpsing the scantily clad young woman lounging on a boardwalk chair to his right, trying not to blush.

"Where you off to in such a rush . . . hey, Danny!" the girl called, but Danny was long past her now, and her last words were muffled by the thuds of his boots on the boardwalk and the clatter of ranch wagons passing on the street to his left.

Danny swung toward the door of his grandfather's office. Not bothering to knock—the door wasn't latched, anyway—he pushed the door open just as the leather goods man, George Henshaw, delivered the punchline to a joke he was telling Danny's grandfather, Town Marshal Kentucky O'Neil: "She screamed, 'My husband's home! My husband's home!'"

Mr. Henshaw swiped one hand across the palm of his other hand and bellowed, "The way Melvin told it, the reverend skinned out that window faster'n a coon with a coyote chewin' its tail, an' avoided a full load of buckshot by *that* much!"

Gramps and Mr. Henshaw leaned forward to convulse with red-faced laughter. When Gramps saw Danny, he tried to compose himself, quickly dropping his boots down from his desk and making his chair squawk. Looking a little guilty, his leathery face still sunset red around his snow-white soup-strainer mustache, he indicated Danny with a jerk of his hand, glanced at the floor, cleared his throat, brushed a fist across his nose, and said a little too loudly, "Oh, hello there, young man. Look there, George—it's my favorite grandson. What you got goin' this fine Nebraska mornin', Danny?"

Mr. Henshaw turned to Danny, tears of humor still shining in his eyes. "You haven't let them girls over to Madam Delacroix's lure you into their cribs yet, have you, Danny boy?" He was still laughing a little from the story he'd been telling, his thick shoulders jerking.

"No, no, no," Gramps said. "He just cuts wood for Madam Delacroix, is all. His mother don't know about that, but what Nancy don't know won't hurt her—right, Danny?"

Gramps winked at the boy.

"Sure, sure," Mr. Henshaw said, dabbing at his eyes with a red cambric hanky. "First they got him cuttin' wood and then he's—"

"So, Danny-boy—what's up?" Gramps broke in quickly, leaning forward, elbows resting on his bony knees. He chuckled once more, the image of the preacher skinning out that window apparently still flashing in his mind.

Danny took three long strides into the office and stopped in front of his grandfather's desk. He drew a breath, trying to slow his racing heart. "You told me to tell you if I seen any suspicious characters get off the train. Well, believe-you-me when I tell you I just seen three of the gnarliest lookin' curly wolves you'll ever wanna meet get off the train not ten minutes ago, Gramps!"

Gramps arched his brows that were the same snowy shade as his mustache. "You don't say!"

He cut a glance at Mr. Henshaw, who smiled a little

and said, "Well, I'll leave you two *lawmen* to confer in private about these curly wolves. I best get back over to my shop before Irma cuts out my coffee breaks altogether." Judging by the flat brown bottle on Gramps's desk, near his stone coffee mug, the two men had been enjoying a little more than coffee.

"All right—see ya, George," Gramps said before returning his gaze to Danny and lacing his hands together between his knees. "Now, suppose you tell me what these *curly wolves* look like and why you think they're trouble."

"One's a tall blond fella, almost red-headed, with crazy-lookin' eyes carryin' one fancy-ass . . . er, I mean . . . a real *nice-lookin'* Henry rifle."

George Henshaw had just started to pull the office door closed behind him when he stopped and frowned back through the opening at Marshal Kentucky O'Neil. O'Neil returned the man's vaguely incredulous gaze then, frowning now with interest at his grandson. Not nearly as much of the customary adult patronization in his eyes as before, he said, "What'd the other two look like?"

"One was nearly as tall as the blond guy with the Henry. He was dark-haired with a dark mustache—one o' them that drop straight down both corners of his mouth. He wore a dark suit with a cream duster over it. The blond fella must fancy himself a greaser . . . you know—a bean-eater or some such?" Danny gave a caustic chuckle, feeling adult enough suddenly to use the parlance used in reference to people of Hispanic heritage he often overheard at Madame Delacroix's. "He sure was dressed like one—a red shirt with fancy stitching and brown leather pants with conchos down the sides. Silver-tipped boots. Yessir, he sure fancies himself a chili-chomper, all right!"

"And the third fella?" the lawman prodded the boy.

"He was short but thick. You know, like one o' them bare-knuckle boxers that fight on Saturday nights out at Votts' barn? Cauliflower ears, both of em. He wore a suit and a wide red necktie. Had a fancy vest like a gambler."

"Full beard?" Henshaw asked, poking his head through the front door.

Danny turned to him, nodded, and brushed an index finger across his cheek. "He wore a coupla tiny little braids down in front of his ears. I never seen the like. Wore two pistols, too. All three wore two pistols in fancy rigs. *Tied down*. The holsters were waxed, just like Bob Wade waxes his holsters."

Bob Wade was a gunslinger who pulled through the country from time to time, usually when one of the local ranchers wanted a man—usually a rival stockman or a nester—killed. Kentucky never worried about Wade. Wade usually did his killing in the country. Kentucky's jurisdiction stopped at the town's limits unless he was pulling part-time duty as a deputy sheriff, which he had done from time to time in the past.

He should probably have notified the county sheriff about Wade, but the county seat was a long ways away and he had no proof that Bob Wade was up to no good. Aside from what everybody knew about Wade, that is. And maybe a long-outstanding warrant or two. Notifying the sheriff all the way in Ogallala and possibly getting the sheriff killed wouldn't be worth taking a bullet from an ambush himself, by one of the ranchers he'd piss-burned by tattling to the sheriff.

He was too damn close to retirement and a twenty-dollar-a-month pension for that kind of nonsense.

"The big fella wore a knife in his boot," Danny continued.

"How do you know that?" Gramps asked. His attention was fully on his grandson now. There was no lingering laughter in his eyes anymore from the story about Reverend Stillwell skinning out Mrs. Doolittle's window. The old laughter was all gone. Now Gramps leaned forward, riveted to every word out of Danny's mouth.

"'Cause I seen the handle stickin' up out of the boot well."

From the doorway, Henshaw said in a low voice, "The knife . . . did it have a . . ."

"One o' them fancy-carved ivory handles." Danny felt a smile raise his mouth corners and the warm blood of a blush rise in his cheeks. "In the curvy form of a naked woman."

He traced the curvy shape in the air with his hands, then dropped his hands to his sides, instantly wishing he hadn't gone that far. But neither of these men chastised him for his indiscretion. They were staring at each other. Neither said anything. Neither really had much of an expression on his face except . . .

Well, they looked scared.

CHAPTER 2

When Kentucky had ushered his grandson out of his office, assuring the boy that, yes, he would vouch for him to Postmaster Wilkes, about why he was late, O'Neil walked up to one of the only two windows in the small building, the one between his desk and the gunrack holding a couple of repeating rifles.

He slid the flour sack curtain back and peered along the street to his left, in the direction of the train station.

George Henshaw walked up beside him, nervously smoothing his green apron over his considerable paunch with his large, red hands. Henshaw was bald and gray-bearded, with a big walrus mustache even more ostentatious than the marshal's soup-strainer. He also wore round, steel-framed spectacles, which winked now in the light angling through the dust-streaked window.

"You think it's them, Kentucky?" Henshaw asked, keeping his voice low though the boy was gone and none of the four jail cells lined up against the building's rear wall held a prisoner. He and Kentucky were alone in the room.

"Hell, yes, I think it's them," the lawman said, gazing

through the dust kicked up by several ranch supply wagons heading toward the train depot. "Don't you?"

"I don't know. I guess . . . I was hoping . . ."

"We knew they'd be back. Someday. We knew it very well."

"Yes, I suppose, but what are we . . . ?"

Henshaw let his voice trail off when he saw his old friend Kentucky narrow his eyes as he continued to gaze toward the depot. The man's leathery red cheeks turned darker from a sudden rush of blood. Henshaw thought he could feel an increase in the heat coming off the pot-bellied lawman's bandy-legged body.

"What is it?" Henshaw said, his heart quickening. He stepped around behind O'Neil and gazed out over the man's left shoulder through the window and down the street to the south.

Kentucky didn't respond. His gaze was riveted on the three men just then stepping off the depot platform and into the street. They were carrying saddles, saddlebags, and rifles. Sure enough—two tall, lean men and one short, stocky one. Not just stocky. Laden with muscle that threatened to split the seams of Kinch Wheeler's checked, brown wool coat. Sure enough, he had a knife poking up from his lace-up boot with fancy deer-hide gaiters. He'd always been a natty dresser. Wheeler must have walked straight out of the prison gates and over to the nearest tailor's shop. Turning big rocks into small rocks for twelve years had added to Wheeler's considerable girth.

Henshaw slid his gaze to the blond man in the Mexican-style red shirt and flared leather pants down the outside legs of which silver conchos glinted. He lowered his hand from his face, wincing as his guts writhed around in his belly with cold, dark dread.

"Christ," Henshaw said over Kentucky's shoulder. "Those twelve years really screamed past."

"They sure did."

"What do you think they came back for?"

O'Neil gave a caustic snort. Henshaw knew what they were doing back in Harveyville as well as Kentucky himself did.

Henshaw nodded slowly in bleak understanding.

O'Neil turned away from the window, retrieved his Smith & Wesson New Model Number 3 from the blotter atop his desk, and returned to the window. Again, he peered out, tracking the three as they slowly moved up the street toward the office. "Oh, Christ," he said, hating the bald fear he heard in his voice. "They're coming here."

"They are?" Henshaw jerked his head back toward the window and drew a sharp breath.

"Of course they are!"

The three men moved up the middle of the street as though they owned the town. Horseback riders and wagons had to swerve wide around them. One horsebacker rode toward them with his head down as though checking a supply list. He raised his head suddenly, saw the three men heading right toward him, and jerked his horse sharply to the left. He turned his horse broadside and yelled angrily at the three men as they passed. The horsebacker's face was creased with exasperation.

While Kentucky hadn't heard the words, he'd heard the anger in the man's tone.

"Easy, now, Ed," he muttered to the man—Ed Simms from the Crosshatch Ranch out on Porcupine Creek.

Noreen must have sent him to town to fill the larder. "Just keep movin', Ed. Just keep movin'"

Ed hadn't been in the country twelve years ago, so he didn't know about the Old Trouble. Hell, a good two-thirds of the people in Harveyville and on the ranches surrounding it hadn't been in the country back then. They wouldn't know about it, either.

But Kentucky knew. He knew all too well. He knew well enough that beads of sweat were rolling down his cheeks and into his white mustache and his knees felt like warm mud.

He was going to die today, he thought as he watched them come. They formed a wedge of sorts, the tall, blond Calico out front, leading the way, like the prow of a ship cleaving the waters with supreme, sublime arrogance. O'Neil didn't know why Calico's return had taken him by such surprise. He'd known this day had been coming for the past ten years.

Hadn't he? Or, like Henshaw, had he lied to himself, telling himself that, no, in spite of what had happened, in spite of O'Neil himself organizing a small posse and taking Calico's trio into custody while they'd been dead drunk in a parlor house—and in spite of what they'd left in the ground nearby when they'd been hauled off to federal court in Denver—they wouldn't return to Harvey-ville.

Well, they had as, deep down, Kentucky knew they would.

The three men, as mismatched a three as Kentucky had ever seen—the tall, blond, dead-eyed Calico flanked by the thick-set punisher, Wheeler, and the dark-haired and mustached Chase Stockton, who'd once been known as "the West Texas Hellion"—kept coming. As they did, Kentucky looked down at the big, heavy pistol in his hands.

He broke it open and filled the chamber he usually kept empty beneath the hammer. When he clicked the Russian closed and looked up again, the three outlaws had veered left and were heading toward the opposite side of the street from the marshal's office.

"Look at that," Henshaw said softly, under his breath. "They're going into the Copper Nickel! You got a reprieve, Kentucky. They're gonna wet their whistles before they come over here and kill you!" He chuckled and hurried to the door. "With that, I bid you adieu!" He stopped at the door and turned back to his old friend, saying with an ominous wince, "Good luck!"

Kentucky raked a thumbnail down his cheek. "Why in the hell are they . . ." The light of understanding shimmered in his eyes. Then his eyes turned dark, remembering. "Oh, no."

Norman Rivers set a bottle of the good stuff on a high shelf behind the bar in the Copper Nickel Saloon. He had to rise up on the toes of his brogans to do so, stretching his arm high and peeling his lips back from his teeth with the effort. As he did, his sixteen-year-old daughter, Mary Kate, ripped out a sudden shriek from where she swept the stairs running up the room's north wall, on Rivers's right.

Rivers jerked with a start, inadvertently dislodging the bottle of the good stuff from the shelf. It tumbled toward him, bashing him in the temple before he managed to grab it and hold it against his chest, or it would have shattered on the floor at his feet—four-and-a-half dollars gone, just like that!

"Gallblastit, Mary Kate—look what you did!" Rivers scolded, turning toward the girl as he held a hand against his throbbing temple. "What's got into you, anyway?"

"That damn rat is back! Scared me!"

"Hold your tongue, damn you! You almost made me break a bottle of the mayor's good stuff!"

"Why do you put it up so high, anyway?" the girl shot back at him from halfway up the stairs. She was a pretty girl, really filling out her simple day frocks nicely, and she knew it and was too often high-headed about it. Her beauty gave her a confidence she otherwise did not deserve. She was sweeping barefoot when if Rivers had told her once, he'd told her a thousand times not to come down here without shoes on.

She didn't used to be this disobedient or mouthy. It had something to do with her mother dying two years ago, and her body filling out.

Rivers held the bottle up, pointing it like a pistol at the insolent child. "I have to put it up so high so you don't mistake it for a bottle of the rotgut and serve it to the raggedy-assed saddle tramps and no-account drifters who stop by here to flirt with you because they know you'll flirt back!"

Color lifted into Mary Kate's ivory cheeks, and she felt her pretty mouth shape a prideful half grin. She shook a lock of her curly blond hair back from her cheek and resumed sweeping the steps. "I can't help it if they think I'm pretty."

"I can't help it if they think I'm purty!" Rivers mocked

the girl. "He pointed the bottle at her again and barked, "You shouldn't be makin' time with such trash. You oughta at least *try* to act like a lady!"

"You mean like the high-and-mighty Carolyn?" Mary Kate said in a scornful singsong as she angrily swept the broom back and forth across the step beneath her, kicking up a roiling cloud of dust. "Look what it got her!"

"Married to a good man!"

The banker's son, no less.

"Hah!" Mary Kate laughed caustically. "Everbody knows prissy Richard leaves her alone at home every night, to tend those three screaming brats, while he—"

"That's enough, Mary Kate! I told you I never wanted to hear those nasty rumors again. And what did I just tell you? *Get some shoes on!*"

Mary Kate stopped at the second step up from the bottom, thrusting the broom back and forth across the first one and shaking her head slowly, hardening her jaws. "Boy, when I'm old enough and have made enough money to flee this back-water cesspool, I'm gonna—"

She looked up when boots thumped on the stoop fronting the Copper Nickel and three men filed into the saloon—two tall men, one blond and quite colorful in his Spanish-style dress. Mary Kate's father, Rivers, had just seen the trio in the backbar mirror and jerked with such a start that the bottle he'd nearly placed, finally, on the high shelf, tilted forward, slammed into his head—the opposite temple from before—and shattered on the floor at his feet.

Mary Kate looked at her father, who held his head, cursing. Then she turned to the tall, red-blond drink of water standing just inside the batwings. The blond man grinned and winked at her.

Mary Kate brought a hand to her mouth and laughed.

Rivers glared at her, then turned his head slowly to regard the three newcomers. He felt a tightness in his chest, as though someone had punched a fist through his ribs and was squeezing all the blood out of his heart. All three men had their heads turned toward Mary Kate. The blond man was smiling at her. She was smiling back at him, still covering her mouth with her hand.

Rivers did not like the expression on the blond man's face. Nor on Mary Kate's. At the moment, however, he felt powerless to speak, let alone do anything to break the trance the blond man—*Ned Calico?!*—seemed to be holding his daughter in.

Finally, the shortest of the three, but also the heaviest and all of that weight appearing to be muscle, which the man's gaudy checked brown suit could barely contain, removed his bowler hat from his head and tossed it onto a table. "I don't know about you fellas," he said in a heavy Scottish accent, "but this feller could use somethin' to cut the trail dust!"

He kicked out a chair and glanced at Rivers, who still held a hand to his freshly injured temple. "Barkeep, we'll take a bottle of the good stuff."

That made Mary Kate snicker through her nose.

The tall, blond man in the Spanish-style duds broadened his smile, slitting his flat blue eyes and curling his upper lip, revealing a chipped, crooked front tooth that took nothing away from his gambler-like handsomeness. He switched his gaze to Rivers and said, "What's the matter, apron? Did you hear my friend here? A bottle of the good stuff!"

He stepped forward and kicked out a chair from the table the big man—what was his name? Wheeler? Yeah, that was it. Kinch Wheeler. The third man was Stockton, a laconic, coldblooded, gimlet-eyed, dark-haired Texan. Rivers hadn't thought of them, he suddenly realized, in a good many years. But for several years after "the Old Trouble," as everyone in town back then had called it, he hadn't been able to get their names . . . as well as their faces . . . out of his head. For years, he'd slept with a loaded shotgun under his bed. Now, just when he'd forgotten them—or hadn't been remembering them, anyway, and having nightmares about them, and when his shotgun was clear over at the other end of the bar—here they were.

One of them, Ned Calico, making eyes at his daughter the same way he'd made eyes at another girl so long ago . . .

And there wasn't a damn thing Rivers could do about it.

"The good stuff—pronto!" barked Stockton, as he stepped up to the table and plopped his crisp black bowler down beside Ned Calico's and Kinch Wheeler's. He scowled across the room at Rivers. His face was broad, dark, and savage, his hair long and oily. Time had passed. Twelve years. There was some gray in the Texan's hair, and his face, just like the faces of the other two men, wore the dissolution of age and prison time. But here they were, looking really no worse for the wear.

For the prison wear.

And now, sure as rats around a privy, all hell was about to break loose.

"That man there," said Ned Calico, leaning against his elbow and pointing an accusing finger at the barman, "is either deaf as a post or dumber'n a boot!"

"I got it, I got it," Mary Kate said, walking toward the bar with her broom and scowling bewilderedly at her father, who was just staring in slack-jawed shock at his customers.

"No," Rivers said, finally finding his tongue. "No, I, uh . . . I got it."

Mary Kate stopped near the bar, scowling at him, baffled by his demeanor.

"No," said Ned Calico. "Let her do it." He looked at Mary Kate again and smiled his devil's smile. "I like her. She's got a way about her, I can tell. Besides that, she's barefoot an' she's pretty."

Mary Kate blushed. She turned to the bar, casting her father a mocking, insouciant smile, and stretched her open hand across the mahogany. "You heard the gentlemen, Pa. A bottle of the good stuff."

Rivers stared at the three spectre-like men lounging in their chairs, smiling at him coldly, savagely, three wolves glowering through the wavering, murky mists of time.

"Mister Rivers, I remember you," Ned Calico said, throwing his head back and laughing. "Did you miss us, you old devil? Wasn't you one o' the townsmen that old lawman roped into helpin' him take us down when we was drunk as Irish gandy dancers on a Saturday night in Wichita? Why, sure it was!"

He laughed and shook his head, though his eyes had now grown cold with admonishing.

"I hope you got a few more bottles of the good stuff

'cause we're gonna be here awhile and it's gonna be a party!"

He looked at Mary Kate. He looked her over really well and blinked those devil's eyes slowly. Again, the girl flushed.

Calico returned his gaze to the barman and said, "Don't that make you happy?"

The three wolves watched Rivers's pale jowls mottle red, and laughed.